WISEGUY IN TRAINING

"I called nine-one-one," Lisa said. "They hung up on me. I just don't get this city."

"You called *them?*" Michael's voice rasped.

"Of course I called them. What kind of person do you think I am?"

"Ssshh!" Michael said sharply into her ear, and his eyes got big and round as he stared at the back of Tony's head. "Never, ever say that aloud again, you hear me?" His lips were nearly pressed against her earlobe. He stayed there for a second, then leaned back, his eyes bulging. "What planet do you come from, Mars?"

"No, Michigan. Remember?" she snapped at him.

"Jesus! I told you what to do."

"Oh, and I'm supposed to follow some thug's advice?"

Tony coughed up front and Lisa moved closer to him on the seat. He looked at her face.

"I'm going to die tonight, aren't I?" she whispered, her face not even an inch away from his.

He stared at her as the tears began to fall.

Lisa felt herself instinctively reach around Michael and take a deep breath. His body seemed to throw off an inordinate amount of heat. She just needed to hold on to someone. He put his arm around her and tightened it against her shoulders. Lisa took another deep breath and laid her head on his chest.

"Aw jeez," Michael said. "I'll think of something."

**NOWHERE TO RUN . . . NOWHERE TO HIDE . . .
ZEBRA'S SUSPENSE WILL *GET* YOU –
AND WILL MAKE YOU BEG FOR MORE!**

NOWHERE TO HIDE (4035, $4.50)
by Joan Hall Hovey
After Ellen Morgan's younger sister has been brutally murdered, the highly respected psychologist appears on the evening news and dares the killer to come after her. After a flood of leads that go nowhere, it happens. A note slipped under her windshield states, "YOU'RE IT." Ellen has woken the hunter from its lair . . . and she is his prey!

SHADOW VENGEANCE (4097, $4.50)
by Wendy Haley
Recently widowed Maris learns that she was adopted. Desperate to find her birth parents, she places "personals" in all the Texas newspapers. She receives a horrible response: "You weren't wanted then, and you aren't wanted now." Not to be daunted, her search for her birth mother – and her only chance to save her dangerously ill child – brings her closer and closer to the truth . . . and to death!

RUN FOR YOUR LIFE (4193, $4.50)
by Ann Brahms
Annik Miller is being stalked by Gibson Spencer, a man she once loved. When Annik inherits a wilderness cabin in Maine, she finally feels free from his constant threats. But then, a note under her windshield wiper, and shadowy form, and a horrific nighttime attack tell Annik that she is still the object of this lovesick madman's obsession . . .

EDGE OF TERROR (4224, $4.50)
by Michael Hammonds
Jessie thought that moving to the peaceful Blue Ridge Mountains would help her recover from her bitter divorce. But instead of providing the tranquility she desires, they cast a shadow of terror. There is a madman out there – and he knows where Jessie lives – and what she has seen . . .

NOWHERE TO RUN (4132, $4.50)
by Pat Warren
Socialite Carly Weston leads a charmed life. Then her father, a celebrated prosecutor, is murdered at the hands of a vengeance-seeking killer. Now he is after Carly . . . watching and waiting and planning. And Carly is running for her life from a crazed murderer who's become judge, jury – and executioner!

Available wherever paperbacks are sold, or order direct from the Publisher. Send cover price plus 50¢ per copy for mailing and handling to Penguin USA, P.O. Box 999, c/o Dept. 17109, Bergenfield, NJ 07621. Residents of New York and Tennessee must include sales tax. DO NOT SEND CASH.

C. Clark Criscuolo

ZEBRA BOOKS
KENSINGTON PUBLISHING CORP.

ZEBRA BOOKs are published by

Kensington Publishing Corp.
850 Third Avenue
New York, NY 10022

First Zebra Printing: January, 1995

Printed in the United States of America

For Gregory,
and to the memories of Johnny and Mary Bush

ACKNOWLEDGMENTS

My agent, Janet Spencer King, for her tireless support and belief in the words. Vince Patrick, who can teach more about writing in a twenty-minute conversation than most people do in years of workshops. Neil Criscuolo and his pals in East Harlem. And finally, my editor, Hope Dellon, and her assistant, Margaret Longbrake, of St. Martin's Press for their input and energy, and for taking a chance on an unpublished writer.

One

We have the time. . . . And sex is not an activity, okay? Mowing the lawn is an activity. Bowling is an activity. Sex is an *event*, Andrew," she called in to him.

His deep laugh echoed off the bathroom tiles and he appeared at the bathroom door and waved a finger at her. She watched his toned naked body in the doorway. Andrew was five ten, muscular, with a flat washboard stomach and perfectly shaped thighs and hips. He was just . . . hard all over and at the same time his skin felt baby-soft.

"You're such a wiseguy, Lisa! I love your sense of humor. Well, whatever sex is, you know me, I'd rather be making money. Now, come on, we don't have the time right now; we're going to be late for work. Tonight, honey." His face disappeared again, almost like the Cheshire cat, leaving only the image of a big smile, and Lisa stretched her arms up over her head and then felt another frown cross her face as she heard the gush of the shower as it was turned on.

"Andrew," she began, "is everything all right?"

"How?" His voice echoed.

"Between us."

In a moment, he had walked back out, leaving the water running in the shower, and was sitting beside her on the bed, the way he did every time they had this discussion. He was staring seriously, and he was silent.

"What are we talking about here?" His voice was low.

"Is everything all right?" she repeated.

"Do you want to leave me, is that it?"

She sat straight up and put her arms around him.

"No. I'm not talking about *that.*"

"Look, Lisa, I know it's been hard the last couple of years. . . ."

"Well, yes. I mean they have you working days, nights, weekends; you couldn't even come home to visit my folks last Christmas." Her voice had a testy edge to it.

"You know how many traders they've let go? You know how bad the economy is? Christ, I'm lucky I have a job on Wall Street." He took a breath. "I know it's been hard and it's going to end, I promise."

"In February," she recited.

"In February. Exactly. Seven months. We will have paid off the loan on this co-op, and you can get out of that terrible job and I can look for something with easier hours."

"But we just have to hold on until we pay off the co-op."

"Right."

"Maybe we should just move back to Michigan. I'm sick of being alone." Her voice rose.

"I know. It's difficult for me, too, but you have to know I love you."

"Yes." She answered the way she did every time.

"Don't I bring you flowers every week?"

"Yes."

"Don't I call you at exactly one-thirty every day from work?"

"Yes."

"Does that sound like someone who doesn't care?"

"No."

"Now come on, or we'll be late." He patted her thigh, and she again got to watch his exquisite body walk naked into the bathroom.

She felt her smile vanish and she slid down onto the bed.

Sex. Was that a rarity these days. It was not only that she couldn't really remember the last time they'd had sex but Lisa couldn't remember the last time they'd had an evening out, or a weekend together.

She sat back up against the pillows and looked at her hands in her lap. She looked at the clock. She was going to be late if she didn't start moving.

Her job. Not wanting to go in. Maybe she *was* just using Andrew's hours as an excuse. Maybe what really was bothering her was that she hated her boss, Henry Foster Morgan, and she hated *Smug Magazine*, and she just couldn't stand to get out of bed in the morning.

She felt that dull depression that was always there these days. Even when she laughed, there was this flatness deep inside her.

Andrew's stupid boss, Jerry. She hated him, almost as much as she hated Henry. Jeez, she was crabby all the time.

God, Lisa couldn't wait until February. Then they could both quit their jobs and she could get away from her boss and Andrew would get to stop working these insane hours. All they had to do was tough it out. And having

Andrew there—*living with Andrew,* she dryly corrected in her head—at least gave her the strength to put up with Henry.

After all, she knew women who didn't have anybody and still had to go to terrible jobs—at least she had someone. She tried to concentrate on something positive.

She thought hard.

This weekend. Lisa swung her legs over the side of the bed and walked into the bathroom. She stood still for a moment and watched him soaping himself in the shower.

She exhaled loudly and then turned and looked at herself in the mirror. Her shoulder-length blond hair was all tousled on top. It emphasized her high cheekbones, which made a rectangle of the upper part of her face and then gently sloped down to a pointed chin. Her squarish nose was dotted with freckles and her generous lips were wet—oddly, it made her eyes seem more green than blue. She looked back at Andrew.

"So what time do you want me to pick you up?"

"Pick me up?"

"Yeah." She grabbed a brush and began brushing her hair.

"For what?"

"We're supposed to go to Connecticut this weekend. Ted and Laurie's engagement party?"

"Oh right! That's *this* weekend?"

Lisa stopped brushing her hair and put her hands on her hips.

"Andrew—"

"All right, all right. I'll tell Jerry I'll take the paperwork with me." He flashed one of his brilliant smiles and leaned over and gave her a wet kiss.

"I want to do something this weekend. Something—I

don't know, unusual, exciting. I want to meet new people." She looked at him.

"There, that's what I like to see. Smiles and no worries."

Tony pulled a pack of Marlboro's out of his jacket pocket, put one in his mouth, and put the pack away. He leaned his arms on the steering wheel and lighted the cigarette, cupping it in his large hands as if there was a wind in the car.

He inhaled deeply, then draped his hand over the steering wheel and exhaled.

He just wanted to see it. Just with his own eyes.

He'd been sitting in the car for hours, parked across the street from the Oceanside Deluxe Apartments out near Coney Island. He'd watched the sun come up over the building, which was an arc of windows rising twenty-five stories, with a big canopy and traffic island with some kind of damn hedge or something. And then, in the center of that was this fountain they lighted up orange at night, like on some wedding cakes at fancy weddings. When he'd first seen it, he thought it was classy, but now he could see it for what it was.

It was a weird-looking building.

He took another deep drag of his cigarette. He'd been staring so hard at the big glass front doors that his eyes hurt.

His chest tightened as the black Porsche drove around and into the traffic circle. His eyes bounced down to his watch.

Eight-thirty in the morning, she was getting home!

His eyes raised immediately to look back across the

street. Doesn't even drive a decent car, he noted. Drives one of them cheap, squishy little foreign jobs.

He sat, staring at the car so hard, he could have set it on fire.

His back arched as he saw the passenger door open, and Angela's long legs stretched into view as she stepped outside.

She went out last night dressed like that?

Her hair was done up high and big on her head and looked like a frosted blond lion's mane. Her eyes were hidden by sunglasses. Her white T-shirt fell off one shoulder and floated down over her breasts, only to be cut off high above her waist. Her tight white leather skirt barely made it down to midthigh; her legs were covered in lace stockings. Her high white heels made her totter, so her hips swung from side to side and made the skirt work its way up even higher on her thighs as she walked around the car to the driver's side.

Tony could feel the breath get sucked out of him, and his torso was now smashed so far into the steering wheel, it felt like it was going to be permanently embedded in his chest.

The door on the driver's side opened and he watched Joe Didero step out onto the curb and reach his hand out to her. She waved him back inside the car and bent way down, and kissed him on the lips quickly. Tony felt his teeth grind together as it looked like her breasts were going to fall down below the shirt. She closed the door and walked around the back of the car on the way to the door of the building.

She darted a look at Tony's car, took another step, then looked back again, and he knew under the dark glasses she blinked. She suddenly stopped and gave her skirt a tug, first one thigh, then the other, so it accentuated how tight it was and at the same time showed off the big diamond ring Tony'd given her five months before. Then she looked back at him, gave him a fuck-you smile and the finger and slowly, exaggerating the swing of her hips, walked around to the driver's side again.

The door was pushed open and she made a big deal out of bending way over so her ass wiggled, and she gave Joey D. a big kiss, then straightened up. The car door closed and Tony silently watched the car pull out and away.

Angela turned and did the slowest, swingiest walk he'd ever seen, up to the front doors, and she disappeared inside.

Only then did he exhale, and he did it hard, through his nose, like a bull ready to charge.

Didn't Ralphie know about this shit? He stared down at the dashboard. He couldn't believe it. Who would let his daughter hang around that lowlife?

Angela had a fuckin' reputation to look after.

He started the engine and sat, pressing his foot down on the accelerator, just to hear the motor groan. So Louie was right. It was Joey D.

Fuckin' scumbag Joey D.

And look at the way she was dressing now. Like a whore. Like one of Solly's whores. Okay, he wasn't going out with her anymore, and he'd heard she'd gotten pretty crazy—but this?

She was making an idiot of herself. And in Tony's mind, it reflected on him, what she was doing, because he'd gone out with her.

Somebody had to straighten her out.

He'd find someone to straighten her out.

Maybe Mikey would do it.

He had to start dating again. Two could play at this game.

Maybe his cousin Mikey could help out here. . . .

And this was *the* day for Mikey, he thought proudly.

The tires screeched as he peeled out of the space. He got to the corner and turned right. He had to pick up Mikey and get over to the union office for Solly's payment. After all, he couldn't leave Giuseppe Geddone hanging there all morning.

Were all moms like this or just his?

Michael Bonello braced himself, wiped his chin with his napkin, and pushed the plate aside as his mother walked into the kitchen carrying an umbrella.

"Whatsa matter with your eggs?"

"Nothin', Ma. I don't want 'em."

"Finish the eggs. You need your stren'th," she said, moving the dish back at him.

He let out a breath as she shook the faded dark umbrella. She walked over to the sink, pulled a wipe out of a basket, and wet it down under the tap. He inhaled the last forkful of eggs and watched her wipe down the umbrella.

"Ma, what are you doing?"

"It's dirty," she said, rolling her eyes at the question.

"It's raining cats and dogs out there. One minute outside, it's not gonna be dirty."

"Yeah, 'cause I'm cleaning it. What time you gonna be home?"

"I don't know. Soon as Solly says." He got up as she began muttering under her breath.

He wasn't sure what was going to happen today, when he was coming home. . . .

Michael took his jacket off the back of the chair and put it on. Even though it was the lightest-weight cotton, it felt heavy and hot in the humid summer weather. His shoulder holster pulled across his chest. He caught sight of his fuzzy outline in the overpolished fridge. His body was in good shape at thirty-two. He was a little on the small side, only five seven, but good-looking—blue-black hair, high cheeks, sharp nose, with olive skin from the southern Italian side of his family.

He remembered a girl he'd dated when he was an undergraduate at NYU. She was an English lit major who kept telling him he had a "swarthy Mediterranean look." He couldn't remember her name.

Those days seemed like a dream now.

He adjusted his tie, leaving the tight collar open at the top. He'd do it for real, right before they picked up Solly.

His stomach tightened. Today was the day.

His mother's mumbling was becoming louder as he rubbed a spot off his black wing-tipped shoe.

"Why he can't give you a time like everybody else?"

" 'Cause he don't work that way. When he don't need me no more, I'll be back."

"You need a raincoat."

"Naw, it's too hot, the umbrella's fine—Ma, stop cleaning it," he said, taking it away from her. "You gonna wipe all the waterproof off."

"Let me get you a raincoat."

"I don't need it. Look, I'm in the car all day."

He walked down the hallway to his bedroom. She'd already hit the room. His bed was made, and he hadn't even been out of it for fifteen minutes.

It had been the guest bedroom when he was growing up. Once he moved back in, after his father died two years ago, he'd settled in here.

There was something soothing about sleeping in the guest room—maybe because it made living back here with his mother a temporary thing.

He looked around the room. The heavy mahogany furniture set from the fifties was so well preserved by her obsessive cleaning, it still looked as good as the day she'd bought it. Only the wallpaper, a creamy background with a light brown trellis dotted with bunches of little rosebuds, had faded. He stared at the large metal crucifix over the bed. She'd polished it so many times in the last two years, the features had begun to wear away. Jesus' face looked like it was melting, with the raised parts overly polished, contrasting with dingy dips in the features. He heard his closet open behind him.

"Here's a nice coat for you to take," she said, handing him a raincoat.

"Ma, I don't—"

"It's a good coat—wear it. Your Aunt Gina paid good money for it. You wear it." She shook it, holding it out for him.

He turned his back on her and opened the top drawer of his dresser and reached inside.

"Okay, where'd you put it?"

"Put what? I din't—" She looked down at the floor.

"Ma, I'm gonna be late," he said, raising his voice a bit.

He followed her down the hall to the kitchen and watched her open the drawer where she kept things like string and scissors. She pulled out his gun and handed it to him.

"I told you I don't want you going through my drawers."

"I was dusting."

"You don't gotta dust inside the drawers." He held the gun in his hand. "I don't want you touching it. It could . . . Where are the bullets?"

"I don't know."

"Aw Jeez—" He looked at his watch: 11:40. "Why you do this to me? Now I'm gonna be late. Where are the bullets?"

"I don't like it when you leave that thing laying around the house. Your father"—she stopped and drew in a breath—"never left his gun laying around."

"Yeah, Pop hid it so you wouldn't find it and take the bullets out."

"You coulda been a lawyer," she said, waving her hands out to him.

He walked back to his bedroom and she followed.

"I can't play this game with you every morning. . . . I gotta pick up Solly in fifteen minutes."

"You coulda finished school."

"They threw me out. Okay?" He glared at her hotly and she looked away.

He breathed out and there was silence for a moment.

"Take the coat," she said, picking it off his bed.

"I don't—" he began as she held it out.

"I'll make you a *trota alla Piemontese* tonight, okay?" she said, helping him on with the coat.

"Fine," he muttered, sticking the gun in his pocket. What the hell, wear the coat, he thought, you're probably going to be dead by tomorrow, anyway.

"Father D'Amico wants to know why you never come to confess no more."

He knew he had to make a run for it now or he'd be there forever.

"I don't got time now." He trotted out to the hallway.

"He misses seeing you there."

"I'm not gettin' up at five-thirty to go tell somebody my sins, okay?" he said, half-running to the front door.

"But if—"

"Ma, you got my bullets, you got me to wear the coat, you got enough this morning. Bye." He kissed her on the cheek.

He bolted from the door, down the front steps, and ran toward the limo parked at the curb. Tony Mac rolled down the window as Michael ran across the lawn.

"We gonna be late," he warned, opening the door.

"I don't want to talk about it," he said, swinging himself into the front seat.

Out of the corner of his eye, he caught sight of his mother, running across the lawn, waving the umbrella at him.

"Start the car," he ordered Tony as he slammed the door.

"Michael! Michael Antonio! You forgot!" she yelled, almost there. Her frame, smaller now since the death of her husband, still bounced up and down. For a sixty-six-year-old, she could run like the wind. He held his hand out for the umbrella as she got to the car.

Her dark blue eyes shone down at him softly. Her bluish white hair was coiffed high, in the same way she'd worn it for the last twenty years, and added to her height. The blackness of her dress, stockings, and shoes was broken only by the floral apron tied around her.

"Okay, Mom, thanks."

"Don't be late. I'm making *trota* and it gets dry. You bring him home early, Anthony?"

"Yes, Aunt Sophia," Tony Mac said, smiling up at her.

"You're a good boy," she said to him, and stepped back.

Tony pulled the car away from the curb so fast, it squealed. He drove to the corner and made a stop at the sign as Mike rested his head on the back of the seat and exhaled loudly.

"I gotta get a place. She drives me crazy." He stared at the dark blue roof. "She means well, but since Pop died . . ." He lifted his head up and looked at Tony.

"Make a right."

Tony grimaced at him.

"She got the bullets again, uh?"

Sophia watched the car turn right at the corner and then roll out of sight. She felt herself sigh and shook her head as she turned to walk back to the house. What could she do? Gina's words kept coming back to her and back to her.

"He's making his bones. Solly's taking care of him. . . ." It had echoed slightly as they left church that morning. It had echoed through her brain as they stopped for pastry and espressos, although Gina would never mention anything that sensitive in a restaurant. All Sophia had heard was that terrible news. And she couldn't even say anything to Gina about it. It would insult her, that her son was giving such a big honor to Michael and Sophia didn't want this at all.

Sophia had planned to talk to him this morning, just as she placed his plate of eggs down, but she had looked into his face and stopped suddenly, shocked by what she saw.

She had seen the fine creases beginning near his eyes, just like Vincent's. She had seen the strands of silver on top of his head, breaking up the blackness of his hair, and she'd felt herself freeze for a moment.

When had this happened? She hadn't noticed it. She stopped to pick a leaf off the lawn and looked at the trees. The tips of all the leaves were beginning to brown. The summer was ending. She continued walking back to the house, staring at the leaf.

It must have happened recently to Michael, the age. It wasn't that growing older shocked her. What shocked her and bothered her was that she hadn't noticed it. She stopped suddenly at the front steps.

She hadn't noticed it. She hadn't noticed anything for two years, since Vincent had died. She breathed out, wondering how many other things she had missed.

Michael felt numb as Tony stopped the car.

"Eh, you come in with me." Tony's voice ordered. Michael nodded and slid outside.

He didn't even bother to look up at the building. Who cared? It was one of the many little errands he and Tony went on that Michael never asked about. Why bother? He sure as hell didn't actually want to know about this stuff.

A creaky elevator took them up to the seventh floor of an old office building. Ancient gold paint on frosted glass formed hand-painted letters in an arc, which read, DYNAMITERS LOCAL 391.

Tony walked inside and Michael quietly followed. He felt himself hanging back near the door as Tony walked up to the reception desk. Tony turned around.

"You coming?"

"Maybe I'll just wait here."

Tony shrugged and leaned over the receptionist's desk. In a minute, he was ushered through a small swinging gate. Tony's large torso obscured the woman from view. Michael heard a knock and watched Tony disappear into an office.

He exhaled. His eyes focused on the door Tony had gone through. Black hand-painted letters on the wood, in the same style as those on the outer door, formed the name G. GEDDONE.

A phone rang and Michael listened to a woman answer.

G. Geddone. Now that name was familiar.

The door to the office reopened and Michael saw a flash of G. Geddone as he quickly shut the door behind Tony.

A dim montage of memory went through Michael's mind, memories of a round, bald man, the kind of person you grow up with as a kid, who shakes your hand too vigorously at weddings and funerals, anniversary parties and retirement banquets. The kind of person you call "uncle" but are never sure if they are actually related to you, but there they are, year after year, telling you, "Look at how big you got!"

Michael felt himself breathe in sharply as Tony walked quickly toward him, slipping an envelope into his breast pocket.

His stomach flip-flopped as he opened the door for Tony. This was *it*—zero hour. He silently followed Tony out into the hallway.

Now they were going to see Solly. Michael would finally find out just what this lunatic was going to give him to do to make his bones.

His mind began assembling a list of the terrible things Solly could come with: breaking parts of guys off, torture . . . If he just knew what it was.

Giuseppe Geddone found himself wiping sweat from his forehead the same way he did every time Tony left his office. Only this morning, his whole suit was soaked. With Tony being so late, he thought something had gone really, really wrong. But Tony didn't seem any different, and he breathed out and stared at the ledger on the desk in front of him.

Giuseppe Geddone carefully entered the pension-interest amount in one ledger and then "adjusted" it in another. He could hear the sounds of the traffic and the city from the open window.

He looked back down at the books, closed one, and stuck it quickly in the safe behind his desk, then took out the big union checkbook ledger.

He opened it up and filled out the deposit stub for the day. Underneath that figure, he placed a withdrawal to the Metropolitan Office Maintenance Company in the amount of the interest in the second ledger, to cover the check he'd just given Tony.

That was for Solly. There had been forty new members in the union this quarter, and the Metropolitan Office Maintenance Company was supposed to get a percentage of all the pension dues, balance, and interest, just as it had done every quarter since 1951.

Only, since Giuseppe had figured out his plan, they'd been short. It had taken him a period of time to see that nobody from Solly's side had even ever asked or was ever going to ask to look at the pay rosters and line them up with the payoffs—not so long as he kept the union rosters looking consistent and kept neither a huge rise in union membership nor a consistent drop.

So it was one for him, one for the Soltanos.

Giuseppe licked his lips and began writing out another check.

That was his. It had taken him the last ten years to make it into this position. He had a nice fat bank account in Zurich. When it was time for him to leave, he was going to take the clothes on his back, drive to the airport, get on a plane, and leave behind the boring, fat, married-for-thirty-years person, known as Giuseppe Geddone, and begin living the way God had intended.

Lisa got to work a little before nine, sweating from the August humidity and wet from the rain that had begun falling.

She shivered as she sat down at her desk. The air-conditioning vent right above her was going full blast. She bent down and pulled off her sneakers and socks, then readjusted her panty hose on her feet. She opened up her bottom drawer and wiggled her feet into a pair of heels.

Back to grim reality, she thought.

Tom appeared by her desk with an armful of galleys from the previous day's work. He dropped them down.

"Ready for the pit beast from hell today?" he quipped, and then leaned down, his voice low. "He wants to see these right away. He's been in since eight-thirty."

"Thanks," she said, as though he had just thrown a sack of snakes down on her desk.

"You should have come out with Lynn and me last night; at least it takes the edge off." She watched him shrug sympathetically and take a step away from her desk. He turned around.

"Oh yeah, Mrs. Morelli in Accounting needs to see you about something," he said, and walked back off down the hall.

That would be an excuse to get out of his office fast. She got up, armed with the pile, and began walking down the hall to his office.

A cold shiver always went through her as she got to his door. But this morning, she felt her teeth begin to grind together angrily. She should—no, she *was* going to say something. She gave two gentle knocks.

"What?" Henry Foster Morgan's deep voice boomed, annoyed.

Her resolve faded into her usual reaction—fear, which was followed by the thought that she just had to make it through until February.

He was sitting at his desk with the *Post* opened to Page Six. A fuzzy photo of him and several "unidentified blondes" was splashed across it. He was on the phone. In front of him sat a glass of tomato juice. He usually poured into it a good dose of vodka from the bottle he kept in his lower drawer. Lisa would sit as he screamed, holding her nose from his breath.

She looked at the other things on the desk. Next to the glass was a half-empty bottle of aspirin and a pack of French cigarettes.

She was going to have to definitely block out any smell coming from him.

"Here are the gal—"

"One moment," he said into the phone, then placed his hand over the receiver. "Where have you been?"

"I just got in."

"When I say I want these on my desk first thing, I mean it. What the hell do we pay you for? Playing around all morning?"

"I'm not due in till nine—"

"Have you proofread these?" He cut her off.

"But I thought you wanted to see them."

"Not if you haven't even proofed them! What the fuck do I want with unproofed text? It's bad enough I have to read this shit at all—now I'm supposed to do your idiot work? What the hell is wrong with you? Sit," he ordered.

She sank down into a chair as he hung up.

He was going to scream for the next five minutes. She stared into his bloodshot left eye, his right being hidden behind a cascade of long hair. Several strands were stuck in a ridiculous pair of glasses he wore.

The odd thing, she thought, was that he didn't need to wear them. She'd looked through them once and there was just plain glass in there.

It was funny—the first time she'd seen him, she thought he was going to be totally different.

He was mouth-dropping gorgeous. Tall, trim, with dark wavy hair, big brown eyes, and golden tanned skin. His face was rectangular, with a strong chin that was gently cleft, and the suit he wore didn't make him look like, well, a suit. He looked like a man with style and grace and charm who knew who he was and where he was going. He had walked past her with what looked like the board of directors, silver-gray-haired men who were all laughing at a joke he'd made.

And he was handsome and charming and gracious—to

anyone who could either do something for him or make his life better in some way.

Boy, do some appearances lie, she thought as the sound of him screaming at her began to intrude.

To the board of directors of the company, Henry was a money-making dream. To the people he worked with and over, Henry was a nightmare.

Her eyes glanced down at the photo in the paper. He always photographed well, more distinguished and intelligent-looking, probably because thirty-one on him looked more like forty-eight on the rest of the world. In the four years she'd worked for him, Henry had begun to fade. He was in the same rumpled pink linen designer suit he'd had on yesterday.

"And when I tell you to do something . . ." She zoned out, staring intently at a crack in the wall and concentrating on the coming weekend.

"I'm going to make your life so miserable, you'll—"

She stared at him. He'd obviously been out all night. That was the only way he ever made it in this early.

"I'm sorry, I thought—"

"I don't pay you to think!" His voice screeched and she felt her face get warm. A lump formed in her throat.

"Get out!"

She stood up abruptly. She made it to the door as the galleys she had dropped on his desk flew over her head. As she bent down to collect the papers, the door was slammed quickly behind her.

She walked down the hall stiffly, trying to hold herself together till she got to the bathroom. She wasn't stupid. She wasn't dumb. She was trying so hard at this. She made it to the first stall as the tears began to flow. She locked the metal swinging door and sat down on the toilet, wishing she was back in bed with Andrew.

It wasn't fair. She'd been so happy when she'd gotten this job as an assistant to the publisher on a big new magazine. She was not going to be sitting outside of someone else's office the rest of her life. *She* was going to have the office and the secretary and a good career.

All she did here was type and file for Mr. Henry Foster Morgan, keep his social calendar straight, and get yelled at and humiliated.

And that was the reality, to have to sit at that desk day after day pretending that this was some great thing. She wiped her eyes with the back of her hand.

She should quit her job. That's what. To hell with waiting until February. She really didn't want to settle in this city for life, anyway. She should stop being so afraid of it and just do it.

She started to feel as if she couldn't breathe in the stall, as if all the oxygen had been sucked from the room while she sat there.

She'd go home tonight and try again to work on her resume. She'd put down anything this time. Another wave of tears drizzled hotly out of her eyes. She knew what would happen the second she'd sit down to do it. Her mind would go blank and she would get all shaky as she'd try to come up with some basic office skills. Stupid skills. Skills she used every day, which she could do in her sleep. But sitting at home, trying to put them down, they seemed to vanish, until it seemed like a miracle that she could walk and talk at the same time.

No. She had to be strong and just put up with it until the stupid loan was paid off. This was just so humiliating.

This weekend, she could think about this weekend. She

should spend the rest of the day concentrating on Connecticut and the engagement party.

Engagement party. Her insides went somewhat cool at the thought of having to go to one of those.

The bathroom rematerialized before her as she heard the door open, and she stood up, wiping her face. She flushed the toilet as she blew her nose to cover up the sound.

She'd feel worse if someone saw her.

She'd just have to get by till 11:30. Maybe he'd go for one of his long lunches today. No, she could bet on it. Half the time, it was when he did his sleeping.

She stared at the tiled wall. Labor Day. That's right. It was next weekend. God, if she was really lucky, he wouldn't come back at all after this weekend, what with some big wedding out in the Hamptons. She was going to stop letting everything get to her, like she had resolved last night. She was going to be strong. All she had to do was make it through the rest of the day.

She ducked into the hallway, avoided looking at anyone directly, and quickly made her way back to Accounting.

She could hear the click of Mrs. Morelli's old adding machine as she approached her desk. Lisa looked at the newer calculator, which the woman had placed on a pile of invoices.

"Mrs. Morelli, why don't you use the calculator?"

"I been using this adding machine thirty-one years, and I ain't gonna change now." Her voice was deep and husky and she spoke with a heavy New York accent. She didn't take her eyes off the machine.

"Be wid youse in a minute," she added.

Lisa shrugged and looked at her as she worked. She

had dyed reddish hair, coiffed in a style that hadn't been popular since the early sixties. Her old faded print dress was frayed and sleeveless. The flesh on her upper arms sagged and flapped as her fingers danced across the keys. The fake pearl and bead string that was attached to a thick pair of glasses swung in tandem with her arms. Smoke from a cigarette, hanging out of one side of her mouth, curled above her. She pulled the handle on the adding machine and looked up at Lisa, smiling.

"Sorry, if I lose my place . . ." she began, then frowned at Lisa. "What's a matter wid youse? You look like shit."

"I just . . . have a cold."

"That bastard's started wid you already?"

"How—"

"Aw, Tom come by here. He said he had bug up his ass from eight-thirty."

She felt the lump returning. As she looked away, Mrs. Morelli placed her hand under her chin and turned her back. Lisa looked down at her lined face, staring at the long ash hanging off her cigarette.

"You don't gotta take shit from nobody, you hear? You shouldn't let him talk to you like he does, you know? You should stick up for yourself."

"I just . . . don't . . . How would you handle it?"

"Me?" She took her hand away, and Lisa watched the cigarette ash fall onto the desk. "You got a husband?"

"No."

"A boyfriend?"

"Yeah."

"Then I'd look at him and say real low, 'You don't ever talk to me like that again, 'cause my boyfriend'll come and break your knees.' Then I'd walk out."

"I couldn't do that."

"Then tell him *you*'ll break his knees."

Lisa stood still for a moment, watched Mrs. Morelli laugh and stub out her cigarette, and then Lisa let out a chuckle.

She began to feel better. This was exactly what she needed to hear.

"You gotta stick up for yourself in this world; otherwise, the bums walk all over youse," she said, and pulled out another cigarette.

"Is that how you do it, Mrs. Morelli? You have a husband who breaks your boss's knees?" she asked, joking.

"Naw, my husband, Gino—may he rest in peace—been dead thirty-three years this past May."

"Oh I'm sorry. . . . What did he die of?"

"He got shot in the neck."

"Oh my God."

Mrs. Morelli lighted her cigarette, shook her head, and looked up at her.

"Well, um, what did you want to see me about?"

"I got some questions about Mr. Foster Morgan's expense account here." She coughed deep in her chest and pulled a sheet out of the pile. "You see here, he's got eighteen hundred charged and the stub reads on a Saturday."

Lisa felt a chill at the base of her stomach. His expenses were always padded. She knew because she was the one who had to fill them out and add them up. When she first started doing it, and really began to look at the charges, she realized what he was doing. And now that Mrs. Morelli knew . . .

"He can't do this here. And you know, I been going

over some of the rest of these, too, and he owes us money back on a lot."

Lisa's stomach went hollow. She wasn't going to be the one to tell him. She couldn't.

"Oh please, couldn't you just," she began in a whisper, then stopped, a bit shocked at herself.

Of course Mrs. Morelli couldn't ignore it. It was fraud, and even if she did ignore it, what if Mrs. Morelli's boss found out about it?

"You look pale."

She focused her eyes on Mrs. Morelli.

"I . . . I just . . ."

"Lissen." Mrs. Morelli's voice dropped. "Normally, I'd look the other way, but they been cracking down on the expenses, and I don't want no trouble. I got four months and eight days before retirement, and I ain't going to lose a cent of that pension."

"Of course not," Lisa whispered. "It's just . . ." She swallowed. Her mouth was dry.

"Look, you want me to talk to him?"

"Would you?" She nearly jumped.

"Sure, sure."

She got up, carrying the paper, and picked up the powder blue sweater that was hanging over the back of her chair. Lisa watched her sling it over her shoulders. She was taller than Lisa had remembered, and wider, too.

Lisa felt a pang of guilt. It wasn't fair for Mrs. Morelli to have to do this. She felt a wave of fear at the idea of confronting her boss with this, and again came the thought that she just had to keep her mouth shut for six more months. Her eyes glanced over at Mrs. Morelli. And after all, she *had* offered, Lisa thought with a certain feeling of relief.

"Why they gotta blast us wid the AC, I don't know," she muttered, and Lisa followed her out into the hall. Mrs. Morelli's slippers made a spongy sound on the linoleum as they walked.

"So, you get in early?" Lisa asked, trying to make conversation.

"In at seven, out by three. My boss said if I watched it, she'd let me do that till I'm gone."

"In just four months, huh?" She smiled. It would be great to retire.

"And eight days. I'll be sixty-five."

"What are you going to do with all that free time?"

"I'm gonna buy me one of those condos down in Florida. I been working my whole life for this. When my Gino died, God bless, he didn't leave me nothin'. That's when I got my job here. All my life, I been planning for this. I got enough saved for the condo, and I figure, with the pension I got coming, I don't gotta do nothin' for nobody."

"Do you have children?"

"Naw, Gino and I never did. My sister's got a son, my godson Tony."

They walked quietly the rest of the way, and Lisa sat down at the desk as Mrs. Morelli tapped on the door. She began proofreading the articles on her desk. After ten minutes, she watched Mrs. Morelli slip out. The older woman gave her a smile and left.

Lisa sat still, feeling a weight lifted off her chest, when she heard Henry's door open.

"Get me Carol Horney on the phone," he barked at her, and slammed his door again.

Lisa felt her shoulders hunch up and her muscles constrict as she reached for the phone list. He had a phone, she thought, as she looked up the number. Was that too much for him to do himself, dial a damned phone? she thought as she dialed the number. This was one of the many things that had somehow become her job description over the past four years. This and coordinating his laundry pickup and his dates and his rent. At this point, she was more of a personal secretary than an editorial assistant.

"Mr. Henry Foster Morgan on the phone for Ms. Horney," she said, and waited for her to come on the line.

She connected the calls and hung up, then picked up her red pencil and began proofreading some stupid, inane story Henry had solicited.

Twenty minutes later, Henry sped out of his office, slamming the door behind him.

"I'll be at lunch," he barked back to her.

She cringed over her desk until he was out of sight.

Henry Foster Morgan had made his way up the publishing ladder the old-fashioned way: His family bought him a job.

At first, Heckett Publishing had him working in their children's book division. In one month, he'd managed to alienate their most successful author so much, he'd switched publishers.

In an effort to keep Henry "working" and soothe the firm's ire, his family had supplied the backing to spruce up a small, floundering magazine called *Scope*.

It had a deadly serious social commentary, which was way above anything Henry wanted to deal with. He renamed it and changed the contents to allow himself the flexibility of not really having to show up and do anything at his office. Henry hated working. He hated offices and the people who worked in them. He resented his family's tiresome insistence that he actually pretend to make a living. The fact was that his "salary," plus anything he could gouge on his expense account, was merely pocket change for his nightly rounds of Manhattan hot spots.

Unaccountably, it had begun to take off.

Smug Magazine had the same persona as Henry: sloppy, hungovery copy, which cared about nothing and no one. It billed itself as *the* magazine for the "young and useless."

Pages of glossy pictures of the Buffys, Biffys, Blaines and Ashleys of this world were featured in every issue. But, unlike the serious society pages, with shots of them demurely being led into their coming-out ball, they were shown with straws stuck up their noses at parties, drunk in clubs, caught in bed with their coke dealers or the business partners of their parents. It was taken as "the inside look at the real world of the CHILDREN OF WEALTH," or COWS, as they were acerbically called by the old *Scope* magazine editors, who hated it.

Henry loved it.

For the first time in his life, he could carouse till six in the morning and say he was "doing research." He had also been brutally pushing out the old *Scope* magazine staff by making life so unpleasant, most of them had quit. This made him the darling of management, who were saving a fortune on unemployment.

It was now 11:30 A.M. Henry was sitting in the corner table at his favorite private club. He ordered a Bellini, lit a cigarette, and waited for Carol.

He was ready for her.

He'd hopped over to his health club from the office,

after telling his dolt of a secretary, or whatever the hell he'd called the position, that he was leaving.

His head hurt. He hadn't been to sleep for a day or two. He tended to lose track of everything at the end of summer. There were so many events to cover before the fall. But within two hours, he'd had a sauna, a rubdown, gotten a new suit. He was back and he was ready. A waitress set down the champagne glass of Moët and fresh peach juice, and he swallowed it in one gulp.

"More. And bring me a bottle of . . . Perrier-Jouët, and some osetra." He winked at the waitress and she flashed a smile at him.

"Aren't you Henry Foster Morgan?" the waitress asked, her eyes wide.

Henry gave her his "embarrassed" smile and nodded.

"Wow." Her voice shook. "I saw your picture in the paper today. . . . I read *Smug* every month. It's my favorite magazine."

"Thank you," he said, and winked at her.

"Well, if you need anything—" she began.

"I'll let you know."

He watched her walk away, her high skirt flapping against her ass. Growing up wealthy was fine, but the perks from fame really allowed him to have anything he wanted. He snapped out of it and went back to his cigarette.

Good, a nice bottle of champagne—not the top of the line, but Carol Horney wouldn't know that—a couple of ounces of caviar—not beluga, but she probably wouldn't know that, either, he thought as he watched the waitress appear with a tray. She set down the caviar platter and champagne bucket, then held out the bottle to Henry.

He nodded as he saw Carol across the room. He waved and stood up as she came over.

Carol was a perfect office machine, impeccably dressed for the corporate world. A cluster of fake gold held the collar of her stiff white shirt together tightly right under her chin, totally concealing any skin. Her large boxy jacket covered her torso and her hips, assuring that no hint of breasts or a waist or any female quality was noticeable. A straight skirt was hemmed to a no-nonsense length at her knees, and her shoes were, as always, black pumps. Her pinched nose was straddled by a pair of silver wire glasses that just screamed, This is the head of an accounting department. Dyed blond hair, her only puzzling concession to femininity, was cropped very short on the sides and top, making her long, bony face look even more parched for food and life.

But there was something under that crisp, correct, sexless exterior that no one but Henry knew about.

Given a couple of drinks, Carol Horney was exactly what her name implied.

As she neared, the memory of last year's office Christmas party—and the two of them alone—trickled through Henry. It was the sight of her in the mail room, lying half-naked and spread-eagled across the Xerox machine, her breasts under her half-unbuttoned shirt moving to the rocking gyrations of the machine as it frantically made copies of her back and ass, that came most vividly to mind.

"Carol," he almost whispered, and held his hand out to her.

"I only came to open the lines of communication on a professional basis between us," she said in that icy voice.

"I know, I know," he said, looking as pathetic as he could.

He noticed that she did take his hand.

"What is this?" Her voice cracked as she sat down.

"I just thought—"

"I have work to do. I cannot—"

"You're right." He slowly raised his hand. "This is a stupid, meaningless way for me to apologize for not having called. I will have them take this away immediately." He lethargically kept his hand up, then winced, let out a whine of pain, and let the hand drop to the table.

"What's wrong with your arm?" she said harshly.

"Oh no, I don't want to discuss me."

"We may not be . . . friends anymore, but I do have human compassion," she said robotically.

"It's just from helping with my mother. She's quite ill."

"I saw her picture in the society pages last week. She looked fine."

"Of course she *looks* fine. Do you think a little thing like the early stages of breast cancer would keep my mother from her fund-raisers? Do you think all those charities give a damn—" He choked bitterly.

Carol Horney took off her glasses.

"Good God, you're serious."

"I need a drink," he said softly.

He watched her pour him a glass and then pause. She poured herself a glass.

He had her, just as easily as he had had her on the Xerox machine. Old Carol was as dependable as a ledger.

"It has just been a nightmare, Carol, these last seven months." His voice was soft and deep as he watched her take a drink of champagne.

By the time lunch came, they had polished off the

better part of a second bottle, and Carol had taken off her jacket and undone her collar and was playing footsies under the table.

"Listen, I have an extra invite to the Sonder wedding in East Hampton this weekend. . . ." Henry slugged back half the glass and looked at Carol's face.

It was wide-eyed.

The Sonder wedding had been front-page news ever since it came out that Mrs. Chase-Upwell, the bride's mother, was having fifty white doves dyed lilac to match the decor. At the crucial "I Do," they were to be set free over the ceremony. And this was just one "little treat to show my daughter I care."

"Do you want to go?"

Carol exhaled from her pinched little mouth.

She gulped at the thought. Henry could see Carol's head spin with the names of New York society who undoubtedly would be thrilled to know her.

"Would I want to go?" She laughed.

He leaned forward, putting his lips as close to her ear as he could.

"Just you, me, a limo, and some champagne," Henry continued. "We'll make a weekend of it. . . . I'll give you a call Saturday when I've set up a limo."

It was his; he could feel it. He smiled at her and kept looking at her lips, which she kept licking.

She was just like him under the skin.

Carol rambled on through a huge lunch of carpaccio, salmon en croute, and endive salad, topped off with two desserts. Henry drank his.

He waited until the check came.

"Oh, Carol?" he said, handing the waitress a gold card, "I need a little favor."

"Anything, Henry. Just you name it."

"There's a woman in your department I want you to get rid of."

"Why?"

"I just don't like her," he oozed.

"Well, who is it?"

"A woman by the name of Morelli."

For a split second, he thought Carol was going to give him a hard time. Her chin fell just slightly, and he could see her searching through her mind to see whether she could personally identify the woman and whether it was someone she would feel hard-pressed to do without.

The golden carrot of the Sonders' wedding invite suddenly loomed large in her eyes.

"Sure, Henry. Consider it done."

"Oh no. But what about the party, Andrew?"

"You know how Jerry is about these end-of-the-month reports."

Lisa pulled the phone away from her ear. She thought seriously about slamming it repeatedly on the desk. She took a deep breath and put the phone back up to her ear.

"I hate that man, Andrew. I hate him."

"I know, I know, but he's right. The figures are all in the computer system and it's just impossible to get the information and take it with me. My little laptop wouldn't even begin to be able to crunch those numbers."

"Well, what do you want me to do?"

"Look, honey, why don't you take the car and you can meet me at the train tomorrow. I know Ted and Laurie would love to have just you. I'll call you there tonight and tell you which train I'll be on in the morning, okay?"

"And you're sure you'll make it?"

"What do you mean? Of course I'll be there."

"You will not let Jerry talk you into another weekend like the last two—"

"Absolutely not. I swear it."

She looked at her watch. It was 1:40, and she had to get to the conference room for an editorial meeting. She put the phone back to her mouth.

"All right."

"Honey, I know you're disappointed."

"Tell Jerry I hope he never gets married and he never has a life." She could hear his deep voice laughing.

"Wiseguy. . . . In February. Love you." Click.

She knew what was going to happen. He was going to call tonight and tell her that he just couldn't make it. And she'd be there, alone again, with his friends, in his old beat-up station wagon.

Maybe she was just being depressed again, but it seemed like things had begun to cool off. And then there were nagging thoughts that hit her—like last week when she and Tom and Lynn had gone out for a drink and there was a man at the bar who kept looking at her and looking at her. And after a couple of drinks, she'd had the thought that she should go over and talk to him.

And then she began to feel guilty about it.

She had thought about Andrew and how she was just not that kind of person and they were just in a tough situation and that everything was going to smooth itself out. All she had to do was hold on and not say or do anything until February. And after that, she'd see what would happen. She'd told herself she shouldn't feel guilty about thinking about picking up some guy in a bar and maybe even taking him home—boy, she was thinking a lot about sex these days. She had really given it a great deal of thought in its absence from her life.

On the other hand, she didn't want to be alone out there.

And as these thoughts were running through her mind, she had watched the guy walk out of the bar.

She slowly stood up and gathered a pad for notes.

She was sitting in the conference room, staring at her pad, thinking about her weekend escape from New York. Andrew's friends had a nice big house and a pool, and they were going to have a big barbecue this evening.

She looked up and watched the new executive editor, who nobody liked, begin his speech by telling everyone in the room that they were incompetent.

Boy, she wouldn't mind getting fired. She could get unemployment. She could take her sweet time looking for another job, maybe even a job with someone human as a boss. She could go on a visit home with Andrew. The summer was almost over and she could be sitting on the porch of her family's hunting lodge, right near the Canadian border, looking at the leaves change around the cool lake, where she and Grandpa fished.

She watched the executive editor's mouth move without a sound. She was still at the lodge.

The meeting seemed to last forever. Every person Henry Foster Morgan had hired recently had nothing but demeaning things to say about anyone who'd worked on *Scope*. Her eyes flashed at Lynn, who was in a losing battle for her job.

"You call that a cover?" Henry bellowed, leaning forward.

"Well I—"

"Look at this. A four-year-old could come up with something better." Henry was snorting at her.

Lynn glared at him, trying to control herself.

"You weren't around to tell me what you wanted."

"Don't give me that. The only thing I have to tell you is that I don't like it."

"Can you at least tell me what it is that bothers you about this one?" Lynn asked, still holding up the board with a perfectly decent cover design.

He'd leaned forward, shaking his head.

"When you give me something, I'll know it."

"I've done eight covers!" she snapped.

"Well do eight more . . . and what the hell is that on the cover?"

"What?"

"That's not the headline. I don't even know what that word means."

Lisa cringed.

"It's dummy type."

"What?"

"It's not a word, it's letters in the right typeface."

"Huh?"

"It's to show placement."

"When the hell did we start doing that?"

"We've always used dummy type."

"Well, why didn't I get a memo on it?"

"Because I didn't think—"

"Well, if you don't think, maybe we'll just have to get someone who can."

The truth of the matter was that the only thing wrong with the cover was that Henry had a friend who wanted Lynn's job.

It was two minutes to five before they were dismissed.

People walked out of the meeting looking as if they had just been interviewed by Torquemada.

Lisa walked tiredly back to her desk and dropped her pad. She plopped down on the chair and kicked off her heels.

At least it was Friday. And Henry had decided to "cover the social scene" from the beach for the rest of next week. He had done this the last two years. At least she could look forward to that.

Lisa leaned over and began tying the laces on her sneakers. She stopped for a moment.

Mrs. Morelli.

Lisa stood up and grabbed her bag. She doubted she'd still be at her desk, but she should at least walk over there. It was nice that they allowed Mrs. Morelli to miss the traffic. She wouldn't want to be almost sixty-five and still being crushed in rush-hour traffic.

She walked down the long hallway. Thank God someone had a decent boss in this place. The vision of Mrs. Morelli going into the office for her appeared in her head.

She owed Mrs. Morelli. The woman had always been nice to her, but standing up to her boss was above and beyond.

She should do something nice for her, bring flowers in on Monday.

She walked into Accounting and over to the desk. She must have gone home. Just as Lisa was turning to leave, she suddenly stared at the desk. Something was not right. She stared at the empty space where the old adding machine had been. Her ashtray was gone. Her chair was left pulled out, and her slippers were nowhere to be seen. She stared at the ghosts of photos and greeting cards that had decorated the woman's wall.

She turned around and stood staring at a young woman who sat across from Mrs. Morelli.

"Where is all of Mrs. Morelli's stuff?"

"Didn't you hear? They fired her this afternoon."

"What?"

"Yeah, can you believe those bastards? Thirty-one years she gave to this company, and one afternoon, wham, it's all gone."

"Oh my God. Why did they fire her? Do you know?"

"Oh, they gave the official reason as leaving early, that she'd left more than three times in the last month. They even came up with memos supposedly showing that she'd been warned about this. I'd told her not to trust Carol. I said all this 'women together' shit would be until you got in her way—she's a barracuda in L'eggs. First, she tells her it's okay and then she fires her by using it as an excuse."

Lisa began to get a sinking feeling.

"What's the real reason?"

"Aw, she says it's 'cause she caught some bigwig padding his expense report and he had her fired for it 'cause she said something."

Lisa stood there frozen as the woman began shaking her head and looking through her handbag.

"You know, you just don't mess with the big guys, I always say. The middle managers you can bring in, but stay away from the big ones. Bastards even took her pension away. . . . Are you feeling okay?"

"I, I . . . can they do that? Take her pension away?"

"It's in the company rules. In the fine print. They don't have to give you nothing, unless you leave in 'good standing.' " She took out a lipstick as Lisa sank into Mrs. Morelli's chair. She watched the woman apply a coat of an odd orange color to her lips, holding up a small mirror as she kept talking.

"Sue the bastards, that's what one guy told her. Take 'em to court and get every cent they got."

"Is she going to do that?" Lisa asked hopefully.

"Ah, I don't think so. It's not worth it. By the time the legal eagles around here get their teeth into it, they could just stall it and stall it. I had a neighbor, fought getting fired in court. Shirley musta been sixty-four when she started the thing. Her old firm's legal department, they dragged it out nine years. By the time she got a settlement, she was seventy-three, owed it all to her lawyers, and she was dead in one week."

Lisa's stomach knotted. It was her fault.

"What a racket, huh?" The woman grimaced, putting the lipstick back in her purse. "You okay?" she asked again.

Lisa nodded as the woman shrugged.

"Well, I gotta get home," the woman said after a moment.

Lisa nodded again and stood up. She walked mechanically to the elevators in silence. The woman next to her kept shaking her head and exhaling.

"How come it only happens to the good people? No husband to look out for her. I'm gonna go over there tonight and see how she is."

"You have her address?" Lisa asked.

"Sure."

"Could you give it to me? I'd really like to go see her."

The elevator door slid open and they both got on as she rifled through her bag for a piece of paper and a pencil.

"Jeez, and on the 'Donahue Show' they can't figure out why there's no company loyalty in America anymore."

Two

That SONOFABEECH. I want him, you hear? I want the sonofabeech dead!"

Rosa Morelli's voice was like nails on a blackboard. It made your fillings hurt.

"He's busy, Rosa—"

"Naw, you don't give me this shit. I want to talk to Solly right now! I want him to send me my Tony."

Ralphie took the phone away from his ear. She'd been calling since three. He exhaled. Rosa was not going to give up until she got through. He knew it. Once she got an idea into her head, she didn't let go. She was like a pit bull when she was angry. Ralphie looked toward the back wall at the closed door. Solly was in a mood today, and getting mixed up with Rosa would be all he needed to take it out on Ralphie.

Ralphie had blown it big that afternoon. He was supposed to meet up with Solly's car in lower Manhattan, then drive to Giuseppe Geddone's union office on account of he was stiffing them on the dues payments. On his way out to meet them, Ralphie had picked up two Channel 11 reporters on his tail and hadn't noticed until

Vesey Street. The bastards had a video camera and everything, and in his heart Ralphie knew there was gonna be another embarrassing "News at Six" report on "Snappy Soltano," New York's "best-dressed don."

Ralphie's mind came back into the club. He could hear Rosa's voice still audible, even through his meaty hand. He was going to have to do something. The way he saw it, he was just as dead if he didn't mention it. He put the phone back to his ear.

". . . and I want his thumbs. And his ears . . ."

"Rosa, whatta you gonna do with his ears?"

"I'm gonna send 'em to his mother. You get him on the phone, or I swear it, I'm gonna make big trouble for you, Ralphie."

He took the phone away. *Stunadze* Sicilian bitch. What's she gonna do? Have little pieces of him torn off, too?

"Rosa, I see what I can do," he said, and smashed the phone down before she could scream back at him.

He stared at Louie behind the bar, watching him brew espresso. The phone rang at once and Louie stared at him. Ralphie shook his head and Louie ignored the ringing.

Ralphie took off his glasses and wiped them with a paper towel. He then wiped his pudgy face. He was sweating now. He stared down at his big pinkie ring and exhaled. He had to do it. He put his glasses back on.

He tapped as gently as he could on the door. After a moment, it was opened and Ralphie walked in. He stood staring at Solly behind his desk. He was on his private line. He crossed his hands respectfully in front of him as Solly placed a hand over the receiver.

"What?" he barked at him.

He cleared his throat. "Rosa Morelli been calling for

two hours. She's real upset. She wants Tony to come up to her house right away."

"So?" he snapped, then immediately added, "What she want with Tony?"

"She wants him to kill some guy at her office and take his thumbs and ears to send to his mother."

Solly's eyes bulged.

"Go," he said, tilting his head.

Ralphie nodded and backed out of the room.

Solly hung up the phone and dialed Rosa. The line was busy. He hung up and stared at the desk.

Son of a bitch. Thirty-three years he'd been paying for Gino's death, and it wasn't even his fault. Gino'd been a hothead, a real jedrool. Go *talk* to the PR on a Hun' four street about selling crap from Nunzio at half price. . . . Gino'd walked in with two pistols. Got himself all shot up on the avenue, and somehow, in Rosa's mind, Solly owed her.

Gino'd been a distant cousin by marriage, and Rosa was his wife, which made her even more removed from the Soltanos, but you wouldn't know it from the way she talked to Solly. You'd think she was blood.

It was the women. She'd gotten in tight with the women. His own wife looked after Rosa better than she did her own sister.

Thirty-three years of phone calls—Con Ed, the phone company, the dry cleaners, the grocer. Every time she got it into her head she'd been done wrong, he was supposed to hack people up for her.

Some days Solly wondered whether Gino hadn't gotten himself blown away just to get away from her.

This afternoon, he didn't need it. He didn't have the time to listen to her scream for an hour, then come up with something that would appease her and all the wives. He couldn't let Tony go up there. Then he'd lose him to her craziness. He needed Tony to run up to Harlem and straighten out Giuseppe Geddone.

Acid began to churn in his stomach as the *agita* set in. Fuckin' Ralphie! That shit shoulda been cleared up this morning. He reached into his desk drawer, took out a roll of Rolaids, and popped two in his mouth. They exploded from the pressure between his teeth.

How could a grown man miss a black van with a Channel 11 logo, three feet high in reflective white lettering?

Some days Solly felt as if he was surrounded by morons. He stared at his nails. He should get Georgie up; he was due for another manicure. Ralphie, Tony Mac . . . His mind flashed on Tony's cousin Michael Bonello.

He swallowed the last of the Rolaids and took out his silk pocket handkerchief, wiped his forehead, then carefully refolded it and put it back in the breast pocket of his Armani suit.

He picked up the phone again and dialed Rosa's. He could see her stomping through her house to get to the phone, her face as red as her hair. Why she dyed her hair red, anyhows?

"Ralphie?"

Solly winced as he heard her voice deep in his fillings.

"Rosa? It's me, Solly. Whadda you scream at Ralphie for, huh?" This was the only way to handle her. Let her know you were annoyed, right from the start.

"Solly . . ." she said, and then she did something that in all the years Solly had known her he'd never heard her do.

She cried.

* * *

If muscles were brains, then Tony Macarelli would've been a Nobel laureate. Standing, he was six foot five and weighed 290. He was a solid walking wall. His body was so built up that he had to have his suits and shirts made for him, as his arms were short, his chest unbelievably wide, and his neck so thick, you swore his shoulders began at his chin. His face was flat, his forehead high, and his nose went off at an angle. He kept his hair cropped short and respectable and carried himself with power.

He was known by the name Tony Macaroni, or Tony Mac, in the neighborhood. He'd always been called that, probably because the stuff didn't seem to make a dent in his voracious appetite. Michael had sat through many a meal as a kid amazed, watching his cousin go through bowls of ziti as if they were water. Five serving bowls later and Tony would be ready for "the meat."

They'd been sitting in the car outside of Solly's club on Mulberry Street for the past two hours. Michael's side of the front seat looked clean and neat. Tony's looked like an explosion in a junk-food factory.

"Jeez, how can you eat that stuff? You know what they put in it?"

"You gotta keep your stren'th up," Tony'd mumbled through his eleventh Ring-Ding.

"So, what do you think he wants us to take care of?" Michael asked, trying to keep his voice steady.

"Ah, I dunno. Probably a little muscle. This is a big chance for you. He don't let just nobody make their bones," Tony said in a voice filled with reverence.

Solly was Tony's idol. East Harlem was not known for producing many rocket scientists or statesmen; you were either a wiseguy, a priest, a cop, or a junkie. Looking at him now, Michael realized that if it hadn't been for Solly, Tony probably would've gone the junkie route. He wasn't schooled enough for the other options.

Michael was a special case—he'd gotten out, gotten an education, he thought, then shuddered, embarrassed. Yeah, he was a special case all right. That's why he was sitting here now, he thought bitterly.

And, good, bad, or whatever, if it hadn't been for Tony, Michael wouldn't have survived in the neighborhood. That fact was part of the reason he was sitting here in all this trouble. His eyes slid over and he watched Tony crumple up another Ring-Ding wrapper. He could pinpoint when all this craziness with Tony and the Soltanos and himself had begun. The memory of a football game sixteen years before came into Michael's mind as if it were yesterday.

Tony had been a tackle on the East Harlem Boys Football team. He was already five foot nine and two hundred pounds then. He was great for the team. On the field with the rest of the normal-sized fifteen- and sixteen-year-olds, Tony looked kind of like Gulliver, playing for the Lilliputians. No one wanted to get near him.

Michael had been short and skinny for fifteen, but he'd been fast as a streak of lightning, short enough to be just below eye level for most players. Michael was almost never touched during a game. He was their ace wide end and safety.

Actually, they'd played very few games, mostly because no one wanted to play the East Harlem Boys Football team as a whole. Winning a game from the team could mean getting stabbed in the locker room, or worse, they'd go after your family. The team motto was "Lose the Game, Win the Fight."

In addition to Tony, the team had been loaded with psychotics like Lead Pipe Raguso. Lead Pipe had played tackle and would tape a piece of pipe to his arm, under his uniform. Then he'd stand still on the field, waiting for some kid to start tearing toward him. He'd never move a muscle. He'd wait until they were two steps in front of him, just till he could see their eyes, and then he'd step aside, stick the arm out, and let the kid break his neck.

In 1975, *Time* magazine had done an article on organized crime, citing the ten most dangerous men in America. Michael recognized eight of them from the team.

It had been an ugly game, informally thrown together before the "real" one during the weekend. There were no referees; they were playing a league from the Bronx that was just as dangerous as they were.

They had been pounded in the last quarter, but they'd tied 8 to 8. They were in the final play; the sun was setting and the temperature had dropped. Michael remembered shivering in his uniform.

They'd broken huddle and gotten into formation for what they called their "tomato surprise" play.

"Hut one, hut two, pass!" Lead Pipe had passed the ball to Michael, who passed it back between his legs and then took off. Lead Pipe stuffed the ball under his shirt as Michael made a wide circle on the right side. Tony barreled ahead, making a clean, body-free path for Michael as everyone ran circles around the other team and made moves like they had the ball.

Lead Pipe circled around to the left, almost unnoticed, bent over and wobbling like he was hurt in order to conceal the ball. He was supposed to wait until Michael got right to the goal line and then toss it to Michael, who'd make the touchdown.

It would've worked, but the Bronx team's tackle, a kid nearly Tony's size, had caught sight of the bulge under Lead Pipe's shirt and took off after Michael. Lead Pipe tossed the ball before he realized the tackle was on to them, and Tony was way the hell on the other side of the field, leaving Michael with no protection.

Michael caught it, and then this huge guy appeared from nowhere. Michael held on to the ball for dear life as he wove and bobbed around the tackle, just out of reach. In a sudden sprint, the tackle charged him; Michael ducked and made it across the goal line.

He was just about to toss the ball up in the air to declare victory when the tackle broadsided him, knocking him down and all of the wind out of him.

"You fuckin' cheater!" The tackle kept screaming as he lay on top of him and punched him in the ribs like a machine, every blow worse and worse until the sharp, splintering pains of cracked ribs followed each blow.

The next thing that happened was just a fuzzy memory for Michael. He remembered Tony screaming, "Mikey, look out!" And suddenly the weight was pulled off of him and the blows stopped. He pulled his sore body up, wheezing, and stared frozenly at Tony.

He and the kid were wrestling for control of a razor. It was the rusty blade of a broken barber's tool, the kind the old men were shaved with in neighborhood shops. The edge had been honed shiny and the handle had been padded with a rag and some electrical tape to make it easier to hold.

Michael couldn't move. He ached, and with every breath the pains grabbed at his chest sharply. He looked around to see whether anyone saw what was going on. Across the street sat Ralphie and Solly's driver, chatting, oblivious.

Just as Michael tried to motion to them, Tony slammed the kid back with one big push, but the kid was like a cat. He bounced back to his feet, razor in hand, and began circling Tony.

"What are you doin' here?" Tony boomed out at the kid.

Suddenly, the kid lunged and got Tony, not deeply enough to cause serious damage but deeply enough to draw blood. Tony looked down at his chest, at the wide opening where the fabric had been cut and was now exposing his skin. Tony felt with his hand and stared, almost puzzled at the blood, as if it wasn't his but something someone had spilled on him.

"You cut me," he said, amazed.

And then something had happened that Michael would never forget. He saw "the look." Tony's eyes slightly crossed and his face scrunched up as if he was in pain, and Michael's blood went cold.

"You tried to cut up my cousin over a touchdown and you cut me—you don't fuckin' do that."

Michael remembered the next couple of moments in that weird way you do when you are frozen with fear—in both slow motion and in the blink of an eye, all at the same time. He'd watched Tony grab the kid, spin him around effortlessly like a dance partner, and, holding one arm up behind his back, he'd grabbed the hand the razor was in and just as effortlessly pulled the blade up to the kid's neck and began to push it into the skin. Michael felt himself tense at the memory of the look on the kid's face:

puzzlement and amazement and absolute terror, then a wince as the blade began to cut his skin.

Tony was just about to pull it across the kid's neck when finally other voices broke through the moment. Michael looked up to see Ralphie and the Soltanos' driver.

"Eh kid, this is a game, *capisce*?"

"He tried to kill my fuckin' cousin. . . ."

"Look, you gotta stop it," Ralphie counseled.

"*Stunadze*, you gonna drop him here? In the middle of a playing field with all these witnesses?" the driver asked.

"I can't do nothin' else," Tony answered matter-of-factly.

Michael watched Ralphie and the driver exchange odd glances and then look back in awe at Tony.

"Drop it or I'll shoot you," the driver said just as matter-of-factly. "Why don't we go somewhere and talk?"

Maybe it was the threat of being shot, or maybe it wasn't, but they watched Tony take the blade away and push the kid down on the ground. The kid scampered off into the crowd that had gathered.

But no matter why Tony had chosen to drop it, the one thing that Michael and Ralphie and the driver knew was that Tony would've had no problem at all cutting the kid's throat and then going home to eat.

There was that look in his face: a steel-cold emptiness behind his eyes, a deadness that could not distinguish a human being from, say, a gnat. It was a frightening glitch in Tony's psyche.

Michael owed him his life from then on. Although Tony never said anything or asked for any favors back, he was owed, and Michael knew the day would come for the payback. But more importantly, it was at that moment,

Michael believed, that he'd watched Tony get hand-picked by the Soltanos.

Solly did appreciate Tony's strength. He was soon giving Tony jobs to make his bones in the business. Run a bag up to the Bronx, visit Mordy Soloman for payments—Tony did it without question.

But the thing that put him in was taking a fall for one of Solly's cousins during a fur heist in Brooklyn.

It had been a walk-through case. The doors to the warehouse had been left unlocked; all they had to do was load the truck. They had just gotten there, hadn't even opened the truck, when Solly's cousin, a real putz, began playing with his gun and hit the alarm box. A patrol car must have been right around the corner, because they were there in what seemed like two seconds.

As everyone scattered, Tony grabbed the guy's gun and yelled at him to run. Tony was left there alone.

And that was when Tony really made his biggest impression on Solly. They couldn't make the robbery charge stick, so they found something else. The unlicensed gun Tony was carrying carried with it a mandatory one-year sentence.

And Tony did the stand-up thing and kept his mouth shut, and did a year at Rikers.

Michael looked at his face, with his weird, off-kilter nose. And that, Michael thought in awe, was the only thing Tony had to show for the whole year—a broken nose, from a guard the first week inside.

Other than that, Tony talked about Rikers the way Michael talked about working in the college cafeteria. Yeah, it was a sewer, and you had to be careful of certain people, and the hours sucked, but if you stuck around long enough, you might learn something.

Tony was "made" by the time he was nineteen. And in his mind, he owed it all to Solly.

He liked driving Solly around. He didn't mind straightening out people for Solly; it came naturally to Tony. In return, Tony now had respect. He earned a good living, had nice clothes, drove a nice car.

So whatever Solly wanted must be right, right?

And that was when the whole mess began.

Michael stared out the window at the little churchyard across from Solly's place. The sun was out, but it was raining. It had to be around five. He stretched his legs out in front of him. Yeah, Solly was good for Tony.

Michael had no idea why he was here.

No, he knew why. It was because two years ago, three things had happened that changed his entire life.

First, he'd screwed up at law school.

The picture of a third-year midterm being waved around a small office materialized in front of his eyes.

"Mr. Bonello, I don't know what you take us for, but this is inexcusable."

"Professor Birnbaum, I really don't know what you mean. That paper is my work—"

He'd tossed it on the desk contemptuously and picked up another blue-covered exam booklet and threw it in front of him. Michael kept his eyes on it.

"Go ahead. Open it up. Read a passage. Almost any passage."

Michael had taken up the booklet and opened it. He pretended to read a page.

"Yes?"

"It's word-for-word in most places. Do you know whose exam this is?"

Michael shook his head.

"It's the work of the woman sitting directly to your left. How do you account for this?"

"Coincidence?"

It wasn't. But it was the only thing he could think of. Of course the work was the same. Jessica had begged him—in bed, out of bed. She'd worn him down one way or another until he finally gave in just to keep her quiet. What would be the harm?

He just hadn't thought it through. And he never, ever expected her to copy word-for-word. Shit, no one was that stupid. He stared up at Professor Birnbaum. She'd been called in an hour earlier, and, judging by the tone of his voice, it had hardly been in defense of him.

He was brought up to a reviewing board to bounce him out of NYU Law so fast, he didn't know what hit him. What it came down to was her word against his, and Jessica Fine's word was taken as true and Michael Bonello's was taken as lying.

Jessica turned out to be a real piece of work. He called her apartment and left crazed, pleading messages with a roommate who seemed to be under the impression that he had copied from Jessica. When that didn't work, he resolved to track her down.

The last time he saw her was a fall afternoon, late. The sun had turned the trees across the street in Washington Square Park a golden red. And Michael sat shivering in the shadow of the NYU law library. He pulled his jacket around him tightly as a cold wind blew against him and watched the peaceful sights of young mothers pushing infants in strollers, being escorted home by dancing older children, excitedly telling them of their day in school.

A woman with familiar dark hair passed quickly, and

Michael jumped off the ledge and grabbed Jessica by the arm.

"What!" she began, and her face went pale as she looked at him. He was rumpled and unshaven.

"You gotta tell them the truth," he said hoarsely.

He watched her face turn from a scared pale to a stony-cold statue's face.

"Leave me alone."

"Jessica, they are going to throw me out this afternoon unless you show up at the meeting."

"So, what do you want me to do?" She shook his hand free.

"Tell them the truth! Damn it, I've worked my whole life for this. My father—" His voice cracked.

"I told them the truth."

His jaw dropped. That was it—it was over.

"You lying bitch," he murmured, scarcely able to inhale.

"You stay away from me, Michael Bonello, or I swear I'll get a lawyer." She turned and walked stiffly away from him, and as she did it was as if Michael was watching his whole life and his last chance to really get out fade with each step she took.

The final meeting, where the board voted unanimously to expel him, seemed to go by in a flash, for something so monumentally life-altering.

He was out and it was put permanently on his record.

Michael walked around New York for a month in a dismal, mostly drunken haze. His whole life had been shot down by a Long Island princess.

He remembered a big bash in New Jersey. His nickname in the neighborhood was "College." He was trotted out in front of Solly with the same pride that Tony was.

That was saying a lot, considering that, as far as Michael knew, his father was little more than a bookkeeper for some of the Soltanos' regular businesses, and Tony helped run the street for the Soltanos.

Michael was going to be the first legit Bonello on American soil. And suddenly, it was all over.

He'd stayed drinking at bars on the Lower West Side—bars where he knew there'd be no chance in hell of running into anyone from the neighborhood. He knew he had to tell his father. He also knew it would destroy him.

That was when the second thing happened.

Michael'd been sleeping one off when the phone call came from his mother.

She was at Brooklyn Memorial. She was crying so hard, she forgot how to speak English. It took him five minutes to connect *padre* and *morte* together.

The first thing he did was throw up. He shaved, put on his best clean shirt, trousers, and jacket. He stopped off for a drink to quell his nausea, and then took a cab to Brooklyn.

It was like walking in on a nightmare as he stood outside the morgue door, staring through a small glass window at his mother, weeping over his father's body. This was just not right. It wasn't right. Everything was happening so fast, so frighteningly fast.

She'd been sitting by her husband in the morgue for a couple of hours by the time Michael showed. It took him fifteen minutes to get her out of the cold tiled place.

That evening, his father was lying in a funeral home, and Michael was sitting at their kitchen table in Brooklyn, surrounded by women, most dressed head to foot in black, swapping widowhood stories in Italian.

He and Tony slipped out, Tony grimacing at him as they walked into a bar.

"Your mother ain't gonna like you drinking, Mikey. It ain't good for you."

"Uh-huh," was all he said as he downed several shots of whiskey.

"So what you gonna do, Mikey?"

"I don't know, Tony. I don't know anything. . . . What do you think I should do?" he asked absentmindedly.

"Maybe I could hook something up for you."

"Yeah, sure, that would be great," he remembered answering—sarcastically, he had thought—but he was on his fifth whiskey in less than an hour.

Sophia Bonello didn't or wouldn't or couldn't speak a word of English for two days. Into the third day of viewing, they were seated in front of the coffin at the Cardarelli funeral home near Oyster Bay.

They were in one of the larger rooms, filled with black folding chairs, the windowless walls covered in brownish red velvet. A red light bulb placed behind the open casket kept your eyes stuck to it.

They'd been staring at this thing that had begun to look like a bizarre table decoration. Michael had stood over it again and again, trying to reconcile the man in the casket with his father.

It didn't look like his father. Pop never had had red, red lips. And he'd never had skin that color. He didn't like cut flowers, either. He'd told Michael once that they reminded him of funerals, and here he was, bathed in them. Among the baskets and bouquets of flowers, a huge cross of snapdragons and white mums stood at the head of the coffin. At the foot, white carnations formed a large horseshoe, onto which was tied a big black satin bow.

Michael had first thought that one was a mistake until he looked at the card.

It was from a bookie who'd owed Pop.

People had filed past them each day from eight in the morning till nine at night, with a special private showing for Solly and his family. Mass cards were everywhere on the black stands on either side of the box. And since that had filled up fast, they had begun tossing them inside and on top of the coffin. The red light reflected off the plastic-coated ones lying on his father's chest, giving him the eerie impression of breathing. There were so many by the end of the thing that Michael figured every church in the metropolitan area was going to be busy blessing Vincent Bonello for the next year.

Why not? Pop was popular in the neighborhood. He'd been a good man. There was always an extra place to be made at his table, always an extra buck if one was needed. Yeah, he was known for being a bit of a pushover on money. But that was part of having a good heart.

He never wanted Michael, his only child, to grow up doing what he did. He wanted him to be main-line American—a lawyer or doctor, something with dignity. He sent him to private schools, made sure he kept his grades up, and kept spoken Italian to a minimum in the house.

The morning of the third day, his mother, puffy-eyed and wearing the black uniform she'd be in for the rest of her life, looked over at Michael and finally spoke English.

"You gonna get in trouble with your school for being out like this?"

"No," he replied flatly.

He took his mother's hands and they both sat in silence as Father D'Amico made the sign of the cross as the mortician's assistants sealed the coffin.

It was all so final, Michael thought. What had happened to the second chances of his childhood? And why was it that when a terrible thing happened in life, it took such an unfeeling split second instead of the long time it should merit because of its importance and ramifications?

Tony silently drove them to the burial site and stayed by the car during the brief ceremony. Mourners returned to their cars, leaving Sophia and Michael holding on to each other's hands in silence.

"Come on, Ma, let's go," he said finally, choking on the words.

She looked up at him, her eyes filled with tears, and silently he dropped her hands and made his way back to the car, giving her time to say her last good-bye to her husband in privacy.

He was weeping when he got to the car, and Tony gave him his handkerchief. They stood leaning against the car as Michael tried to pull himself together.

"I don't know what I'm going to do," he murmured, and glanced at Tony.

A big smile moved across Tony's face, and that was when the third thing happened.

"Don't worry, Mikey, I got you taken care of. Solly says take some days, then come in when you're ready."

"What?" he asked, not following.

"You said you needed a job in the bar. . . . I had to pull a lot of strings, but I got it okayed." Tony put an arm around Michael's back and gave a quick hug that nearly dislocated his shoulder. "I'm gonna teach you everything I know. You got a job. Solly's gonna take care of you, just like he does me."

So now he owed Tony twice—once for his life and now for his "new career."

Michael sat dumbfounded as Tony drove them back to the city. He thought he'd been sarcastic. He never expected Tony to take him seriously. He felt his palms get wet, and he began to think about it. What were his options? He was going to tell someone who kills for a living that he didn't want this "favor"? After all, if he didn't accept and Tony was made to look like a jerk . . . He couldn't think about that.

By the time they reached New York, Michael was resigned to having to accept Tony's offer, at least for now. He'd just be real smart about it. He'd keep a low profile, ride with Tony for a couple of weeks, and then slide out of it. After all, his father had never gotten deeply mired. He'd managed to dance on the outside. If Pop could weave and dodge not getting involved with the dirty side of the business, he certainly could. He could prove he was Vincent's son.

That had been two years ago.

A tap on the window brought him back to the present. He rolled down his window and looked up at Ralphie.

"He wants to see youse now."

Lisa threw a bathing suit into her small overnight bag and went into the bathroom. She took down all the stuff Andrew referred to as "that face crap" and tossed it into a plastic Gristede's supermarket bag. She walked back into the bedroom and dropped the bag into the overnight case. She zipped up the whole thing and carried it into the living room. She should set the answering machine. Otherwise, she'd never hear the end of it from Andrew.

She leaned over it and was just about to press the message record button when instead she went over to her handbag and took out a piece of paper. She picked up the receiver and began to dial the smeary number the woman at the office had given her. A rough, coughing voice came over the line.

"Yeah?"

"Mrs. Morelli, please."

"Who's this?"

"Mrs. Morelli? This is Lisa Johnson, Henry Foster Morgan's secretary . . . from the office?"

"Yeah . . ."

"I just heard. I am so sorry. . . . I was wondering if you'd mind if I dropped by for a moment this evening?"

There was a muted sound on the other end.

"All right. When you think you gonna be here?"

"Within the hour."

"All right." The line clicked dead.

Lisa hung up and then stared at a photo of Andrew and her on vacation four years before. She stared at Andrew's face.

He had piercing blue eyes and sandy blond hair. He was wearing a Lacoste shirt, British navy shorts, and Top-Siders. He looked like a walking ad for Ralph Lauren.

On to Connecticut, she thought. She turned on the answering machine and left the apartment.

Getting out this weekend was going to do her a world of good, Lisa thought as she waited by the elevator. It was going to be fun to be around new people and do something besides sit inside and watch television. And barbecues were her favorite. The elevator opened and Lisa got on, and for the first time all day she really gave herself a smile in anticipation of two whole days of pools and trees and hamburgers and fun people.

* * *

Rosa Morelli lit a cigarette and took a swig from the glass of cola in front of her. She stared up, red-eyed, at her nephew—her wonderful godson Tony.

"She's comin' up here in the hour." She nodded to Tony and then darted a glance over to his cousin Michael. "She'll lead you to the sonofabeech."

Lisa took the car out of the garage on Seventy-fourth Street and stared at the address.

One nineteen Pleasant Avenue.

She drove the car up the ramp. She was going to tell her how sorry she was.

She should buy flowers.

She pulled up at a red light on Third and Eightieth and looked over at a Korean fruit stand on the corner. A nice large bunch of speckled tiger lilies caught her eye. By the time the light had turned green, she had the bunch lying next to her on the front seat. She continued driving, stop and start in the heavy traffic.

The flowers began to bother her.

Well, Lisa thought, she'll get another job and . . . Then it hit her. Where was a sixty-four-year-old woman going to find a job? Who was going to hire someone only a few months away from retirement?

She had no family except for some godson. Who knew if the kid even lived nearby. She was all alone. Seriously, Lisa speculated, how was she going to get along?

And then Lisa felt even worse, realizing just what kind of a sacrifice had been made because she was too scared or too cowardly or . . . guilty. She was feeling guilty.

Flowers were not going to cut it.

Money. What she had to do was offer her money—without making her sound like a charity case. And she could darn well do other things—maybe help her around the house, do her resume. Lisa made a list in her head.

She swung back around to First Avenue. The woman from the office had assured her that Pleasant Avenue was up here, on the East Side, and she could easily find it.

She had five hundred dollars in her savings account. How could she offer it to Mrs. Morelli?

Maybe if she just said it was a loan?

That was always what her mom did with her Uncle Joe, and heck, he never paid back a cent, or at least that's what her dad always said.

The neighborhood began to change as she left the nineties. Tall, low-income housing projects mushroomed along the littered streets. The sun was beginning to set and she just wanted to find Pleasant Avenue. Three tattered men pulled aside a piece of tin covering the doorway of a burned-out building, and Lisa watched them slip inside. She shivered slightly as she caught sight of a fat gray rat foraging in a pile of garbage near a fire hydrant. The hydrant was open, lazily splashing water over an old mattress.

All right, so where am I? she thought, trying to take her mind off the devastation she was seeing.

Okay, she could say, "You know, I have this extra money just sitting around, not doing anything, and you could probably use a little something—until you get another job."

Another job. She felt herself wince. No, better not bring that up.

Her mind snapped back to the streets. Rows of burned-out buildings were separated by vacant lots with garbage piled high. It reminded her a little of pictures she'd seen of London during the Blitz.

Okay, so she wouldn't go see her family this winter. She swallowed. At least she had Andrew. Well, five hundred was all she could afford to offer her, but at least it was something—certainly better than a lousy bunch of tiger lilies.

She turned down a street next to a small park to get onto Pleasant Avenue but got stopped behind a car. As her eyes began to focus on the block, she felt a bit startled.

At the far end, there were several quaint little houses, some with garages and little yards out front. The street was packed with limousines: three, four, five, eight of them, parked and double-parked.

She stared at a small, beat-up-looking church.

There must be a wedding, with all these expensive cars lined up. Or a funeral . . .

She was looking for the hearse when a man in a dark suit, who'd been leaning against one of the limos ahead of her, walked over to the car. He tapped on the window and she rolled it down.

"This street's closed," he announced in an accent that sounded exactly like Mrs. Morelli's.

"Funeral?" she asked.

"Street's closed," he repeated testily.

"Well, fine. I'm looking for Pleasant Avenue?"

"Go across a Hun' sixteen," he barked, and then walked away.

Lisa backed out onto First Avenue. She lucked out and found a spot right in front of the building. She took the flowers and looked at her overnight bag in the front seat. Her eyes darted around the street. Oh well, she'd only be inside a couple of minutes, and who would break into a car in daylight? She locked the doors and made her way to the building.

She was standing in the airless foyer of the tenement building where Mrs. Morelli lived. She peeked outside the scraped-up piece of plastic someone had glued into the front door. Her car was still there.

"Mrs. Morelli?" Lisa screamed into a staticky intercom.

"Who wants her?" a voice barked back.

"It's Lisa Johnson, from her office."

The box clicked off and she waited, holding the flowers.

Nothing had prepared her for the inside of the building. Here she was in the middle of this run-down, dangerous neighborhood, and all the apartment doors had big glass windows in them, some with lace curtains, others covered with old wooden venetian blinds. The halls were spotless. Flat white paint with a shiny green border looked new. There was not a speck of grit, not even in the cracks of the old blue and white tile floor. A huge skylight poured sunshine down the center shaft of the building, flooding the white marble stairs with light.

The smells of pine cleaner mixed with smells of cooking. Aromas of tomato sauces, boiling pasta, roast beef, and chicken wafted out from behind the doors and hovered in the center of the stairwell.

A few eerie notes, picked out on piano keys, began playing as she stepped on the first step. The swingy, smooth sound of a Frank Sinatra recording filled the hallway. She continued up the stairs as horns kicked in. Sinatra's voice rang out as she reached the second-floor landing.

She felt a little fluttery as she continued her climb, listening hard to the song.

"The best is yet to come, come the day you're mine, and you're *gonna* be mine . . ."

She was finding the lyrics slightly menacing, and his voice faded away as she reached the third-floor landing.

She rapped on the door. It was opened a crack and Lisa looked up at a steel-toned eye.

"Who?"

"I'm Lisa Johnson. . . . I'm . . . I'm looking for Mrs. Morelli," she stammered.

The door was shut. She heard voices inside but couldn't make them out. After a moment or two, the door was opened again. She stared up at the largest human being she'd ever seen up close.

He was massive. There had been a guy in college on the basketball team who was probably taller, but no one bigger. His chest blocked her view of the entire apartment.

"What do you want?"

"I came to—is Mrs. Morelli here?" she asked, half-hoping she had the wrong apartment.

"Tony, let her in," Mrs. Morelli's voice said, and he stepped aside.

They were standing in the kitchen of a railroad apartment. Blue teapots and little cups adorned the wallpaper. Venetian blinds covered by ruffled plastic window curtains decorated the windows. An old circular fan sat on the sill, agedly blowing in air from the opened window. There was a cold cast to the room from a lone circular fluorescent light set in the middle of a stamped tin ceiling. A clock ticked loudly above a pillowy old-fashioned refrigerator.

Mrs. Morelli had a handkerchief in her hand. She was sitting at a small old Formica table, the kind with flecks of gold suspended in a blood red background. Lisa walked over to the table and set the flowers down.

Mrs. Morelli looked terrible. Her eyes were puffy and her face was red. An overflowing ashtray sat in front of her, alongside a half-empty gallon bottle of Coca-cola.

"Oh Mrs. Morelli, I don't . . . I'm *so* sorry."

"Sit," she said, motioning.

Lisa sank down into the chair opposite her, then heard a cough. She twisted around and stared at a second man, standing in the darkened living room. He was smaller than the big man. He was normal-sized.

She turned back to Mrs. Morelli and cleared her throat.

"I'm responsible for this, I know," Lisa began, feeling stupid. "If only I'd have gone in there. If only I wasn't so scared of him. I hate myself for what happened."

"Who'd have known the bastard would . . ." Mrs. Morelli's voice trailed off.

"You want me to get you something to eat, Aunt Rosa?" Tony asked, leaning down over her.

He almost made her seem pale and delicate.

"No, Tony. I don't want nothing. I ain't hungry. I ain't hungry. I ain't ever gonna be hungry again!" she said, her voice rising as she got up. "He sentenced me to a life of poverty! My last years, my golden years, spent in shame, trying to feed myself. I wanna die! I wanna die! He stole my money—that SONOFABEECH."

It was the damnedest thing: Lisa's fillings hurt.

Guilt overwhelmed her. Even if she offended Mrs. Morelli, she had to try to offer her some money.

"It's all my fault. Oh God. Listen, whatever I can do,

just tell me. I could help you do your resume or help out around the house." She swallowed. "Look, I don't want to offend you, but do you need money?"

Mrs. Morelli looked at her oddly. "Whatta you talking about?"

Lisa brightened a bit.

"Well, I was thinking, you probably need some money to tide you over, and I have five hundred dollars in my savings account." She watched Mrs. Morelli's eyes dart to her nephew. She said something in Italian to him, and the other man came up behind her.

"I don't want your money! I want the bastard dead!" she snapped.

"Believe me, I know. People like that don't deserve to live. If you knew how many times I wished he'd . . . he'd get run over or something, just die, so I don't have to listen to him. . . . I mean, why does he have the right to do things like this, huh? Why? Because he's wealthy? I'll tell you something, if he was dying on a street corner, I don't think I'd bend over to help him. I'd let him just bleed to death in the gutter. Some days, I think . . . I think about sending him a really nasty letter. . . . I—" Lisa stopped as she caught sight of the smaller man trying desperately to stifle a smirk. "What's so funny?" she demanded.

"Nothing," Michael said quietly.

His accent was softer than the others'.

"Well, I'm angry," she snapped.

"I know you are."

Lisa turned back to Mrs. Morelli, embarrassed. She'd flown off the handle. The tension of the last couple of days seemed to well up inside her and burst. She exhaled and sat down.

"Anything I can do to help, please, please, tell me."

Mrs. Morelli shot a glance up at Tony.

"Anything? You'd do anything to help me?"

"Just name it. Just you name it," she said, leaning forward in her chair.

"You know where he'll be tonight?"

"Well . . . not offhand."

"Could you find out for me?"

Lisa stared at her. "Are you going to go talk to him?"

"My godson Tony and his cousin Michael gonna talk to him," she said calmly. "Now, you tell us where he'll be at."

"Well, I'd have to look in his appointment book. What are you going to say to him?" she asked, looking at Tony.

"I'm gonna tell him to give my Aunt Rosa back her full pension," Tony said, blinking down at her.

There was an odd look to his eyes. They almost looked crossed, or as if they didn't really focus on anything.

"You don't know Henry Foster Morgan. He's a pretty nasty man. What if, you know," she said, lowering her voice, "he doesn't *do* it?"

Tony slowly leaned down over her, and she suddenly felt herself sinking lower and lower in her folding chair, feeling as if she was very small as his oversized face got close to hers.

" 'Cause I'm gonna kill him on the spot if he don't."

Lisa sat in the kind of silent confusion you feel when you hear something so outrageously out of the realm of what you consider possible that your brain temporarily gets derailed. She looked at Mrs. Morelli, who stared at her calmly as she squashed out her cigarette in the ashtray. She couldn't see the other man. She looked back at Tony. It was as if his eyes were dead.

"Um," she squeaked. "What makes you think he'll keep his word?"

" 'Cause we're going back to his office, and he gonna put through the paperwork and sign a check over for all the trouble he caused." Tony's breath was hot against her cheek and smelled faintly of chocolate.

"He could just . . . cancel the check and tear up the paper on Monday," she said with a flutter.

"I don't think so."

"Why?"

"He's gonna have a accident right after he signs."

Her neck craned back as he straightened up, and she felt a little dizzy. She stared straight ahead at his belt buckle and then stared over at Mrs. Morelli and the other man. Her mind raced through what was being said. Of course, over the years she'd joked around about killing her boss, just the way everybody did who had a boss like hers, but there was something about the way these people were talking . . .

She stood up.

"I know just how you feel," she said, pointing a finger at Mrs. Morelli. She picked up her bag. "And he really deserves it, too. Well, my car's illegally parked and I have to be in Connecticut tonight for a barbecue and—"

Tony blocked the front door and the other man stood, his arms crossed, staring at her.

They were not laughing.

"Where is this appointment book you was talking about?" Mrs. Morelli snapped. Her voice was harsh.

"Look, you can't be serious. I mean, you can't kill a man because he fired you."

She felt Tony's large hands rest heavily on her shoulders. She wiggled free and looked up at him and then over at Mrs. Morelli.

"He deserves it. You said so yourself. 'Cause he's bad for people."

"Yes, but . . . you could take him to court, get a lawyer—"

"I'll be dead before they give it back to me. Where's the book?" she demanded, motioning to Tony.

She felt his huge hands wrap easily around her upper arms, like manacles.

"Hey, wait one darned minute." She struggled.

"Tell us where the book is," the other man ordered, stepping in front of her.

She stared into his eyes and he looked away quickly, as if he was embarrassed. Tony tightened his grip on her until all the blood seemed to get cut off from her lower arms.

"Where is it?" the other man demanded, carefully avoiding her look.

"It's in his lower desk drawer, but it's locked!" she yelled at them.

Tony loosened his grip. They were all silent.

"What do we do now, Aunt Rosa?" Tony asked in a deep voice after a moment.

"What are you? *Stunadze?* Take her to the office. She got the keys for all them drawers," Rosa snapped.

"Okay, Aunt Rosa," Tony said as the other man opened the apartment door.

Lisa found herself being lifted off the floor like a rag doll and swung toward the door. Suddenly, Tony turned back to Mrs. Morelli, and Lisa felt her feet swinging out.

"Don' you worry, Aunt Rosa. I'm gonna take care of

you. I love you. I'll be back wid what he owes . . . and the rat bastard's ears so you can send 'em to his mutha."

Lisa looked in horror at Mrs. Morelli, then at the other man, who turned his face away.

Michael held his gun up right below her chin as they sped down Fifth Avenue in the Cadillac. He could feel her whole body shaking as he held one arm. She began squirming, and he looked over into her eyes. They were pretty green eyes. They were filled with terror and disgust at him. He looked away.

He was frantically having conversations with Vincent in his head, thinking, Pop, Pop, how did you do it? How did you dance on the edge with these guys for so long without becoming one of them? Where did you find that line?

He kept going back to when he was a kid. His father's pie-plate-shaped face appeared slightly above his eye level. His crown of dark hair, cropped to less than half an inch on his head, his steady dark eyes, straight nose, rounded and spread out at the nostrils, and Santa Claus cheeks stared deadpan back at Michael.

"Your father's a bookkeeper." His mother's voice floated past the two of them, and Michael again saw his father slowly nod up and down, keeping Michael's eyes on him. And at the time, being a child, he didn't question anything. But there had been a hint of something in his father's eyes, something a nine-year-old couldn't put his finger on.

Now he knew what had been in his father's eyes. It had been embarrassment and shame. Maybe he hadn't carried it on his sleeve each day, but at that moment, having to lie to his own son, it must have bubbled up in him, because Michael suddenly remembered that it was not long after that he was transferred to a school outside of the neighborhood.

And suddenly, Michael realized that he'd been kidding himself. Kidding himself that he wasn't really a hoodlum, that his father was merely a bookkeeper, and that a college education had raised him above all this.

What was he doing here? What was he trying to prove? Chauffeuring Solly around was one thing—but this? Why had he done this?

His mind bounced to the last two days. He should have bowed out. He should have looked Solly straight in the eye and told him he didn't mind the car rides but that was as far as he wanted to go. That he really didn't want to make his bones. He was comfortable on the outside. He would've understood.

Yeah, right.

They'd been led into Solly's office two days ago. Michael knew something was not right, because *he* was in there, the inner sanctum of Enrico Soltano's power base.

"You done good, Mikey. I asked Tony and he thinks it's time."

"Time for what . . . padrino?"

Solly had laughed at that and punched him in the arm.

"Hey, just like in the fuckin' movies, eh? From now on, you start making your bones."

"How?" Michael swallowed when he should've walked.

"Eh, you don't ask," Solly warned, and then softened a bit, coddling him. "Just some small favors. You don't worry about that; I'll let you know when it's time."

That was enough for him. Michael began backing out

of the room, when he felt Tony crushing his upper arm, his eyes popping out at him.

He stared at Tony's face. It was the first time he'd seen Tony go pale, and Michael realized that his cousin, his big, dumb, stupid ox of a cousin, had *manufactured* this. It had been his idea. *He* had laid it on the line again for Michael, and now Michael was supposed to—No, he *had* to do the stand-up thing and lay it on the line for him.

What else could he do? He knew just enough about their business to make him dangerous enough for Tony to kill on the spot if he didn't say yes. Plus, it would bring on that dumb gumbah Sicilian loss of respect crap for Tony, who would be dishonored. Would they throw him out over Michael? Was he that important? Probably not, but it would put Tony in a bad position.

And it wasn't like Tony could pick and choose careers. It wasn't like Tony could survive in the real world. Michael knew he was in way over his head. He knew he'd been in over his head for some time. Why had he done this in the first place?

He took a deep breath. "Whatever you say, Solly. It would be an honor." Michael's knees had almost buckled as he wobbled his way out of the club.

And two horrible days had passed, and then, two hours ago, it came: the favor.

It was Geddone. Oh Jesus! Someone he *knew*. The guy who shook his arm off at family gatherings. The guy whose office Tony and he had visited that morning.

Tony had almost had to carry him to the car as Michael grabbed at straws.

"But Giuseppe Geddone? Kill Giuseppe Geddone? He's—he's an accountant, for Christ's sake. How dangerous could he be?"

"That ain't the point. He's a rat-bastard thief, been on the take from Solly. Jeez, Mikey, why you think we went up there this morning? Don't you see nothing that goes on in fronta your face?"

No, he didn't. He hadn't seen anything that had gone on in front of his face, not for two years.

Tony had helped him into the front seat of the car and Michael had sat there shaking like a leaf.

It was penance. Penance. He knew that now. For screwing up law school. For betraying his father for a Long Island princess. Penance for his father's death, which was his fault, too, because deep in his heart he knew that if he hadn't died from the coronary, he'd have been killed off by Michael's news.

Michael's eyes focused back on the shivering woman next to him. He stared at the woman's blond hair and felt the muscle of her upper arm twitch beneath his fingers, and somehow it came to rest in his head. No matter what kind of man his father had been, this was not the sort of man he'd been brought up to be. And after tonight, after this . . . and the bone-making task Solly had told him to do, he'd be drowned in this life forever.

Tony sneezed, and ran through the intersection at Fifty-ninth.

Fuckin' Angela. Now where was he gonna find someone to date?

Tony's stomach began to growl.

Meatballs. Maybe his mother was making her meatballs for him tonight. . . .

* * *

Lisa stared at the man holding the gun. She couldn't stop shaking. She couldn't stop crying.

She should have gone to Connecticut. Anywhere but Mrs. Morelli's. What had she done? They were going to force her to get the appointment book, and then what? Were they going to leave her there? Just walk out to go shoot her boss?

For a split second, she thought about it: being there to see Mr. Henry Foster Morgan grovel in front of them.

Oh she hated him, really hated him . . .

The man coughed and she snapped back. She couldn't believe this was happening. Okay, so she'd joked about pushing him out a window in the bar last week, but it was a *joke.* And besides, could she actually take pleasure in the knowledge that these men were going to kill him?

Well . . .

He coughed again, and she looked into his eyes. He seemed upset by all this. His eyes weren't like the other one's. They focused. The car hit a pothole and they bounced up and down on the seat. The gun slammed into her chin and she gave a yelp.

"Ow, you're hurting me," she said, holding her chin with her free hand.

"Hey, Tony, slow down, huh?"

"Mikey, we gotta lot to do tonight, you know? Solly's counting on us."

It didn't seem fair. What had she done to bring this on? She'd just tried to get through life like everybody else. And now here she was, with a gun at her head.

A gun . . .

As a day in September up near her family's lodge came into her mind, she felt her body freeze rigid. How old had she been? Fourteen? Was that right? Her grandpa had gotten her up right before dawn. The house had remained quiet, with not a stir from their sleeping family. She remembered the sound the door had made when he'd clicked it closed and how the boards on the porch had creaked and clacked from their weight as they'd walked across it.

He'd brought along two rifles from the locked cabinet in his study. It had been cold and gray, right before the first snowfall, and that burning smell was in the air.

She remembered the long, brownish grass and the whistle from her brown corduroys as she walked behind him. She'd zippered her sleeveless down vest. She'd worn a red plaid chamois shirt underneath. They got to a place out by the lake and climbed into a dinghy.

She watched him, his gray beard, and his arms and shoulders, still powerful for a man in his seventies, row, dipping the oars into the water soundlessly. She watched the water drip off the ends when he held them perfectly perpendicular to the water and let the dinghy glide over the glassy lake.

They rowed down a ways, near where the reeds were, and the water became shallow. They came to a stop and he threw out a small anchor to keep them there.

He loaded the guns and gave one to her silently, flashing a smile. Out of his pocket came a small wooden whistle.

"Now, you're going to see how it's done," he said, and winked at her.

The whistle gave off a duck noise. He blew twice, very fast. They both looked up into the sky. It was quiet and peaceful.

They sat very still for about twenty minutes. He blew

again and suddenly she heard the flap of feathers, and an answer.

She looked up and saw them. There were three of them, a mother, a father, and a little one.

Up on his feet, shaking the boat back and forth, he aimed before she knew what had happened.

CRA-A-A-CK.

Oh God, she watched the little one's body snap back from the force and begin to fall. She could still see a wing moving as it shot toward earth and she heard the splash where it had hit.

Most of the neck was blown away and its dark brown feathers dripped bloodred.

The car jolted to a halt and her eyes, terrified, looked out at her office building. She watched Tony turn his head around and stare at her.

"Okay, you don't give us no trouble."

She shook her head as the image of the duck hovered in her mind.

Three

Just have to get something for Mr. Foster Morgan," she yelled loudly at the security guard.

He hadn't even looked up from his paper. Her heart sank. That was going to have been her escape.

Tony pushed her into the elevator and they rode up to the office. Only the emergency lights were on. The air conditioning had been shut off as well, and a stuffiness had begun to set in. She dropped the keys, trying to get them into the lock. Tony grimaced at her and pulled the gun out for her to see.

The other man, the one Tony called Michael, hovered behind Tony. Tony pushed the door open and shoved her inside with so much force that she tripped and fell against the receptionist's desk. Lisa stared down at the phone. It was just an inch away from her hand.

"Okay, where's the book?" Tony said, pulling her away from the desk.

Michael stepped in between them.

"Let me take care of this," he said, and turned to her. "Show us the office."

She looked into his eyes and nodded. She was giving

up. They had her here. It was hopeless. She was going to give them the book, then they were going to shoot her boss.

This was not going to look good on a resume—and if they shot him, she'd have to face writing one. What could she say? Under *Skills*—she could see it now—"typing, filing, provided boss's schedule to hit man for successful mob hit . . . knows some WordPerfect 5.1." And this was provided she lived long enough to ever write one again.

She led Michael down the hall. It was hot and airless. They walked past the secretarial pool, which smelled of old coffee, past the art department, which smelled of melting wax. It was from the machine they used to stick copy to the cardboard layout boards, which Henry Foster Morgan never liked and now, thanks to her, would never again have the opportunity to dislike. She began to walk quickly, in rhythm with her thumping heart, and Michael slipped his arm around hers, but gently.

She looked up at him and he kept his eyes focused straight ahead. Behind her, she could hear Tony's heavy steps.

Michael kept his arm around her loosely as thoughts went racing through his mind. Sure, they were going to get the book, then what?

He knew what. He knew what Tony's first reaction—only reaction—would be.

Whack her.

It was the only solution. Aw Christ! He couldn't do that. Look at her.

"Where're you from?" he asked quietly.

"Michigan," she answered in a shaky, thin voice.

All right, he had to do Giuseppe Geddone. He had to stop his stomach from doing these somersaults every time he thought about Geddone. He was honor-bound. But he was not honor-bound to have this extra blood on his hands.

He had to come up with some reasoning Tony would go for between now and the time Michigan here got out the appointment book.

Henry awoke at 7:30, hung over as sin. He stared at the clock radio next to his bed, simply because that was the only place his eyes seemed able to focus. The clock hands were little papier-maché faces of Andy Warhol being dunked in liquid.

He sat up and his head spun around. It was not fair. It was his job to do this to his body. He waited for the room to stop its annoying dance. When it finally did, he slowly got up off the bed and began to slip on the mountain of laundry in his bedroom. Where was that dumb bitch he'd hired to take care of things like this? he thought as his landing was cushioned by a pile of designer jackets.

That's right. He'd fired her. She annoyed him no end, snooping around in his drawers, out of his drawers, and never in the right drawers. He struggled back up to his feet and made a run to the bathroom.

Once he'd thrown up, he'd feel better. Vomit was nature's way of making you ready for the next round.

When he finally pulled himself up from the toilet, he was ready to bathe.

Showers made him feel almost human. God, how he needed a vacation. All right, so he'd taken one in July. They just didn't understand the extent to which he *gave* for his career.

He shuffled out into his living room and walked over to

a purple and lime green credenza his interior designer had insisted he must have.

His apartment was a Memphis nightmare.

The credenza tilted at a rushy angle. It always looked to Henry as if it were caught in a fierce wind that was smearing it across the wall. He rummaged through all the drawers. Nothing.

On the amoeba-shaped coffee table, he saw the packet, lying next to a mirror and straw.

A sniff or two later and he was ready to pull it together.

There was a flurry of invites for this evening, all of which he'd accepted, half of which he'd never go near, job or no job. It helped keep the paparazzi off balance. There was a thing at the Palladium for dying children, or something equally wrenching, a party at the Met for a blood disease. A cancer dinner was at the Plaza. Jesus! It looked like a subscription to the disease-of-the-month club. He sifted through them all. Which disease would be the best?

AIDS. That was the one. That would attract the most of his set. AIDS, or starving children in Africa were always good.

Really, who died of just plain cancer anymore?

Okay, the AIDS cocktail party, which was already going on. He could get in and out of that by ten. Drop by for a bite to eat at some dismal little campaign fund-raiser he was supposed to attend. He'd never voted in his life. He wasn't even registered. Why should he care who was in office? His family was rich.

He did another line and stared for the longest time at a zigzagged chair that absolutely looked too dangerous to sit on. This room had actually been featured in *Architectural Digest.* He could not recall the name of the designer who'd done this, but if he ever did remember . . .

* * *

"C'mon on, C'mon. I ain't got all night." Tony was standing over her as she tried key after key in Henry's lower desk drawer.

Michael was standing at the door, looking out, just to make sure they weren't interrupted by janitors or a night cleaning woman. That was all he needed to turn this entire night into one big bloodbath.

"I'm going as fast as I can!" she snapped at him.

Tony glanced over at Michael, who shrugged. Tony was just turning his head back when the clock radio on the desk snapped on, blasting the room with noise.

Tony shot it.

It flew off the desk as Lisa gave a yelp. Michael glared at him and bent down to pick it up. He'd gotten it clean. It was stopped at quarter to eight. Jeez, they were behind schedule with all this craziness. He heard the desk drawer click open and he dropped the clock into the wastepaper basket, then thought better of it and picked it up, shoving it into the pocket of his raincoat.

She shakily handed the book to Tony, who opened it and began tearing through the pages.

"What the hell is this here?" Tony asked, staring down at the date.

"What?" Michael asked, taking the book from him. There were twenty entries.

"I can't go running all around lookin' for this fruitcake!" Tony began to complain.

"He goes to all these places each night?" Michael interrupted.

"No. It's for accounting. And to keep the press off his back. He usually picks a couple and goes there."

"Mikey, whadda we gonna do? We gotta go, you know, for Solly," Tony said, motioning with his gun, which was something Michael wished he wouldn't do.

He looked down at Lisa.

"You have any idea which ones he'd go to?"

She shook her head automatically.

Michael looked up at Tony. "I don't know. He's got four cocktail parties he's supposed to be at right now—"

"Oh, he won't be there," she offered, then shut her mouth so fast, she could hear her teeth knock together as Michael looked down at her.

"Why not?"

She shook her head, and he shook her by the arms.

"Because he never goes anywhere before eight-thirty," she blurted out. Michael looked at Tony.

"Okay, so where is he now?"

"Home," she whispered.

Michael straightened up as Tony came over.

"Okay, let's go," he said, picking her off the chair.

"Wait, wait," Michael said, and motioned him over to the corner of the office.

Tony dropped her back down onto the chair as if he was dropping a package and walked over to Michael. Michael exhaled.

"Whadda you doing?" Michael began.

"We take the girl to the house, and then wees can clip 'em both and still get to Giuseppe Geddone's by eight-fifteen and back to meet up with Solly by nine."

"Naw, naw, why waste a bullet on the girl?" Michael said, slipping into his heaviest street accent.

"But, Mikey, she knows who we are. She knows the plan."

"She don't know nothin'. Look at her. Looky there.

She ain't gonna talk to nobody. She don't even come from this city. Lissena this," Michael said, and broke huddle.

"Aay, honey. Where you from?"

"Michigan."

Back to the huddle. "There, you see, she's from Michigan."

"Where?"

"It's one of them cold places up near the Canadian border."

"She's *foreign*?"

"No, no. Our side of the border. Lissen, Tony, she's not gonna say nothin'. Look at the way she's shaking. We leave her here, what's she gonna do?"

"She goes to the cops."

It was time to bring out the ammo.

"Tony," he began, lowering his voice, "remember the hit at Freddo's restaurant on the Upper East Side?"

"Yeah."

"You did the guy on a Wednesday night, in fronta one hundred people. Did anybody say anything to the cops?"

"Naw . . ."

"Not even the guys saw you walk into the kitchen and back out, right? Not even an entire dining room of customers? Not even the guys who left the back door open for you in the kitchen, right?"

Michael waited for, and finally got, the reaction he'd wanted from Tony. Tony's eyes got unfocused and began to cross slightly, and he squinted, wrinkling up his mouth and nose in pain.

Tony was *thinking*.

"Nobody said nothing," he said after a minute.

"And why not?"

"They was scared."

"That's right. You made 'em so scared, they didn't talk. Look at the way she's shaking."

Tony's eyes slid over to the girl, then back to Michael.

"Yeah, but she's from outta town—"

"So she's double-scared. We do a number on Michigan over there—you know, tie her up loose, shake her around, tell her she's dead, and I guarantee she ain't gonna do nothing. And, it's less of a trace if we don't leave bodies laying all over New York tonight. We don't want the boss hit where it looks planned, right? We just want him to disappear after we get Rosa's stuff straightened out."

"Yeah?" Tony said, unfurling his face. There was a glint in his eyes as he stared at Mike. "Solly said you was to call the shots tonight. . . . So this is the way you wanna go with it?"

"Aayyy."

It took them ten minutes to tie up Michigan, most of it spent finding something to tie her up with. They bound her with a roll of masking tape to the swivel chair in the office and stuffed a wad of cheap paper towels into her mouth.

Tony Mac waved his gun around at her, told her she'd be shot and her thumbs would be cut off and sent to her family as a warning to other presumptuous out-of-towners.

Michael discreetly cut a slit in the masking tape over her hands as Tony did his number.

He didn't want Michigan stuck here all weekend.

It wasn't her fault she'd gotten mixed up in this. She should've gone to her barbecue in Connecticut. But no, she'd come to offer Rosa what she could spare—a lousy five hundred dollars. Jeez, they must work for slave wages in magazines, Michael thought as he wiped down the desk and the door.

She was a good woman. She had nice eyes, he thought as Tony walked out of the room. He liked her face, too. She was pretty. Nordic-looking, though. She had a nice figure and . . .

He snapped back together as he looked down at her frightened eyes. Yeah, she was a good-looking woman, all right. She'd look real good on the stand in court, fingering him for all this. 'Cause Michael knew, when it came right down to it, if she talked, she would not look upon him as the one who got her off the hook.

"C'mon, Mikey!" Tony's voice boomed from the hall.

He leaned down, and she pulled away, as if he was going to hit her.

"Count to one hundred slowly, then pull your hands free and get out of here. Don't ever tell anyone about this, 'cause if you do, we'll tell them you hired us. Don't forget, you gave us his book and your fingerprints are all over it," he whispered. Then he stood up and walked to the door.

He turned and gave one last look, just to make sure it had sunk in. She nodded to him, and he closed the door.

He walked over to the elevator banks, where Tony was holding the door. They rode down in silence.

He'd won this round. He'd convinced Tony to spare Michigan. His eyes slid over to him and he saw Tony watch the floor numbers light up as the elevator descended.

If he could save Michigan, what about her boss?

That would take more careful planning, and it would be one less murder he'd be in on. . . .

His stomach suddenly went cold.

Giuseppe Geddone. He couldn't get out of that. But

how could he do it? He wasn't a killer. Not only wasn't he a killer but to get payment for it—that's what Solly had thrown in, more for Tony than for him. If Tony was in on it and he didn't get his usual "bonus," he'd get all confused, and Solly didn't want that.

Michael didn't want that.

Tony was more likely to go off half-cocked when he was confused.

Jesus Christ! Why had Giuseppe done this? Michael couldn't imagine he'd been skimming so much. Knowing Solly, it probably wouldn't even buy him a suit each month, but it was "the principle of the thing."

Still, Geddone should've known better.

Michael caught himself wincing. Two years with these guys and he was already beginning to think like them. They were talking about a human life here. This was something that seemed to elude these people. He needed a plan.

They walked silently through the lobby. The guard was off somewhere.

They walked out to the car and got in.

"We're going to SoHo," he said, and Tony grunted as he started the car.

"How you wanna do this?"

"It's up to you."

"Look, you gotta call it. You wanna get him in his apartment or on the street?"

It was ten past eight. Henry walked into his closet and sorted through a rack of clothes he'd never worn. He selected a Bijan outfit, with a matching shirt that had never even been out of the bag it came in.

Once he had realized that if he continually bought new clothes, he would never have to do laundry, life became a pleasure. God! Expense accounts were great!

He stood, adjusting his tie and combing his hair, which dramatically fell into the same place every time. He should get it trimmed, but just a tiny bit. He liked the overgrown look. It read, Henry felt, like a man who was too dedicated and busy to get a haircut. Of course, he had to pay his stylist one hundred bucks a visit to maintain this degree of sloppiness, but he looked so devoted on Page Six.

He rummaged through a box with eyeglasses in it. This was another affectation of which he was fond: the hard-working head of a magazine so staunch, his eyes were going on him. It added to the aura.

He chose a large pair with Calvin Klein frames. He couldn't remember who'd taught him the trick about plain glass in the frames. A lot of his memory seemed faulty these days. Even though he suspected it was his night-prowling schedule—a schedule he'd perfected at twenty-one and not changed even though he'd aged a decade—he preferred to think it was because he worked for a living.

He left his hair loose—it wouldn't do to have another picture of him with it pulled back, in case he ran into the press again—and stared at his reflection in the floor-to-ceiling mirror in the closet. This would be fine. And he could really let loose because, after all, this was Friday night.

Forty-five.

Forty-six.

Lisa squirmed and tried to concentrate on the count. The paper in her mouth was making her gag and the tape on her wrists was slightly pulling some hair on her arm, so it felt as if she was removing a Band-Aid horribly slowly. Her shoulders were all hunched up and pulled back by the chair. It was frighteningly uncomfortable.

Forty-seven.

Forty-eight. She continued counting in her head as she coughed on the towels.

"Okay, so we wait for him to come outta the building and we grab him, and, if we need to, we take him back to that office to do the paperwork, right?" Tony asked.

Michael nodded and they both looked up at the third-floor window of a large loft on Grand Street in SoHo.

Michael's stomach began to gurgle and Tony shot him a glance.

"I'm hungry."

"You shoulda had some of my Ring-Dings."

"Well, I didn't think we were going to be out all night," Michael said, and they listened to his stomach gurgle again.

"I saw a deli around the corner on West Broadway," Michael insisted.

Tony shook his head.

"I can't go all night without anything in my stomach."

"All right already! So go get a sandwich. I'll grab the guy as he comes out."

Michael opened the door and the bell-like door warning went off, sounding like a department-store sale.

"You have the picture of him from the office?"

Tony held up the fuzzy photo they'd ripped out of the newspaper after Michigan pointed it out to them.

"Good. I'll be back in a minute," Michael said, and walked toward West Broadway.

"Eh, get me some Cheez Doodles?" Tony's voice echoed back to him.

Seventy-seven.

Seventy-eight.

Seventy-nine.

Lisa spit out the wad of paper towels in her mouth. She froze and looked at the door. . . . Oh God, she'd lost count!

She sat still for two minutes, shaking.

One.

Two.

Three.

This is ridiculous.

She stopped.

The fact of the matter was that Henry, thanks to her, was going to die tonight. All right. He was not a nice man. She certainly didn't merit the abuse she took from this spoiled, illiterate brat. But did he really deserve to die for it? Did any human being deserve to die for cutting off a sixty-four-year-old's pension? There was a snap, and she felt the tape holding her hands together break apart.

It was close but . . . no. No one deserved that, even if it was obvious that Mrs. Morelli was hardly the sweet little old lady Lisa'd thought she was. What could she do, though?

She put her hands up to her chin and rested her head

on them. Her eyes focused on her right thumb and a chill went through her.

That was it. She was going to call the police.

She put her hand on the phone and Michael's words came into her head. They had the appointment book. Her fingerprints were all over it. They were going to tell them that she had organized this whole thing. Would they believe two thugs over her?

She picked up the phone and dialed 911.

"Nine-one-one," a voice responded.

"I—I need to report a crime."

"Where?"

"Um . . ." she stammered. Well, now what was she going to say?

"Ma'am?" the voice prompted.

"Um, SoHo. Grand Street."

"Where on Grand?"

"Nineteen Grand, off West Broadway."

"Can you see what's going on?"

"What?"

"Is the crime still in progress?"

"No. It hasn't happened yet."

"What?" The voice sounded annoyed.

"Look, there are two men who are going to kidnap Henry Foster Morgan, the editor-in-chief of *Smug Magazine,* and kill him."

"The head of *Smug*? That stupid magazine that's always getting sued?"

"Er, yes."

"We was wondering when someone was going to have the brains to do that—come on, lady! Look, this line is for *emergencies.* This is not some kind of party line for your Friday night!"

Click.

Lisa felt her mouth drop open. Good God, the police weren't interested? Who the heck else did they expect you to call in this city?

This is nuts.

A human being was going to die. Her stomach went queasy. All right, she had to get a grip on herself. She breathed deeply.

Maybe she could handle this by herself. No, she *had* to handle this herself. She could not just sit up in Connecticut knowing her boss was going to get killed or go thumbless. She swallowed as the odd image of Henry Foster Morgan trying to open his bottle of aspirin with no thumbs came into her head.

He'd probably just hire someone to do whatever it was that he did with his thumbs. Or, more likely, it would end up as part of her job description.

No, she had to do something. She was a competent person; she could think her way out of this.

She found herself pacing, hunched over in the office.

Well, she'd called the police, and that got her a big nothing, and she certainly didn't want to run into those two guys again. So what could she do?

She stood straight up.

She could warn him.

That's what she could do. Warn Henry Foster Morgan not to go out, not to leave his building. Just stay inside. Hide there until they got tired of waiting and gave up. Then he could take a long vacation. He wouldn't mind that.

She was jolted back into the room as she gazed at the torn masking tape on her wrists.

She quickly peeled it off, cringing as she pulled. It felt

like a hundred Band-Aids, and it made her angry. She rubbed the skin and picked up all the tape and threw it in the basket.

She left Henry's office. She'd get a cab and get over there as fast as possible. She stopped short at the elevator.

What was she *doing*?

She should get her car and get the hell away from here is what she should do. God, she'd probably missed the barbecue, she thought, looking at her watch.

She paced in a circle.

Should she do the right thing and warn him? Or the safe thing and go to Connecticut?

She stopped still for a moment.

What a dummy! She could *call* him. Then she wouldn't have to go all the way downtown, and she wouldn't have to run into those guys, and she could get her car out of Harlem and go to Connecticut!

When the phone rang in the living room, Henry was in the process of getting himself a Bloody Mary to get him to the cocktail party. He was just about to take his first sip. He hated telephones when he had to answer them. He loved them when someone else had to answer them. He stalked into the living room and grabbed the phone.

"What!" he yelled.

Lisa sat on the other end, frozen. It was that tone of voice humiliating her, just like he did every morning. Well, he was still alive. She guessed there was some good in that. Maybe she should go to Connecticut. Leave him to that Tony guy.

"Answer, goddamn it!" his voice snarled.

"Mr. Foster Morgan?" she said, dropping her voice to try to disguise it.

"Who is this?"

She took a breath.

"Never mind. You're in danger. Don't go out tonight. There are men trying to kill you."

There was a long pause, and she heard him exhale, and this odd gulping noise.

"Okay, who is this? Is this Mindy?"

"I'm telling you for your safety. Do not leave your apartment, or you'll be killed. Wait until tomorrow morning and then get out of town as fast as you can."

There was a pause and an odd slurping noise.

"How did you get this number? Who the hell do you think you are, calling me like this? I mean, what the fuck do you think I am? Stupid?"

"No, I— I—"

"Listen, you dumb bitch, you ever call this number again and I'll have you arrested." *Click.*

Zero for two. Lisa went numb. Now what was she going to do?

Michael got on line at the deli behind a woman who seemed to be ordering enough food for forty. What luck. This always happened to him. At bank machines for instance, he always got stuck behind the whack who had seventy transactions and couldn't figure out how to use a bank card.

He needed to get away from Tony for a moment. Part of the problem with his stomach was Tony. Michael knew that Tony hadn't liked his solution about Michigan. He'd wanted to ice her. Make it clean and neat. But he'd gone along with Michael's reasoning. Aw God, he felt awful. They'd kill this guy, then Tony would drive him up to

Giuseppe Geddone's and watch him kill the guy. They'd go back down to Solly's and collect the envelopes.

Fourteen thousand, that was his cut.

He stared at the salads and pastas behind the glass counter. The woman moved off and Michael finally ordered his sandwich.

He had to figure a way out of this whole mess. He couldn't shoot somebody. He just couldn't do it. He got to the checkout, grabbed a bag of Cheez Doodles for Tony, and went back to the car. His appetite seemed gone as he tossed the bag into the front seat.

"He come out yet?"

"Naw," Tony said, and ripped open the bag with his teeth.

They'd been sitting very still, eating. Michael had just been looking down at the morning's *Daily News* when Tony nudged him. He looked up, across the street at the doorway.

Standing in front of it was a guy who had on a long white coat. He was searching in his pocket for something. He looked like a doctor.

Tony held up the Page Six photo, his eyes bouncing from the windshield to the blurry photo.

"That's him," Tony proclaimed. "C'mon."

Michael thought quickly.

"Naw, that's not him," he said lazily, then took a bite of his sandwich.

"Mikey, look. It's the same guy." He held up the paper.

"No, look at the picture. That's an older guy there. A guy about fifty. The one across the street's young," he said, waving the sandwich.

They watched the man take off his regular glasses and put on a pair of jet black sunglasses.

"I dunno, looks the same to me."

"No. Look, the guy in the photo has short hair."

"Yeah," Tony said warily. "But what if it's him? He's getting away."

"Look, it's *not* him. Fahcrissake, let me eat in peace," Michael snapped, and looked down at his paper.

His eyes slid over to Tony, who was watching Henry Foster Morgan like a hound dog.

The man was standing there, looking east. Goddamn it, why didn't he move? The sooner he walked away, the sooner Tony could go back to his Cheez Doodles and the sooner Michael could sit in peace, planning how to get around Rosa's revenge contract.

His eyes bounced back up to Henry, and Michael's stomach relaxed a little as he started strolling east down the street. His back was to them. He felt Tony sink back on the seat.

"Yeah, I guess that's not the guy," Tony conceded.

A cab screeched in from behind them, and Michael looked back to the *Daily News.* Suddenly, Tony shot straight up in his seat.

"Mikey, look, it's Michigan."

His mouth froze around the sandwich and his eyes opened so wide, he thought he was never going to get them back to normal. He watched as she stood, holding the door to the cab and calling and waving down the street.

"Madonna! That's the guy." Tony started the car.

Michael couldn't believe it. What the hell was she doing here? She must have some kind of a death wish. The schmuck. The jedrool.

Before Michael knew what was happening, she was back in the cab. It pulled out, blocking the street, just as

Tony hit the accelerator. There was a screech as he floored the brake pedal and stopped just short of the cab.

A barrage of Haitian came out of the cabdriver, and a barrage of Sicilian was pouring out of Tony. Michael stared at the back window, at Michigan's face. Her mouth had dropped open and her eyes were huge and she was frozen and staring back at him through the glass. His eyes shifted up the street and he watched Henry Foster Morgan stop at the corner, glance back at them to see what all the racket was about, and then disappear down the street.

His heart sank as he felt Tony's weight spring off the seat. In a second, he was out of the car. Michael opened his door and spit out the sandwich. Tony was standing, screaming at the cabdriver. Michael ran up next to the two of them, leaned down, and stuck his head in the back window, watching her squash herself against the opposite door.

"What the fuck's the matter with you? You want to die?"

She bit her puffy lower lip and he watched her grab the door handle and bolt.

Before he turned around, he heard Tony yell, "Hey, you get back here!"

Michael turned in time to see the gun come out of Tony's shoulder holster. The cabbie shut up, raised his hands, and backed off as Tony took off after Michigan.

"Shit," Michael said under his breath as he began to run after the two of them.

He followed Tony's figure as it rushed in and out of the street lamps, down Grand Street. He sped around the corner of Green, to the right, toward Canal, with Michael following. His heart was pounding, the alarm clock in his pocket that Tony had shot was banging against his thigh as he ran.

He rounded the corner as the cab sped out past him. Halfway down the center of the street, he stopped and saw Tony pointing his gun out, in his aiming position, at Michigan, who was shaking with her hands above her.

"Tony, no!" Michael screamed, and hurled himself down the street.

He came up to them and looked at Tony.

"Yeah, she ain't gonna say nothin' to nobody! Then what's she doin' here, huh, Mikey?" He was angry now.

"I don't know."

"I shoulda blowed her away back there."

Michael couldn't talk. He didn't know what to do now. He couldn't believe this woman. What the hell could have been going on in Michigan's mind? He'd gotten her off the hook once. He didn't think it was going to happen twice. What—

"All right. You're comin' wid us," Tony said, waving the gun at her.

Michael exhaled. He wasn't carried away enough to try and whack her in the middle of a Manhattan street. They walked silently to the car and Tony opened the back door.

"Get in. You get in back wid her. I'm troo lissenin' here."

They both ducked in the back and Tony slammed the door so forcefully, the car rocked from side to side.

"What—"

"Shut up. Just shut up!" Michael snapped as Tony opened his door and swung himself inside.

The *bong, bong, bong* of the door alarm went off and Tony slammed the door shut, which silenced it. He started the car and the windy sound of the air conditioning began to hum.

Michael could feel her staring at him as they went east, across Grand Street.

"Where are we going?" he asked, leaning forward.

"It's almost nine."

"So?"

"We gotta meet Solly." He grunted.

Michael's eyes got large.

"We're taking her to Solly's?" He leaned forward and dropped his voice. "You think that's a good idea, she sees Solly's?"

"I don't think it's gonna be a problem what she sees after tonight." Tony shook his head. "The whole evening's screwed-up now," he muttered.

They drove in silence. Michael's mind was like a fuse blowing. No thoughts came in clear and loud, just frantic half messages, half-finished thoughts. They were going back to see Solly. They were fucked. He was fucked.

Lisa sat dazed. This was not what was supposed to happen. She was just going to lean out of the cab and warn him and that was it.

He didn't even look around when she'd called his name!

And what was going to happen now? It was one thing to try and prevent a crime, it was another to wind up as the victim with her neck on the line. She couldn't believe it. And for whom? Henry Foster Morgan? That was adding insult to injury.

Okay, she'd decided that she could handle it, take a stand and be brave. Now she was in real trouble. Now it was *her* thumbs on the line.

Tony knew he'd never make it home in time for dinner,

so now he'd be stuck heating up the meatballs in the microwave. He was sure his mother was making meatballs because he'd seen ground beef and pork and veal in the refrigerator before he'd left this morning.

He didn't like heating things up in the microwave. They got cold too quick.

He also wanted to go back to Angela's.

They turned down onto Mulberry Street in silence. Several limos were parked out in front of the dark doorway. The club had at one time been a legitimate storefront. In the big picture windows, meant to show off the latest in canned goods and groceries, now sat two dusty statues—one of San Gennaro, the other one of the Virgin Mary.

Tony got out quickly and opened the back door.

"You, get out."

Michael and Michigan got out as Tony knocked on the door of the club. It was opened by Ralphie. Michael held on to Michigan's arm and they went inside.

"Keep a eye on her," Tony ordered Ralphie, and Michael angrily pushed her into a chair.

It took a couple of minutes before they were beckoned into the inner room.

Lisa had a bad feeling about this.

She looked around, trying to figure out where they were.

There was a long bar at the end, near the door that Michael and Tony had gone through. A man behind the bar, short, balding, with greased back hair, was standing near a machine, waiting for coffee to drip out into a tiny porcelain cup. The smell of dark, strong espresso mixed with cigar smoke from a table where three old men were sitting.

Odd fake wood paneling lined the wall, up to a whitewashed stamped tin ceiling. Fluorescent lights slatted the ceiling. A large wooden crucifix was hung in the center of the back wall, over the bar. Four six-foot Formica tables sat in the room in front of the bar. Empty folding chairs were aligned at them.

She looked at the table of men, all staring silently at her, as though they'd never seen a woman before. Above their table, on the wall, an elaborately robed doll of the Virgin Mary holding baby Jesus was covered with a dirty clear plastic bag.

She stared back at the men and then watched the man behind the bar come around carrying the two cups. He was also staring at her. He stumbled on something, and she heard an odd yelp from the floor.

There was a huge black dog lying at the foot of one of the old men.

"Stunadze!" The old man growled, and Lisa thought the waiter was going to drop the cups, he was shaking so hard. The man raised his hand to the waiter and then she noticed the oddest thing. Her eyes focused on what the old man was wearing. He was in a brown and white striped bathrobe and faded pale blue pajamas with small brown V's on it. Her eyes darted curiously down to the floor. He had on brown leather slippers. She looked back up at his face and was startled to see him staring angrily at her, as though it was a sin to notice his attire.

Another old man, wearing a faded white cap, a windbreaker, a plaid shirt, and a green pair of pants took a cane around front and leaned his arms and chin on it. His eyes were hypnotic, not blinking at her. He did not so much as glance up as the waiter put down the cup, nor when he went back behind the bar and came out with a bottle and two little glasses. She watched him shakily pour the clear liquid into each glass, and the one staring at her, without taking his eyes off her, waved him away.

She looked and gave them a weak smile, watching all three of them grimace, puzzled. Two of them began chewing on their fat cigars, looking her up and down. There was something obscene about what they were doing, and she looked away.

She looked up at Ralphie. He was also fat and balding, but younger, in his fifties, with big brown-tinted glasses in gold frames. His hair was slicked down, with several long strands combed across the bald crown. He wore a dark blue three-piece suit, light blue shirt, and solid dark tie. He leaned down, putting a hand on the table she was sitting at, and her eyes stuck on his large gold pinkie ring. It had an immense diamond in the center, surrounded by rubies in the shape of a horseshoe.

The waiter came over and hovered behind Ralphie, and she looked up at him. He licked his lips and she stared at the floor as hard as she could.

Yep, she definitely had a bad feeling about this.

Solly was popping Rolaids right and left as he listened to Tony talk. His eyes would get round and then narrow. They bulged when Tony got to the part where Michael had convinced him not to whack Michigan.

"So then, Solly, the girl took off an—"

He waved him quiet, and Tony stepped back.

"Aw right, aw right, enough already. You tellin' me you ain't taken care of Giuseppe Geddone yet? Is that what you saying?"

"Yes, Solly," Tony whispered, looking at the floor. He shot Michael a glare.

"Whatta you *crazy*? I tell you to do somethin', you do that!" Solly screamed, slamming his fist on the table.

"Well you told us to help my aunt Rosa an—"

"Rosa! *Rosa!* Who you work for, me or Rosa, huh?" Solly stood up and Michael felt his knees begin to go.

"You, Solly—"

"Fahcrissake! Whatsa matta wid you? Get Geddone *now*. I don't care about Rosa."

"Okay. We're gonna do it right now. Right this minute. We gonna go up to Harlem—"

"He ain't there no more. He got in his car, and Ralphie's people says he went to his office. He's probably halfway outta the country with my money. I don't believe it. I don't believe none of this."

"Look, maybe he's still there. I'll find him, I swear. I'll find him tonight."

"Yeah, that's right you'll find him tonight. If you don't, you don't come back here. You hear me, Tony?" he said, walking around the desk.

"I promise I'll make it right," Tony stammered, and began to back out.

He turned after a moment.

"Whatta we do with the girl?"

"What girl?"

"Michigan."

"Why, whatta you care?"

Tony swallowed, and Michael stared at the floor.

"She's out front."

"You brought her *here*?" Solly's face was so red, Michael thought he was going to strangle in his collar.

They watched him walk around Tony, getting close to his face.

"You screwed this up, Tony. It ain't like you. Maybe your cousin here, the *smart* one," he said, smacking the word *smart* like it was a disease, "maybe he got you all mixed up. . . . You listen to me, and you do everything in the order I say. First, you gonna get the girl the hell out of here. Then, you gonna track down Geddone and get my money back, and then you gonna settle with him for me. You hear?"

They both nodded.

"You do whatever you gotta do for Rosa later, *capisce*?"

They nodded, and Michael turned to the door.

"And the girl, Solly? What about the girl?" he heard Tony say.

"Whack her."

Rosa Morelli positioned herself at her bedroom window, which faced the street. She had a high folding chair, which was her favorite for watching from the window. She'd taken a big pillow and laid it across the sill to pad her thick elbows from the hard wooden surface. An ashtray was balanced on the edge of the pillow and a liter bottle of cola sat on the floor next to her chair.

Her eyes followed the traffic on the avenue as she waited for Tony to come to her. Down below the sound of smashing glass drew her attention. She watched two men breaking into an old rusty station wagon parked in front of her building. They quickly pulled an overnight bag off the front seat and took off around the corner before she could blink her eyes.

What asshole would leave a car parked in this neighborhood with a bag on the front seat? she thought.

Must be one of them people from outta town, she concluded. She reached down and grabbed the soda bottle, then looked back down the avenue for signs of Tony.

Sophia's eyes were stuck on the kitchen clock, ticking away loudly in the silence of the room. There was a bad feeling in the pit of her stomach as she watched the big hand move to five past nine. The *trota* was wrapped and sat on the counter, like a beacon to the fact her son had not come home.

Why hadn't she said something that morning?

She began to drum her fingers on the kitchen table, trying to drown out the sound of the clock. She couldn't stand looking at the plate with the fish on it, so she got up and put it into the refrigerator. She looked tensely around the kitchen. All the dishes had been done, the floors and surfaces had been washed; she couldn't start washing the walls this time of night.

She sat down again and drummed her fingertips to the ticking as the words of the priest—she knew which one—went through her head again.

The dark confessional chamber of that morning came back to her and she was there.

"Forgive me, Father, for I have sinned. . . ." It had begun normally.

"How long has it been since your last confession?"

"Yesterday afternoon," she'd answered quickly.

She had detected a sigh from the other side of the partition.

"And what are your confessions, my child?"

"I . . ." she had wavered. "I have neglected my child." The words cut through her like a knife.

"In what way?" the familiar voice asked.

"I have been . . . grieving for my husband and I have neglected my child." Her voice broke on the word *child.*

"Mummhuh."

"I heard some disturbing things this morning, Father D'Amico. About my son, my only son," she said, breaking the anonymity of the confessional. She waited to hear him reply.

He did not.

"I had my son late," she began. "I was already thirty ah . . ." She let her voice trail off, not wishing to add the exact age. "And he was the only child I had, we had, Vincent and me. We agreed, Vincent and me, that he would not be a common criminal, and now I find . . ."

She couldn't continue the thought.

"And now you have found . . ." he prodded her.

"He is in with very bad people—" She caught herself, as even explaining this to a priest was iffy. "Just people which his father and I had hoped would not be in his life, would not be his employers." She groped for the words.

"And what do these people want him to do?"

"Something, something bad, I don't know what."

"If you don't know what, how can you say it is bad?"

"I know these people, I know it is bad. These are not good people. He's doing this because he has no focus in his life. And he is being led through this confusion and I don't know what to do," she said, then exhaled sharply.

"And what do you blame this on?"

She exhaled and then drew a sharp breath.

"Me."

There was a long pause, and she could see the outlines

of Father D'Amico as he rubbed his chin, the way he did when there was something he had to say. She waited and waited. At last, she heard him cough.

"Sophia, you have been coming to my church for the last two years."

"Yes."

"And while I'm not in the habit of discouraging regular attendees, I can honestly say that you've been here sometimes more than my nuns have."

"I wish to be a good Christian," she defended herself quickly.

"Yes, and you are, you are a good Christian, Sophia Bonello, but"—he gave a sigh—"for twenty-eight years I see you for the holidays maybe, and that is all, but since the tragic death of your husband two years ago, now, all I see is you. I am not ungrateful, understand me, but you are not a nun, and here you are always, every morning when I come in, and every evening when I leave."

"I know," she said near tears. "I *know.*" She began to weep.

"Grieving death is a necessary and good thing. We must do it; we must remember our dead and all the joy that they brought to us but . . ." His voice trailed off.

"But what?" she asked almost frantically.

"But there comes a time when you have to say, 'I am alive, I am still here, and I must continue on and have a life which the good Lord wants.' Otherwise, he would have taken you, too. To make yourself no life on this earth is to spit in God's face, Sophia. I watch you here, day after day, and believe me, I wish I had as many people as dedicated, but you are masking your life with this grief. I watch you at the candles, lighting them for hours. After you have gone for your cannoli and your chitchat, you come flying back here!"

She bowed her head, nodding in recognition. Yes, she did that. She did that for a stupid, superstitious reason.

It was just after Vincent died. She couldn't eat. She would lie in bed, eventually falling into a light sleep for a moment or two and then would wake with a start.

"Vincent? Vincent? I had the worst nightmare," she would begin, half in a dream state, and grope beside her in the empty bed, until a thunderbolt would go through her as she realized it was not a dream, that he really was gone. After so many years with this man, she could not sleep without his familiar weight sagging down the mattress next to her, the rhythm of his snoring lulling her to sleep. It was now dark and quiet, empty and alone in her bed.

In church, she felt better, and that was when the eerie thing began to happen. She would light candles for him, trying to light up every candle on the eight-tiered rack. The first time she got all the candles lighted, she stood back, watching them, and suddenly they began to flicker, and a cold breeze hit the back of her neck, like a cold hand gently caressing her, as if Vincent was standing behind her, caressing her. She had turned quickly and the feeling had gone away. The odd thing was that she had been all alone in the church; there were no open doors or windows.

She began to light candles every day, waiting for the breeze.

She thought back with scorn to her mother's warnings when she'd announced her intention to marry him.

Her mother was Piedmontese, high Italian, who scorned Vincent because of his ancestry. His people were from Vico Equense, not quite as bad as Naples in her mother's eyes, but unthinkable still as a marriage partner.

"You never go with them. They will bring you many years of unhappiness. They are all crooks and murderers," she'd said, dismissing the thought. That was all a near-Neapolitan merited. "The people in the south, they have no education, no sense of beauty or style. They eat all those red sauces, which ruin their stomachs—the only people worse are Sicilian; they are the true pigs of the earth." The words still rang as clearly in Sophia's ears this day as the day her mother had said them.

But Sophia was an old woman by neighborhood standards—she was past her prime—and there were no dashing young men of Piedmontese background waiting to marry her in East Harlem.

And then came Vincent.

He had seen her in the marketplace and on her way to church in the mornings. After awhile, he made a point of standing watch across the street from church. He would look down or away when she came out, but he was always there. She knew him from his comings and goings at the Soltanos' house on a Hun' fourteen, which whet her interest enough for her to find out exactly what he did for the Soltanos.

She remembered literally breathing a sigh of relief when she was told he was nothing more than a bookkeeper. A full-fledged wiseguy, she didn't want. They lived too fast and died too young.

The first time they spoke was at a dance given in the church's basement for Valentine's Day. She and her best friend, Maria, had gotten dressed in beautiful silk dresses. Hers was light pink, with lace on the front. They had made a special journey and bought them in a shop in midtown. In midtown, it was a "frock," bought from a "frock shop," not just a dress.

It had been cold that night, and her teeth were chattering as they started down the basement steps. Music echoed up the long, dark passageway, lighted at the bottom like a tunnel. And as they walked down, the air got warmer and warmer, taking the chill off of her.

And there was Vincent, standing at the bottom of the steps, guarding the door. He'd gotten a job as bouncer, using the Soltanos' name.

Only she knew, or thought she knew, that if anything really happened, the worst he could do was probably run for cover.

The dance was beautiful, decorated with paper hearts and doilies, red streamers and pink balloons. Maria found someone to dance with, and Sophia found herself hovering near the front door. They made conversation, talking about the neighborhood, when their parents had come over, how long they'd been here, the doings of the neighborhood—meaningless chatter of two people who wanted to know each other and didn't know how. The dance was coming to an end.

"I should be finding Maria," Sophia said, looking around.

"You gotta go now?"

And then she said something that came out kind of nasty, even though she meant it as a tease.

"I should stand around here talking to some wiseguy all night?" She sniffed and turned to walk away.

That was the first time he touched her. It sent shivers up her spine as his fingers easily curled around her forearm and he whirled her back around and they stood, so close she could feel his chest expand and contract with each breath. It seemed so long that they stood quietly and began leaning against each other tighter and tighter, never letting go of each other's gaze. Her body was tingling all over.

"For months I watch you going in and out of church and all I can think is, How do I talk to Sophia? . . . I got this job so I could speak to you. I'm no wiseguy, Sophia. I just didn't know any other way to talk to you. I'm an accountant."

She melted on the spot.

She also knew he was lying through his teeth about not being a wiseguy.

And that was the first reason she'd decided to marry him. After all, this was a man she understood. And no matter how many lies he told or how craftily he thought he was pulling one over on her, she would know. She would know every moment of the day where he was and what he was up to, because she could look right through him into his soul.

The other reason she'd decided that Vincent Bonello was the right man was because she knew he had a reputation in the neighborhood for having a good heart, and, she reasoned, any hoodlum with a good heart was not going to be a hoodlum for long.

A couple of years of marriage, let him get it out of his system, a child or two, and he'd soon be walking the straight and narrow with a little help from her.

They were married soon after, and quickly after that she was happily pregnant and distracted enough not to say anything about it. He was out till three in the morning, then they would sleep till three in the afternoon, and she would get up and make him black coffee, and he would lovingly rub her growing belly, then go out to get a shave and a haircut.

That was the first thing that had tipped her mother off—the fact he never shaved himself.

"All the hoodlums go to that barber!" her mother had lectured while he was gone. She wouldn't come into the house when he was home.

"So? I shop at the same *salumeria* as Gina Soltano, that makes me some mobster's wife?" she'd countered.

And she remembered her mother shaking her head sadly at what a jerk for a daughter she'd raised. And she *was* being stupid; she needed to be. She was finally married to a dashing, mysterious man who worshiped her and had given her a baby. And she was confident in the fact that when it came time to face him on his chosen profession that she would win. Besides, what was she going to do? Move back in with her mother?

As the months passed and the baby came, the hours and the rumors begin to gnaw at her, and the strangeness with money, and how things like rugs or silverware would suddenly appear.

And one week, the money stopped and all hell broke loose. Vincent announced that there was trouble and they had to leave town for awhile. It was then that she'd confronted him, and that was when she'd found out how deeply she'd been lied to, and, according to her mother, tricked into marrying him.

Because the truth of the matter was, while Vincent was not proud of what he did, he wasn't ashamed of it, either. It held a certain fascination for him, and the fact was, he was good at it. He was good at running the numbers, he was a good controller, good at running the crap games, and he never had to break anyone's knees because of the shylocking. He was good at being a hood, and would be till the end of his days.

It was then that they'd had the first in a long line of fights, she remembered angrily.

Being angry at the dead, she chided herself, then realized that she hadn't thought about this, about the bad times with Vincent, in the entire past two years.

Her eyes focused back in on the clock. It was 9:30, and it jarred her back into the kitchen. The reality of the time sank in.

Oh God, she thought, where is my son?

Four

They rode in silence across the Brooklyn Bridge. Periodically, Tony would grunt, and Michael could hear Michigan draw shivery breaths.

That was it. There were going to be three murders tonight, and he'd be in on all of them.

This made litigation law look like a piece of cake.

Giuseppe Geddone's union office was just on the other side of the Brooklyn Bridge. It was a small union, which had been supplying dynamiters for the local construction sites of city buildings since the thirties, and skim for the Soltanos since the fifties.

Giuseppe Geddone stood, inhaling from his cigar and staring out the window at the lights in Manhattan. It had been a rough day for him. He'd been told Solly was going to visit him in person. So that was it. It was over, after all this time.

He'd paced about the floor, wondering what to do. Should he make a run for it right then? That was when the call had come in from Ralphie.

"Solly's comin' to see you."

"Yeah?" he'd said calmly, even though he broke into a sweat at the name. "Whatsa matter, Ralphie?"

"Aw nothin'. He just wants to talk some things over with youse. You know Solly, he likes to keep in touch with his people," Ralphie'd said easily.

Yeah, Giuseppe knew Solly all right. This was the same guy he'd grown up with, the same guy who by the time he was seven was shaking down the whole first grade for their milk money at Our Lady of the Holy Virgin.

"When he's coming?"

"Ho, tomorrow sometime. Why you gotta ask?"

"No reason, just want to make the place neat-looking, that's all. This is a big honor for me, Ralphie."

He'd hung up and stared at the phone. That was the call. That was Ralphie trying to assure him he wasn't gonna be murdered, so when he did send someone over, he'd be there to kill. Of course Giuseppe knew they didn't have a hope in hell of finding him here in the morning. He'd heard that they'd picked up two Channel 11 reporters, so he figured he was okay for the day at least. Okay, he'd work the rest of the day, just like normal, then go home, eat, come back to work overtime, just like normal, and then get the hell out to the airport in time for the flight to take off.

By 5:30 P.M., he shut off his light, took his briefcase, and went home. He made it through a leisurely dinner, laughing out loud at the TV report showing Solly, Ralphie, and Tony Mac knocking the camera out of the cameraman's hands. Then he sat in the living room, watching "Bowling for Dollars," trying to tune out the heavy-metal music coming from his son's room.

He took a Havana out of his humidor and smoked it

down. This was the last time he'd do this, he thought. Then he went over to the box and stuffed several cigars he'd been saving for the right occasion into his briefcase.

About 8:00 P.M., he told his wife he was going back to the office to do a little overtime. She was on the phone and barely looked up at him as he left the kitchen. He stood at the front door, looking at the front hall, the dark living room, and listening to the sounds of his wife in the kitchen. He walked back into the living room and took a picture of his family—his daughter, Gina, his son, Alphonse, and his wife—off the mantel and shoved it underneath his raincoat.

He walked out of the building, down the tiny front walk, and closed the gate silently behind him. He stood staring at the small town house for a moment, then turned and stared at the softball field in the park across the street on a Hun' fourteen.

The high-pitched sounds of boys at play mingled with the crack of a ball hitting a bat as childhood games he'd played in the park materialized in his mind. He stared at the park hard as figures of people, some long dead, filled it.

He got into his car, puffing from the exertion of fitting his big belly behind the steering wheel, and tried to etch the sights into his brain.

This would be the last time he'd ever see this place. This would be the last day he'd ever be called Giuseppe Geddone. A small pang of homesickness went through him, surprising him that it was there at all.

He drove to his office and opened up the safe. He took out the ledgers and a passport he'd had made. A fuzzy picture of himself in a dark wig stared out, and next to it was typed the name Myron Baxter.

He'd spent one week writing out the name, trying it different ways until he was satisfied with it.

He wrote one last check to Myron Baxter for $100,000 and signed it Giuseppe Geddone at the bottom. He put the check and the passport in his briefcase next to his airplane ticket and snapped it shut. He lighted a cigar and stared out at the view from the window for one last time. He had four hours to kill before his plane took off. He figured he'd make his way slowly and easily out to the airport, maybe stop somewhere for a bite to eat, then check in.

He caught himself smiling as the homesickness vanished forever. Now it was his turn—no wife, no screaming daughter, no basket case of a son.

No. Myron Baxter's first order of the day was gonna be to rent himself a yacht and sail around for awhile.

Women. He could have women again—young, beautiful European women. They wouldn't care that he was fifty pounds overweight, bald, and short.

He was a rich American, a rich WASP American aboard his yacht—out for a journey, a little sail, while other people worked like dogs in offices.

He could imagine himself, his yacht moored on the French Riviera or in Marbella on the Costa del Sol. And, after a couple months of sailing, he'd find himself a place to live, probably in one of them Latin countries with no extradition.

Of course, at this point, the law was the least of his problems.

* * *

"What are you, some kind of loony?" Michael whispered hoarsely into Michigan's ear, so close, he brushed her earlobe.

"Me?" she whispered back. "What did you expect me to do? Just sit there, knowing you're going to kill my boss?"

Tony Mac coughed up front and they both shut up for a moment. He turned the radio up louder and began to hum to the music and think about Angela and that dip Joey D. and dating. Veal scaloppini.

"Who do you think you are? Fuckin' Joan of Arc? We're in a city where solid citizens step over poor starving people in the street, where you can shoot someone in front of one hundred people in a restaurant and nobody'll see a thing—"

"Tell me about it. The cops weren't even interested."

"What do you mean?"

"I called nine-one-one. They hung up on me. I just don't get this city."

"You called *them*?" his voice rasped.

"Of course I called them. What kind of a person do you think I am?"

"Ssshh!" Michael said sharply into her ear, and his eyes got big and round as he stared at the back of Tony's head. "Never, ever say that aloud again, you hear me?" His lips were nearly pressed against her earlobe. He stayed there for a second, then leaned back, his eyes bulging.

He was flabbergasted. How naïve could she be? Not only had she called the cops but she was telling the guy with the gun that she had?

"What planet do you come from, Mars?"

"No, Michigan. Remember?" she snapped at him.

"Jesus! I told you what to do."

"Oh, and I'm supposed to follow some thug's advice? I might not have done the best thing, but at least I tried to do the right thing, don't you understand?"

He stared her right in the eyes. "I got you off the hook back there. Don't you understand? I told you to count to one hundred and then get the hell out of the office. Go to your tea party in Boston."

"Barbecue in Connecticut," she said hotly.

"Connecticut," he spat back at her. "Well, I hope you're satisfied. You're going to die now. But hell, you did the right thing!"

He watched her mouth fall, and she sat back and clasped her hands tightly. They both watched her mangle her fingers until Michael couldn't stand it anymore and grabbed her hand and held it. He could feel her shivering next to him.

"When nine-one-one hung up on me, I . . . just thought . . ." Her voice dropped down to nothing and she stared out the window.

Michael dropped her hand, and she stared back at him as he looked at the floor. Now he felt badly about being that blunt.

"What is it? Do you have a thing for this guy?" Michael asked quietly.

He heard her blow out a breath.

"Are you *kidding*?" she said, whispering close to his ear. "I hate him. And I'll tell you something right now, if I get out of this alive? I'm going in and quit. I don't need this. Life is too short to have to put up with someone like him. I've had enough of this city, and everybody in it. I want to go *home*," she said, her voice cracking on the word. She brushed his earlobe with her lips.

He felt a tingle go down his neck, and he turned and looked at her, feeling her close to him.

He stared at her lips. . . .

Tony coughed up front, and Michael snapped back into things. Jeez, this was weird. He swore he was beginning to want this woman. This naïve, upright, honest—he moved away from her on the seat. What would she want with someone like him? A man who'd held a gun to her head and tied her up? Not to mention the fact that he was a failure, which was why he was running around New York doing stupid things like this.

Lisa moved closer to him on the seat, and he looked at her face, seeing it appear clearly and then vanish into shadows as they went in and out of the bridge lights. He could feel the tires of the car running over the mesh roadway of the bridge. It created an odd hum and a small vibration on the seat. He could feel her pressing herself against his body and staring up at him, her eyes big and watery.

"I am going to die tonight, aren't I?" she whispered, her face not even an inch away from his.

He stared at her as the tears began to fall.

She felt herself instinctively reach around him and take a deep breath. His body seemed to throw off an inordinate amount of heat. She just needed to hold on to someone. He put his arm around her and tightened it against her shoulders. She took another deep breath and laid her head on his chest.

It felt good, being held. It had been so long since anyone had touched him.

"Aw jeez," he said. "I'll think of something."

* * *

Giuseppe Geddone stubbed out his cigar and looked at his watch. It was ten. Time to get out to Idlewild—no, Kennedy. For some reason, that airport still stuck in his head as Idlewild.

He was just about to open his briefcase for one last look when a sharp itchy feeling went up his back, straightening it as flat as a board. His ears pricked up. He was straining as he stood there, not even breathing, so he could hear better.

Off in the distance of the outer office, there was a small creak of the outer office door.

He swore he heard it. He snapped off the lamp quickly, walked around the desk, and ducked down. He exhaled from stooping and was having trouble catching his breath. He would lose a little weight in Europe, he thought, trying to keep his mind sharp and on his prize. He carefully slid out his bottom drawer, felt around. His fingers wrapped themselves around the old dusty pistol and pulled it out. He put the safety off, cocked it, and shifted his weight onto one foot so he could get at his belt. He stuffed it in at the waistband.

He hoped to hell it was loaded. He hadn't looked at it in ten years, since the first time they showed to him, his first day there at work.

A floorboard creaked, closer to his office door, and he centered himself on both feet, trying to run down what would be the best thing to do. He could hear whispering.

BAM.

The door to his office swung open and bounced off the wall, then shut itself. He took a breath.

WHAM. It swung open again, but less hard this time, and he peered over the desktop, looking at the empty doorway. He saw a flash of light on metal, along the barrel of a gun being held up by a hand, on one side of the door.

"We know youse in there, Giuseppe," he heard Tony Mac's voice call into the room. "We seen the light on when we come in."

So that was it. They'd sent Tony Macaroni to do the job.

Fuckin' Ralphie. Lyin' rat bastard—

"Why don't you make it easy on yourself and come outta there?" a second voice said, and Giuseppe bobbed his head up over the desk, puzzled.

He didn't recognize the second voice at all.

Madonna.

Solly'd sent *two* people to do him. Little Giuseppe Geddone, CPA, rated *two* hitters?

"Where are we?" a third voice whispered.

"Ssshhhh."

"What are we doing here?"

"Would you shut her up?" Tony Mac's voice whispered.

"Sshhh!"

"Well, I'm just asking a question—"

"For God's sake, shut her up!" Tony's voice boomed.

Lisa felt her mouth drop as she huddled in the dark next to Michael. They were in some kind of office building. She took a step forward to try to see what Tony was doing, and the sight of him holding a gun up made her bite her bottom lip hard. Michael's hand squeezed hers and he drew it around his stomach. She felt her pressing herself, pressing against his back, and realized that they had been hanging on to one another since the car. She was just about his height, she noticed.

Giuseppe crouched, trying to breathe, in back of his

fortress, the desk. Three hitters? Three people to get a poor little accountant who was just trying to make a buck like the rest of America?

And a woman, no less.

God, it was like Solly'd hired a whole fuckin' army to wipe him out. Okay, one person, maybe he could take, but three?

"C'mon, Giusepp', we got you here. Why's make it hard on everybody?"

Snap.

The overhead lights went on, and Giuseppe squinted in the light and slowly stood up, his arms in the air, as Tony Mac entered fully, his gun pointed at Giuseppe's head. He was followed by a woman Giuseppe didn't recognize at all, being pushed inside by Vincent Bonello's kid, Michael.

"Mikey? That you?"

"Yeah, Giusepp', it's me."

"What you doing here? I thought you was a lawyer."

Michael swallowed, but his mouth was bone-dry. Tony grabbed Michigan's arm and pushed her over next to Giuseppe. He came back to stand beside Michael.

Tony Mac grunted and broke in. "Solly's very angry wid youse."

"Why?"

"You been skimming off his money."

"Me?"

"C'mon, c'mon, we want the money—"

"What money?"

"The *money*, now!" Tony Mac boomed, and he made it across the floor in one step.

Michael stared at Michigan, who was shaking and staring at him as she realized which side of the room she was standing in. Tony raised the handle of the gun and grabbed Giuseppe by the collar. He lifted him up until Geddone's toes were barely touching the floor.

"Give me the fuckin' money now," he said, and raised the gun back, ready to swing it into Giuseppe's jaw.

"The briefcase. There are two passbooks—"

Tony Mac dropped him down, went to the briefcase, and began trying to open the locked case. After a moment, he slammed the top with his fist and shot it.

The thud of the case on the floor was mingled with a whine from Michigan, who began to cry and looked as if she was going to pass out. She was shaking uncontrollably and her knees began to buckle. She felt herself falling back against a filing cabinet for support.

Tony Mac emptied the case out on the floor and sifted through it as Michael kept his gun centered on Giuseppe. He picked up two passbooks, the plane ticket, and the passport. Geddone looked over at Michael.

"Mikey, why? You was a good—"

"Shut your face," Tony ordered, flipping the passport open with his free hand while the other was pointed at Geddone. He grimaced and stared at the signature.

"You gonna sign this over to Solly," he ordered, and Giuseppe nodded.

Lisa kept her eyes on Michael as Tony and Giuseppe took care of the paperwork. She kept shaking her head at him, feeling as if she was going to get sick. She relaxed a second when he mouthed to her to be calm. Tony then ordered Giuseppe back against the wall, with his arms raised.

"Tony, please, I knew your father."

"Yeah, Pop hated you. Nobody steals from the Soltanos. You shoulda known that. Everything you have is because of Solly. You shoulda remembered that, Giuseppe," Tony finished, then stepped back next to Michael.

They all stood in silence for a moment until Tony looked over at Michael.

"What you waiting for, Mikey?" Tony snapped.

"I—I just . . ." Michael stammered.

"You got the fuckin' safety on," Tony said, and he grabbed the gun from him, clicked it off, cocked it, and handed it back. "You gotta get the hang of this better, Mikey," he scolded.

Lisa looked over next to her. Giuseppe Geddone's hands were raised over his head, with his jacket waving loosely around his big belly. She looked back at Michael, who was holding the gun out, pointing it at Giuseppe.

"C'mon, Mikey, I'm hungry," Tony said, and waited another second.

"Shoot him now."

"I CAN'T," Michael screamed.

"What?"

"I can't do it, Tony." He lowered the gun, shaking. "I can't shoot him. I'm not a killer. I don't know how to kill him."

"Whadda you talkin'? You just aim the gun and squeeze. It's easy—anyone can do it."

"Well, I can't!"

"Mikey, come," Tony said, pulling him back a couple of steps. He turned his back to Lisa and Giuseppe and lowered his voice.

"You promised *Solly.*"

"I know, but I just can't do it."

"You gotta."

"Why?"

" 'Cause otherwise, I gotta shoot you."

"What?"

Lisa glanced over next to her at Giuseppe and then, suddenly, looked down as something caught her eye. He moved his arms back and she stood, staring at the gun stuck in his waistband. Her stomach began to knot up and she looked back over at Michael and Tony.

"Because it's morally wrong," Michael was saying.

"But Solly *wants* this."

"So? You do everything Solly says?"

"Yeah."

"Why?"

"He *got* me this job—"

Lisa heard Giuseppe exhale next to her, and she knew, deep down, he was deciding whether this was his chance. She stared back at the gun, then raised her eyes and looked up at his face. He was glaring at her. Suddenly, it sank in: There was going to be a gunfight. She felt her chin drop as she realized that if Tony didn't shoot her, this guy would. She had to do something.

In a second, she watched Giuseppe's hands begin to drop, and without thinking she made a grab for the gun. He grabbed her arms as she tried to pull it free, but his ample stomach kept rolling over it, trapping her fingers in the waistband like a vise of flesh as they struggled.

"What the—" was all Lisa heard of Tony's voice as Giuseppe yanked hard on her arms.

Her hands tightened suddenly and she got a grip on the handle and pulled it free. It sent her reeling back against the filing cabinet. The metal sounded like a clap of thunder going off next to her ear.

"Give me the gun," Giuseppe growled, motioning with his fingers as he began to take steps toward her.

She began backing out toward the window, shaking her head as he stalked her.

"Give me the fuckin' gun," he growled louder.

"Don't come any closer," she squeaked, and felt a breeze from the window.

"Give it to me NOW," he screamed, and lunged.

When she opened her eyes, she was flat on her back, staring at a crack in the ceiling that looked like a rabbit. The back of her head hurt where she had hit it against the open window sash. She stayed there, perfectly still, finally hearing the voices.

"She got him clean all right, lookit this, Mikey."

"My God."

"Jeez, that's clean, one shot, almost perfectly centered, right between the eyes."

She slowly, reluctantly lifted her head in time to see Michael back away to the desk and lean down. She could see him swallowing hard, trying to control himself.

Tony's voice floated back down to her as she tried to concentrate on the crack.

"I could'na done it better myself. She's a good shot, Mikey. Not a great shot, but a good one. A little training and she could be valuable."

Lisa groaned, and Michael looked over at her. He looked down and dropped his gun on the desk and went over to where she was. She looked up at him, and he fell to his knees.

"Are you okay?" he asked, his voice quivering slightly.

"No."

"Are you hurt?"

"What have I done?" she whispered.

He gave her a hand, and she stood up, wobbling like a

new calf. She gaped at the body and realized her lower lip was bleeding.

Michael looked over at Tony, who was now busy stuffing the passbooks into his pockets and wiping down the table with his handkerchief. Michael looked back down to her, and suddenly everything fell into place. He began to exhale, as though fifty-ton weights had been taken off his chest.

It was over. Giuseppe was dead, and *he* hadn't shot him. Michigan had done it, in self-defense. All he had to do now was go back to Solly's, pick up the bonus, and figure out how to get her out of this whole mess, or how to calm down Rosa Morelli's bloodthirst. Everything would be all right now. He'd have time to back out now, get away from the Soltanos and Tony Mac.

What a gift he'd gotten from her. He was off the hook.

"What have I done?" she repeated, and he suddenly focused in on her. She was riveted to the body, and shaking, and he realized that she was going to lose it.

"Oh *my* God! Oh my *God*!" Her eyes were stuck on the body and her neck seemed to have been bolted into place, so she could look neither up, nor down, nor sideways. And there was this shouting feeling of panic across her torso as the hair on her head seemed to stand on end, and the bloody face of the body began mixing itself with the last image she had had of his face as he lunged at her. Of his eyes and nose and face, when he was a living human being. And the face was coming closer and closer and she again saw him lunging at her and his voice saying, "Give it to me NOW." "GIVE IT TO ME NOW" boomed over her like a thunderstorm and Lisa suddenly felt herself put her hands over her ears as though to block him out, and she heard the echoes of her own screams desperately trying to drown out the sounds of the man inside her own head. My God, I *shot* and *killed* another human being! Good God Almighty. "I took someone's life," she heard herself screaming.

Tony ran over to her.

"We gotta get her out of here," he ordered.

Tony took one arm and Michael took the other. They carried her, still screaming, down and out of the building. Tony exhaled as they stood on the street, with her screams echoing off the empty buildings. He dropped his keys, spun around, and gave her a wallop with the back of his hand.

Lisa grabbed her cheek with the side of her hand and stared at him.

"Shut the fuck up! Whatta you makin' a fuckin' big deal outta nothin', fahcrissakes?"

He opened the car and unlocked the doors.

Tony got in front and Michael took his usual position next to her. She slid down in the seat, holding her stomach as Tony started the car.

"Anybody hungry?" Tony asked after a moment.

They both stared at him incredulously. He turned back and put the car into first, and drove to the corner.

"I gotta get something to eat. Let's see if Forlini's is open, huh, Mikey?"

"I don't know, Tony. I don't know if I could eat right now."

Tony grunted and then looked back over his shoulder at Michigan.

"What about you? You hungry, Michigan?"

"Aw God, I think I'm going to be sick," she said, and covered her mouth with one hand.

"Well *I*'m hungry here, so I'm taking us down to Forlini's," Tony said forcefully, and began to drive up the ramp to the Brooklyn Bridge.

"And after I get something in my stomach, we can decide what to do," he added.

"Do about what?"

"What to tell Solly."

"Solly?" Michael asked, leaning forward. "What do you mean? We did it. We got his money, and . . . did it. All we have to do is go there and pick up the bonus."

Tony got onto the bridge as Lisa sat up and stared grimly at the bright city lights.

"Now, Mikey, that ain't exactly true."

"What are you talking about, Tony?"

"Well, we got the money to give him when we go there, but the rest of it, it din't go down the way Solly wanted," Tony said quietly. "You can't pick up that bonus, Mikey, it ain't fair."

"What?"

"Well, Mikey, Michigan was the one did him. That fourteen should be hers, and we gotta tell Solly, so he can give you something else to do to make your bones."

Michael fell back in his seat and darted a glance over at Michigan.

She was Jell-O.

He stared back up at Tony.

"You can't tell him that some girl we picked up did the hit for him," Michael began. "He'd . . ." Michael's voice trailed off.

"But he owes Michigan the money. She done the hit—she get the payment."

"Tony, this is crazy. You can't tell him what really happened. . . ."

"You want me to *lie*? Lie to Solly?" His voice was

booming with indignation. "I can't do that, Mikey. Besides, you gotta do something real to make your bones. That's what it's all about. He gotta get something on you, see? That way, you gotta be loyal to the family or it's your ass, and you ain't done nothin'."

"I was in on a murder," he offered.

"Yeah, but that don't count. You gotta pull the trigger."

"You're all confused."

"I ain't confused, Mikey. You're the one confused. Solly owes Michigan fourteen bills for the hit and you ain't made your bones."

Michael sat back again and stared down at her. She didn't seem to be moving or listening at all. What could he say?

"But she wouldn't have done it if we hadn't brought her there, would she?"

Tony was silent for a moment, and Michael could feel him twisting his face up into his painful thinking expression. The truth was, he didn't give a damn about the money, but he didn't want to be there when Solly was told, and he certainly didn't want to be given *another* task. This one was enough.

He pulled the car down the ramp and headed over to Little Italy.

"We discuss it over dinner at the restaurant," he said finally.

Lisa closed her eyes and the horrible sight of the man lying there came into her head, as if it was on instant rewind on a VCR. She had stopped screaming, that was true. After Tony's slap, this eerie numbness had overtaken her. She opened her eyes again, wondering how long the sight was going to stay with her. Would she always see the body?

Guilt began to gnaw at her. She'd just left some poor man lying in a pool of blood, and the only thing she could think of was when would the picture in her mind fade.

She thought about going back home to Bliss, Michigan. And she thought about church. In all her years at the end of the sermons, when they were supposed to reflect upon their sins, like an unspoken confession, just about the worst she'd ever come up with was sleeping with some guy or cheating on her tax return. That was enough for the Presbyterians to sentence her to eternal hell.

She could hear it now: "I lived with a man for four years in an unmarried state and I shot some guy to death in an office in Brooklyn."

She couldn't imagine where she'd get sent for murder, and she didn't want to know.

And then the thought occurred to her that it didn't matter anyway, because she was never going to see Bliss again.

This had all just gone far enough. The fact was that she should have called the police back, or at least someone *else* in the police department. There must have been someone out there who would have taken her seriously. I could handle this: The pious thought she had had echoed in her head. Who had she been kidding? These guys had guns. But had she even thought about that? Had she even considered it? No! Instead, she just went off on some fantasy. She was reprimanding herself, and then it settled in her head; it was enough. This all was going to end right now.

She cleared her throat. Michael looked over at her. She looked at him with an odd expression.

"You can drop me at the police station."

"What?" he said.

"I didn't hear that. What she want?" Tony asked.

"Drop me at a police station. I'm going to turn myself in."

Lisa was thrown against Michael as Tony veered the car onto the sidewalk and slammed on the brakes. As she pushed Michael off, Tony turned around, switched on the overhead light, and stared at her like she was from outer space.

"What you say?"

"I'm going to turn myself in."

"Fahcrissakes, why?" Tony asked, obviously mystified.

She stared back at him with the same incredulous expression. "I just killed a man."

"Yeah . . ." Tony said, waiting for her to continue.

"I just *killed* someone."

Tony blinked.

"I can't do this anymore. I don't want to cause any more pain than I have. I don't want to have the police looking for me. I just want to turn myself in."

"Mikey, help me on this," Tony said, staring at him.

Michael looked over at her and finally cleared his voice. "Don't you think it was self-defense?" he offered weakly.

"Aw-what?" Tony groaned and stared at him, then turned back to Michigan. "Look, honey, you got him fair and square. You done good. He was nothin' but a no-good thief—"

"I shot him—"

"Yeah, yeah, like I said, you done good. Now you can't turn yourself *in* to the cops. You'd insult them. And you'd set a bad example. They wouldn't know what to do wid youse, *capisce?*"

"No," she said after a moment.

"Aw Christ, don't you understand nothin'? Look, their job is to catch you, right?"

"Yeah—"

"That's how they feed their families, see?"

She nodded and glanced at Michael, confused. He shrugged, and they both looked back to Tony, whose face was all tied up into an expression that could only be described as agony.

"So what happens to their families if everybody who did somethin' turned themselves in, huh? They'd be out jobs. Their kids would starve; they'd have to move out to the country. It would be a mess. Plus, if you just turn yourself in, it'd be like you didn't think they was smart enough to catch you on their own, see? So now, you got 'em unemployed, and *insulted* 'cause you gonna turn yourself in for killin' a rat-bastard thief?" Tony shook his head at her.

"I . . . " she murmured. "I didn't think . . ." Her voice trailed off. Michael sat silent, trying to run through Tony's logic.

Tony turned back around front and pulled the car back into the street.

"Well, we all can't think of everything, right, Mikey? As long as you got it straight now. Jeez, turn yourself in . . . that's crazy. You know how many of them guys would be unemployed in this city? Must be a hundred thousand of 'em."

He muttered to himself, shaking his head, and turned the car down to Hester Street and parked. He swung himself out, walked around, and opened the door for Michigan. She darted a glance at Michael and allowed

Tony to help her out of the car. Michael walked behind them, watching Tony carefully.

"You like braciola?"

"I don't know what it is," she said, confused, and suddenly she felt very tired. Michael grimaced as Tony put his arm through hers as they walked down the small, winding street toward Forlini's.

"They don't have braciola where you come from? Jeez. What do youse people eat up there in Canada?"

They walked along to the restaurant, Tony almost holding Lisa up and Michael walking silently behind.

Tony pulled a chair out for Michigan and made sure she was comfortable. Michael watched him intensely. There was something brewing in Tony's mind about her. It was something that Michael was not too thrilled with.

"You want a nice antipast'?" he asked, smiling at her.

"I really don't think I could—"

"You'll feel better if you eat. I'll order a hot and a cold for youse to try."

"Tony, I don't think she's hungry—" Michael began, but he was cut off by Tony's glare.

"Don't you gotta call your mother?" Tony asked, leaning forward.

"What?"

"Wasn't your mother makin' *trota* for youse?"

"Yeah . . ."

"Jeez, ain't you got no manners? I told her I'd have you home early," Tony said, motioning with his head that he wanted Michael to leave the table.

Michael glanced at Michigan, who moved her head ever so slightly and looked panicked, as though if he left her alone with Tony, she would die.

"Mikey, call you mother," Tony ordered. "It's ten o'-clock at night."

Michael shrugged and stood up. Lisa watched, terrified, as he walked away. Tony looked back at her and smiled.

"You got good aim. Where you say you come from?" he asked softly, smiling at her.

Michael went over to the maître d' and asked for the phones. He was directed to the small entryway. He stood in front of a phone and looked at his watch. Through the plate-glass doorway, he could see Michigan and Tony at the table. He watched the waiter bring over two glasses of what he knew was cola. He stared at Tony, who was talking and smiling at her.

That was all he needed. He walked back inside the restaurant and over to the table. He leaned down and looked at Tony.

"My mother wants to talk to you," he said quietly.

Tony looked up, stunned. "Your mother wants to talk to me? What I do?" Tony stood up and looked at Michigan. "Youse don't go anywhere. We'll be right over there," he said, pointing to the phone.

They walked back out to the entryway. Before he could stop him, Tony had picked up the receiver.

"They ain't nobody on the other end," Tony said, hanging up the phone.

"I just wanted to talk to you. Listen, what are we going to do about Michigan?"

"Whadda you mean? We gonna give Solly the stuff we got from Giuseppe, and, when they discover the body, she'll collect the money and you'll—"

"I'm not doing any more, Tony."

"What?" he asked, staring at him.

"I'm not making my bones. I can't do it. You saw me back there. I don't belong."

There was a stunned silence from Tony.

"Aw, he's not gonna like that."

"Can you fix it?"

Tony's eyes crossed.

"I don't know, Mikey, you know a lot. . . . I never asked nothin' like this of Solly before."

Michael stood silently.

"Maybe you're being too hard on yourself," Tony offered. "Maybe you just need some practice."

Michael shook his head.

"I thought you liked ridin' wid me," Tony said after a moment.

Michael stared up at him.

"I like riding with you fine, Tony. But I just can't do what you do. . . . What are we gonna do about Michigan?"

"Whadda you mean?"

"Solly said to whack her, remember?"

Tony's jaw dropped, and Michael watched him look through the glass to where she was.

"Madonna, I forgot."

He watched Tony turn and stare at her in silence for a moment.

"Jeez, everything's all screwed up, huh, Mikey?"

"Yeah. . . . Look, I was thinking. We were supposed to ice her along with Giuseppe, right? So she couldn't tell anyone I shot him, right?" Tony nodded. "But then she shot him, so . . . how could she rat on herself?"

It seemed to make perfect sense to Tony.

"That's right. She got nothing on us. Now, we got something on her. And as long as she's straightened out on how the cops work . . ."

"So why don't we just call it even, and Solly won't be the worse for wear, huh? It's not like we're going to lie to him; we just won't mention the girl. Solly probably won't even remember about her."

Tony looked back inside and then back at Michael.

Lisa sat through dinner, watching Tony eat, and periodically looking over at Michael. She began to assess them both.

She liked looking at Michael. She had felt oddly safe with him from the moment he had looked away, embarrassed, in Mrs. Morelli's apartment and on the Brooklyn Bridge. Even in the office, when Tony was trying to force Michael to shoot, she knew he wouldn't do it. She didn't know how he'd gotten mixed up in all this, but he was either a very decent human being or an unbelievably incompetent gangster. She felt strangely attracted to him and . . .

She stopped herself, feeling her jaw tighten. Attractive or not, this man had held a gun on her. Now what? Maybe she was turning into one of those sick women who liked that sort of thing. . . . Naw. Her eyes darted to Tony.

Tony, on the other hand, was from another planet. Tony's reasoning about turning herself in had just about worn her down mentally. Michael was right, it had been self-defense, but . . . It was as if she didn't care anymore. Screw the mortgage. She was going to quit her job and get as far away from this city as possible.

Tony excused himself, finally, and Lisa looked over at Michael.

"What are you going to do now?" she asked tiredly.

Michael smiled at her. "We're going to go back to Mulberry Street, and then I think we'll let you go. You have to promise never to say a word about this."

She looked at him and took a deep breath. As she exhaled, every single worry and thought about Henry Foster Morgan vanished. He was on his own. They had worn her down. She just wanted to get back home and be quiet. She was definitely leaving this city forever on Monday.

"All right, you have my word," she said, and looked at him. She gave him a weak smile. "Thank you for protecting me back there."

Tony threw the passbooks down on Solly's desk, and Michael watched him pick them up, smirk, and look back up to Tony. He took the passport out of his pocket and added it to the pile. Solly picked it up. His stocky face and bulbous nose were the vision of sheer enjoyment. Solly was savoring the kill as though he had personally pulled the trigger. He then looked over at Michael.

"You done good. Where you leave him?"

"In his office."

Solly sat back in his chair, touching his fingertips together. "Okay. That's good. It'll be a warning. . . . You done good, Mikey," he said, and leaned forward in his chair.

He slid open his desk drawer and threw an envelope on the table. He nodded to Tony, who picked it up.

"Half. Until they find the body," he added as Tony opened it up.

They nodded and began to turn to leave.

"Now you take care of Rosa's problem."

Tony's eyes slid over to Michael, who looked at him. He turned back to Solly.

"I, uh . . ." Tony stammered.

"What did you do with the girl's body?" Solly added, and Tony began to rock slowly back and forth.

"Well, um . . ."

Michael watched Solly's smile turn into a frown as he leaned forward.

"You did take care of the girl, right, Tony?"

"Well, you see, Solly—" Tony began, but Michael broke in.

"Look, Solly—"

"Mikey didn't exactly shoot Giuseppe," Tony broke in.

"What are you sayin' to me? Giuseppe ain't dead?" Solly asked loudly, and stood up.

"No, no, he's dead. Dead as a dog. It's just that . . . Mikey didn't exactly—"

"Say what you're saying," he ordered.

"I didn't shoot him—the girl did," Michael said quickly, and they watched Solly's eyes get large and popping and then narrow as he sat back down.

"Say this again?"

"Well, I was getting ready to shoot him—"

"He was, he was, Solly. He just forgot to take the safety off—"

"And that's when we seen Michigan—"

"Who?"

"The girl, that's when she seen he had a gun on him, and she grabbed it and shot him."

A roll of Rolaids appeared from the desk drawer and Solly stared at them both.

"Who the hell is this broad?"

"She's nobody. She's from outta town."

"WHATSA MATTER WID YOUSE? Outta town or not, she's gotta go, and you, Mikey . . ." he began, snatching the envelope out of Tony's hands.

"But—"

"You tried to pull a fast one, and I don't like it. I know this ain't Tony's idea, College, and I'll let you slide on account of Vincent was your father, but now you owe me, Mikey. . . . Go take care of the sonofabeech for Rosa and then I'll decide what happens. Where is the girl?"

"They brought her out front, Solly," Ralphie informed him.

"Take care of her."

"But, Solly," Michael began, and took a deep breath, "we need her to get to the boss."

"Fine, then get to the boss, do 'em both, and I don't wanna hear no more."

Tony was just about to say something when Ralphie came up behind him and opened the door.

They walked out stiffly and Michigan stood up. She followed Michael out the door. He shot a glance back inside, in time to see Louie whispering something in Tony's ear. He watched Tony's chin drop and his eyes bulge. Something Tony'd just been told was making him irate. It was hard to tell from Tony's face that he was burning up, but Michael knew it from all his years with his cousin.

"Goddamn it!" Tony was tearing down Mulberry toward Grand, with Michael following him, and pulling Michigan by the hand.

"Tony—"

"A-fah-na-bla! Fourteen grand—"

"Tony—"

"SHUT UP," he yelled, and unlocked the car door.

"What's happening?" Lisa asked as she was pushed back inside. "Can I go?"

Michael just stared at her, and she looked down. "Oh."

The car squealed out of the parking space. They were all quiet for a moment.

"All right, where the fuck will what's-his-name be?" Tony barked, driving across Canal toward Sixth Avenue.

"I won't tell you," she said quietly.

"Fine, Mikey, we're going to every place on the list."

"Aw come on, Tony, it'll take all night."

"Listen, did you hear Solly back there? He ain't happy, and when he ain't happy, I ain't happy. It's only midnight. Now, where's that book?"

"Right here."

"What's the first place on the list?"

"Some political thing."

"Good, what's the address?"

"It's on Fourteenth Street, a place called Maude's."

"Maude's?" Lisa said, then caught herself. She sat back in the seat.

"What do you know about this place?"

"Nothing—"

"Tell me now," he ordered, and Michael looked into the backseat at her.

"Fine. I'll tell you what I know about Maude's. You'll never get in there, so I wouldn't even try," Lisa heard herself snap.

"Yeah? Why not?"

"They have these huge guys at the door who don't let

anyone inside. You have to have a membership or know someone to get in."

"Yeah? Well, I know someone."

Tony pulled the car up in front of the unmarked building on Fourteenth Street by making a screeching U-turn. A long line of people, very dressed up and some looking bored, others angry, stared out at the car. If it hadn't been for the line, there wouldn't have been anyone on the block.

Tony got out, and Michael came around to get Lisa.

"I'm sorry. It almost worked," he began to explain softly as he got her out of the car.

"Just leave me alone." Her voice was terse and strained.

"Come on, I really did try, Michigan—"

She stopped and glared. "My name is Lisa. All right?"

He stared at her in her small print dress, still in her sneakers and the socks with the little pom-poms on the heel, and he suddenly felt cowed by her.

"All right, Lisa."

"Thank you," she said curtly.

She was feeling too tired to be afraid anymore.

Tony stopped at the front of the line.

"Oh Jeez," Michael said, grabbing her by the arm. "Here we go."

Tony banged with his fist on the black door, and after a minute it slammed open and a muscle-bound man in a large white T-shirt, stomped out.

"Who did that?" he demanded.

Tony pushed him backward through the open door as Michael and Lisa followed. Michael closed the door behind them and they stood in the dark hallway to the club. Tony towered over the man in the T-shirt.

"We're going inside to look for someone, *capisce*?" he said, pulling the bouncer up by his shirt.

"You've got to be joking. No one but members—"

Tony pulled his gun out, then cocked it while the barrel was against the bouncer's temple.

"This is my membership. Now, you stay quiet a couple of minutes and no one gets hurt," he said, and pushed inside.

Lisa and Michael followed. She stood, staring at the place in wonder as Tony began walking through the crowded club.

"Are you okay?" Michael asked.

"Yes. My God, this is what it looks like in here." Her voice had the ring of just having landed in Oz.

"Yeah, right, come on, let's find Tony before the cops get here," Michael said, trying to take her by the arm.

She walked by a round upholstered bench, staring in wonder at the huge fresh flower arrangement on top of it. The walls were covered in red velvet and all the furniture looked like something out of an old English movie she'd seen. Chicly dressed people mulled around talking to one another, some staring at her strangely, and Lisa consciously ran her hands across her print dress, which looked as out of place here as a snowsuit on a beach in August.

"You know, Andrew and I tried to get in here once, but they wouldn't let us," she said in a respectful whisper.

"Who's Andrew?" Michael asked, stopping in the middle of the floor.

She stared up at him and shut her mouth quickly. She'd goofed.

"Is he your boyfriend?"

She began to walk around him, and he wrapped his hand around her arm. "You have a boyfriend?"

Henry's limo pulled up outside the club. He bent over a small mirror and snorted loudly. He was down to almost no blow. That was all right—he was finally here, the place where for eighteen hundred dollars a year he could call home. He stepped out of the limo and looked at the chauffeur. She was a small blond woman. All his drivers were women. It was considered a necessity these days.

"Pick me up around three," he said, staring down at her.

She nodded and he watched her drive away. He turned and walked up to the black door, which was open. He barely glanced at the lines of nobodies down the street.

"Hey, wait a minute. I've been here for three hours!" he heard an outraged voice yell as he slipped through the door.

"Yeah, that's what I said, a big, big guy with a gun." Rodney, the bouncer, was on the phone, seemingly agitated. He waved Henry inside and went back to his conversation.

Henry made a beeline for the rest room.

Michael spotted Tony looking around in a small cubicle with more of the low, heavy Victorian furniture.

"I see him," he said to Lisa.

"It's great, isn't it?" she said as Michael pulled her over into the cubicle Tony was standing in.

"I can't see a thing in here. Did you see him?" Tony asked as they came up to him.

"No. Listen, Tony, we got to get out of here. They're probably calling the cops right now," Michael said.

"Yeah, yeah. Jeez, this dump looks like a horror show, huh, Mikey?" Tony said, grimacing at the furniture. "I mean, you gotta be some kinda midget or something to sit on this crap."

"I think it's perfect," Lisa chimed in. "It's atmosphere that they're going for. And look at all these people. I can't figure out their names, but I know they're famous. Just look at . . ." her voice trailed off and she froze where she was.

She blinked and stared again at a man and a woman in the corner. The woman was sitting on the man's lap, and they were laughing and sharing a glass of champagne.

"Come on, let's go. There's gotta be a better way," Tony announced, and began to walk off.

Michael followed, felt around for Lisa, then turned around and went back over to her.

Lisa was beginning to have trouble breathing as she watched the man begin to rub the woman's fishnetted leg up and down, pushing her short black skirt even higher up on her thigh. The woman laughed and craned her head around and they went into a long, passionate kiss.

"Come on, we've got to—" Michael began, and then looked at her. "What's wrong?"

Tears were running down Lisa's face as she stood staring at Andrew and the woman he'd brought over for dinner several times in the last two years.

Michael's eyes scanned the room and followed her stare to a man and woman across the floor. He watched them for a moment, then looked down at her.

"Who is that?"

She opened her mouth slightly, though no sound came out. She couldn't take her eyes off of them.

"That's Andrew," she said mechanically, not even looking up at him. "He's the guy I live with."

Five

Lisa slid down in the backseat of the car. All right, she was admitting it—she'd been playing this game of "see no evil" with Andrew for years. As long as it wasn't smacking her in the face, she didn't feel she had to do anything.

Well, she'd just gotten slapped.

She stared out the window at Michael, talking to Tony Mac, arguing with him. She didn't care. She didn't care about anyone or anything. She shouldn't have gotten out of bed this morning.

What had she done wrong? She paid half the rent; she kept the place clean; she did his laundry; she cooked—used to—for him. Maybe that was it, maybe if she had cooked more, maybe if she'd been more like . . .

Her breathing became shallow and tears spilled down her face. She felt stupid and foolish.

Tony and Michael got into the car silently. Tony started it up and drove over to Tenth Avenue. In the rearview mirror was the flashing reflection of police lights, stopping in front of the club.

"Where you live at?" Tony said quietly.

"Why?" she whispered.

"You're goin' home."

"Seventy-second."

"I couldn't believe it when I heard. Someone actually was so desperate to get in here, they pulled a gun on Rodney?" Henry was asking as he leaned against the sink in the bathroom.

"That's right," Morris said, sifting through a Baggie of gram and half-gram packets of coke. He dug in and handed Henry three.

He pocketed them immediately.

"Good God, you mean this place has been infected with the tread of a *nobody*?"

"And there were some other guys with him, huge guys, Rodney said."

"And Rodney couldn't take care of him?" Henry said, and began to back toward the door.

"I heard the guy was about seven feet tall and—don't you owe me something, Henry?" he asked, holding out his hand.

"Really, Morris, how droll—" Henry began.

"No, no more of this shit. You're into me for fourteen hundred, and I want it."

"The whole thing?"

"That's right. And I want it tonight, Henry."

"Are you threatening me?" Henry asked, standing up as straight as he could.

"Yup," Morris said, walking over near him and staring him in the face. "I don't do this out of the goodness of my heart."

"You *know* I'm good for it."

"Uh-huh. That why you stopped going to the Palladium?"

Henry stood still and watched Morris begin to circle him.

"Oh, I got a real rundown on you, Henry. There are beginning to be lots and lots of places you can't go back to, aren't there?"

"I don't know what—"

"There are a lot of people in New York who can tell me things."

"What's the matter, Morris, have a bad week on the Street?" Henry said as Morris backed him into a sink.

"Naw, we're not going to play this game. You get me my money—tonight," he said, and Henry made a move toward the door. Morris pulled a stiletto out of his pocket and clicked it open under Henry's jaw. He held it there while he dug the three gram packets out of Henry's coat pocket.

"Now, you go get me that money, or you won't be able to come back here to cover the 'scene' for that sucky little magazine you pretend to publish."

"But—"

"And if per chance you don't make it back here, or I wind up in a story? You're a dead man," he said. "Now you have an hour."

Tony pulled the car up in front of Lisa's building and Michael helped her out.

"I pick youse up around ten," Tony said, and took off.

Lisa stared up at Michael.

"What?" she asked, tensely.

"I'm . . . supposed to keep an eye on you tonight, and

then tomorrow we're going to his apartment," Michael stammered.

"I don't need this," she said, and walked into the building.

She opened the door to the apartment and turned on the lights. She walked away, into the bedroom, without even looking at Michael. It was as if he didn't even exist right now. He felt uncomfortable as hell here.

He looked around the room. It was a pretty one, very neat, he thought. He dropped his raincoat on the gray couch and loosened his tie.

His eyes landed on a lace-covered side table. Under a Tiffany-type lamp were a phone and picture frames. His eyes darted back to the bedroom. It was shut. He walked over to the table, picked up the phone, and got a dial tone. He placed it silently back on the cradle. He turned on the lamp and picked up an oval silver frame.

The sandy-haired man he'd seen with the girl on his lap at the club was standing with his arm around Michigan—Lisa, he corrected himself. She was smiling; he had this odd expression on his face. Michael couldn't quite make it out. It wasn't exactly a smile.

He was good-looking . . . if you went in for that sort of Robert Redford thing.

"What are you doing?" Lisa's voice was choked, and he looked up in time to see her rush across the floor.

She grabbed the picture out of his hand and stared at it, red-eyed.

"My *boy*friend," she said tartly, and looked back up at Michael. She began to move toward him, waving the frame at him. "The man I moved to New York to be with. The man I left my family for, because I *knew* deep down that he loved me and was going to marry me."

"You must—"

"The man I was going have children with. Do you hear me? *Do you think this is funny?* I'll show you funny!" she said, and winged the thing against the wall behind him, nearly glomming Michael in the head.

He felt the color drain from his face.

"Hey, wait—"

"Men! You're all nothing but self-centered *idiots*!" she said, turning back to the table of photos. She snapped her arm out, sweeping it across the table. The lamp and photos smashed to the floor, and she held her arm in pain. Michael felt himself press against the wall. He noticed his reflection in the window and was a bit shocked at how frightened he looked on the outside. He tried closing his mouth and looking angry. He did not want to be here. This was scaring the hell out of him.

"Four years I've blown on this stupid . . . lying . . . dumbhead . . ." The words were getting tangled up in her throat as something snapped inside her. She no longer cared whether she had *done* something or *not done* something. Andrew had betrayed her. He had made her feel that all her suspicions were silly, just a figment of her imagination. He'd told her that what she was really upset about was her job. That her job was what was wrong with her life. Her job, not him. And, once he'd convinced her of that, she'd felt so foolish and doubtful about her own fears that she stopped asking questions. She'd stopped *herself* from bringing up the late hours and the missed weekends. He had played her for a jerk.

Suddenly, this feeling began at the base of her stomach. It rose up her spine, as if she was in some kind of vat that was quickly filling with water and in a moment would be over her head and she'd be drowning in it. Her entire body was hot and tight as this strange emotion overtook her for the first time in her life.

The flatness and the dull depression was gone. Lisa was enraged.

"Now, look, you gotta—"

"Shut up. I'm through listening! I'm through being some nice little woman who is lied to. DO YOU HEAR ME?" she yelled, and stooped down, grabbing the picture of them at Yellowstone National Park. "I've been kidnapped, tied up, I killed someone—I've had enough, do you hear me?" she screeched, and sent the picture hurling. The sound of smashing glass tinkled and chimed as the picture smashed through the shut window Michael had been looking at his reflection in. It did not even slow her down.

"Hey, wait a minute—" Michael began.

"I want a drink," she said, storming away.

As she stomped into the kitchen, he dashed over to the broken window and opened it up. He stared down and breathed out. No one was lying on the sidewalk.

"Four years! Four miserable, rotten years!" he could hear her rant in the kitchen.

He stood for a brief second wondering what to do. She was like a crazy woman. This mild-mannered woman, with her freckled nose and her petit floral dress and little pom-pom socks, was like blasting putty that had been hit with a hammer.

He listened to her slam something against the counter, muttering incoherently.

He should go in there. His body leaned toward the kitchen, but his legs did not move.

No, he shouldn't. . . . He stared at his raincoat on the couch. He *did* have a gun, if it came down to it.

"GODDAMN IT." The sound cut through the kitchen walls.

That was it, he was not going to spend the night ducking furniture.

"WHAT ARE YOU DOING?" he screamed, walking into the kitchen.

She turned around with a large carving knife, and his hands immediately raised. She looked up at him, tears streaming down her face.

"I can't reach the liquor."

"Okay, let me do it," he said, and calmly took the knife from her. "Where is it?"

She pointed up into a built-in shelf above the refrigerator. "What do you want?"

"I want the most expensive thing he's got," she answered, and dumped ice into a glass.

Michael shoved the Stolichnaya bottle aside and hunted around. The cabinet was very impressive—Chivas Regal, several bottles of cognac he recognized as good. A bottle of twenty-seven-year-old Glenlivet caught his eye. He could use a drink, too. He took the bottle down.

"You sure this is the best stuff?" she demanded.

"Well . . ."

"I want the best—I—no, I want you to bring down everything."

He stared at her.

"Can I have a drink?" he asked, gazing at her steadily.

"Will you bring down the bottles?"

"Are you gonna throw more stuff out the window?"

"No . . . I'm going to pour it down the drain."

He exhaled. "Fine." He turned and began taking down the bottles. She uncapped the Stoly and he watched it splash down the drain. He quickly grabbed the Glenlivet and began hunting for a glass.

As she finished pouring the cognacs down the drain, he put a couple of ice cubes into a glass and poured himself a stiff drink. He sipped it, feeling it warm his tongue slightly, then turn peppery and smoky at the back of his throat. He watched a 1961 Armagnac splash down the drain, and at the last minute grabbed the bottle from her. She glared at him, and he looked at her and gave a weak smile.

"I gotta taste this one," he apologized.

He took a swig, and then a second, and swirled it around his tongue. It tasted like liquid velvet. He gave it back to her and stood in the doorway, sipping his Glenlivet.

"There any particular reason you're destroying this stuff?" he asked.

"I've had a bad day," she replied tersely, and they both watched the Armagnac splash down, turning the white porcelain maroon in the sink.

"This is his. All his. I wasn't even allowed to go into his goddammed liquor cabinet. It was too good for *me* to drink," she said, and stood very still for a moment, holding the empty bottle.

She dropped it and stared at the stained sink and the broken glass and began to cry. He put down his drink and came up behind her. She spun around and began to cry into his chest. He raised his arms to put them around her, then dropped them. She continued to cry until he wrapped his arms around her shoulders.

"She came over to dinner. *I* tried to make friends with her. . . . They were laughing at me," she mumbled. "I've never done anything wrong to anybody, you know? God, my life wasn't supposed to turn out like this."

He stood there gently rocking her in his arms. She felt nice there, and he began to feel guilty as his mind wandered about her body.

God, he was lonely. He hadn't felt it until today. Back over the Brooklyn Bridge, then again at the restaurant, and now . . .

He brought himself back and gently pushed her shoulders away.

"Look, let's go into the living room and take it easy for a moment, okay?"

She nodded and he led her out into the living room and sat her down on the couch. He walked back into the kitchen and grabbed both their drinks and a paper towel. He handed her the paper towel and she blew her nose. Then he sat next to her and handed her the drink. She took a sip of his and coughed. The cut on her lower lip burned.

"This stuff's vile," she said, her mouth puckering. "Isn't there anything sweet in there?"

Michael went back into the kitchen and brought down a bottle of Chambord and poured her a snifter, filling it generously.

He watched her sipping on the drink and drying the tears with the paper towel.

"I guess I knew he had women on the side, you know? But I really thought I'd . . . I don't know, grow on him or something. If I loved him enough, he'd come around sooner or later. Jesus, I've never admitted that before."

Michael sat across from her and winced.

"Grow on him? You make yourself sound like some kind of pet dog or something."

She stood up angrily. "Well, *excuse* me! I'm not one of your sophisticated New York women. I don't want to be the head of AT&T—I wanted to be a wife and a mother, and maybe an editor. Now it's all over. Don't you understand?"

"No, I don't. So you'll find someone else to marry you and—"

"Yeah, sure! You think anyone's going to marry me now? I killed a man tonight. You think that makes me good wife material?"

"Well, it depends—"

"Well, it doesn't hold water in Michigan, Michael! My life is over. I can't live here anymore. I can't work here anymore. I should have killed myself years ago. That's it, I should turn myself in. They'll do it for me."

"We don't have capital punishment in New York."

"Jesus Christ, I don't understand this city! Then I'll turn myself in someplace where they do. Just one bolt of electricity and—"

Her voice was rising, and Michael stood up and grabbed her shoulders and gave them a shake.

"Stop it! This isn't about paying for killing a guy," he said loudly, and she stared up at him. "First of all, you shot someone who was running at you to take the gun away and shoot all of us. It was self-defense, don't you understand?"

"I—"

"And how come you have no self-respect? Huh? Is that what they teach women in Michigan? To lie down like a dog just so a man will marry you? This guy you've been living with sounds like a lowlife, and you're stomping around here wrecking things, not because he's an idiot but because you're gonna actually have to take a *stand,* face him and stick up for yourself. You're no weakling. You're a good, strong woman, and the second you start believing that, then the second you'll be able to do something for yourself instead of whimpering that this jerk isn't going to marry you."

He grabbed her shoulders with his hands and stared into her eyes.

God, he wanted to kiss her.

She looked up at him and her eyes slid down to his lips. A confused look crossed her face. He gave her a shake, then pulled her in and gave her a quick squeeze, and she finally nodded up at him. His arms lingered around her until he let go, catching himself again.

"Now, what do you want to do?" he said, rubbing his forehead with one hand and staring at the carpet for a moment to calm down.

"I want to go someplace safe where I can think things through."

"Fine, I know a place."

She nodded and silently went into the bedroom. A couple of minutes went by. The phone rang, and she appeared so quickly at the bedroom door, he was surprised. She had changed into a pair of jeans and a shirt and was twisting the strap on a purse around in her hands as the phone rang again. His chest felt tight, as though they'd been caught.

They both listened, frozen, as the taped voice of Andrew droned out the message.

Beep.

"Andrew?" an annoyed female voice began.

In a blur of a second, Michael watched Lisa rip the machine out of the wall. He watched her open the top and take out the cassette. There was a slight whirring sound as she pulled the shiny brown tape out of its casing: *whir, whir, whir,* till a ribbony pile lay at her feet. She dropped the cassette ceremoniously on top of the pile, exhaled, strangely satisfied, and looked at him.

"We can go now?" he asked.

She nodded and he followed her out the door.

Henry Foster Morgan hit the sidewalk, ignoring the line out front. He loosened his collar and stared up and down the block for his limo. Goddamn it! Why had he told the fucking chauffeur that he'd be there till three? He stepped off the curb. If he hurried, he could be out at the Hamptons for the Sonders' wedding by dawn. That would give him enough time to go buy some clothes, find some coke, and get cleaned up.

Tony silently walked up the steps of his mother's row house in Brooklyn. Everything was dark as he entered the hallway. He took off his jacket, holster, and gun, dropped them onto the sofa in the living room, and walked on into the kitchen. A large aluminum saucepan had been left on the stove. He lifted the lid and looked inside: meatballs in gravy.

Next to the pot was a pot of water for pasta. He opened the bread box on the counter and ripped off half a loaf of Italian bread. He stuck it in the sauce pot, like a spoon, and began stirring the gravy. When he was sure it had soaked into the end, he took a large bite, and stood in the dark room, chewing. His mother's homemade tomato sauce filled his mouth. He thought over the day. . . .

Louie'd told him that Angela was out running around

again tonight with Joey D. His stomach tightened at that.

He should date. Beat Angela at her own game.

Find a nice woman, someone who could understand what he did, who'd stay at home, raise children. . . . He wasn't getting any younger.

He dipped the half loaf back into the gravy.

Understanding what he did—that was the trouble. It wasn't like he could just tell someone, like he was a mechanic or something.

His mind flashed through everyone he knew. There weren't too many unmarried women his age left in the neighborhood.

Fucking Angela again. The problem with Ralphie's daughter was that she understood exactly what he did, and it didn't matter to her. As long as he kept givin' her things—cars, furs, diamonds. In the year and a half they'd been together, the woman had sucked through his salary like a high-powered vacuum cleaner.

So he'd been working overtime for Solly, any job and every job. Yeah, sure it was good for his career—he was now in a better position with the Soltanos than he'd ever dreamed—but still, she was never satisfied.

So the end had finally come in the Cadillac two months ago. She'd just been to the beauty parlor and her hair, now all blond, was done up real high on her head. Her long fingernails were bright red with little black stripes painted across and little sapphire chips glued on. She'd been leaning on him for an hour about doin' an extra job so she could get a pair of diamond studs. He'd watched the five-carat diamond he had given her glint as she waved her hand around angrily. Then he'd watched her pull around her shoulders the mink jacket he'd given her for their four-week anniversary.

"And I don' unnerstand why you can't do this one little thing for me!"

"It ain't my hit—"

"Pop said if you wanted it, you could have it. What do you want me to do? Show up without earrings? To Gino's birthday party? What do you think I am? Cheap?"

"I ain't gonna do no hit on Perrino. He was like a uncle to me when I was growin' up an—"

"So, whatta you care? Someone's gonna get him, and it mi'se well be you."

"Aw, nice, Angela, nice way for a woman to talk."

"Don't give me this sainthood crap, Tony Macarelli. I know what you do, when you do it, an' how many times you do it."

"Hey, you shut your mouth." He glared at her. "You don't talk about my business. . . . You're talkin' about a man's life here! I should kill a man so you could get a pair of earrings?"

"He's gonna die anyway, so I mi'se well be the one who gets from it," she snapped, and began drumming her nails on the car door, just loudly enough to drive him crazy. Her pointy nostrils were flaring and her thin lips, painted a raspberry red, were twitching back and forth. They sat silently as Tony drove toward Mill Basin.

"You know, I could *make* you do it," she said quietly.

Tony's eyes narrowed as they turned onto Ralphie's block.

"What did you say?"

"You heard me. I could make you do it. I could tell my father to make you do it."

He pulled the car over, leaned across her, and pushed her door open.

"Wha—"

"Get out!"

"What?"

"Get the fuck outta my car, now."

She was still screaming as he slammed the door closed. He slid over to the window and rolled it down.

"I'm gonna tell my father," she screeched.

"You go ahead, Angela, you tell him what you been sayin'. I don't care if you show up at Gino's without no clothes on, 'cause I'm not gonna be there wid youse! I had enough. I don't wanna see you no more."

He slid back over and started the car. She stood on the curb, temporarily dazed. As he drove away, he could hear her screaming for Ralphie and he heard the thud on the trunk from her handbag hitting as he drove off.

Of course, it had taken six weeks to straighten it out with Ralphie. It turned out Angela had been looking at wedding gowns for two months. Her whole family and the neighborhood had been told they were engaged. And Angela'd hinted that she was in the family way, which was the kiss of death for Tony. Then Ralphie woulda gone to Solly and *made* him marry her.

Tony had thought back on that long and hard, trying to remember when he'd said anything about being engaged. There hadn't been one word—he was sure of that.

So now Angela was dating Joey D.—lowlife scumbag who sold crap for the Soltanos. Ralphie couldn't know about this. Tony swallowed the mouthful of bread and gravy and then shot a glance at his watch. It was 2:30. Driving at this hour, he could be parked outside of Angela's in forty-five minutes.

He sank the remaining end of the bread into the gravy, and the memory of Angela that day ran through his mind again. Yeah, Angela understood his business all right, but she didn't care that he chopped people up.

That wasn't right for a woman.

All she was after was every dime she could get. And besides, Tony felt that the mother of his children should care that he hacked people up.

Not *do* anything about it, but care he did it.

Michael waved his arm and the cab made a U-turn across Seventy-second and came to a stop in the street in front of them. Lisa came running off the curb and got in as he held the door open for her. He slid in next to her and closed the door. He sat, staring at the torn seatback for a moment.

"Where to?" the cabbie asked in a heavy Chinese accent.

"Michael?" Lisa asked, looking at him.

"The Plaza."

Henry stuck his card into the bank-machine slot and pressed in his pin number. A man weaved over to him and held his hand out as Henry pressed in the amount of the withdrawal.

"Spare some change?"

"Get real," Henry snapped, and the man moved slowly off, walking in an S pattern along the sidewalk.

The drawer opened and Henry took out eight hundred dollars, then snatched his card back and took his receipt. He jammed them into his pocket and stepped out to the sidewalk and hailed a cab.

A battered taxi pulled up and he got inside.

"Vhere you go to?" a thick Polish accent grunted as the cab pulled away from the curb.

"East Hampton."

The car came to a screeching halt, which threw Henry against the divider.

"Vhat you say?" the man said, leaning his arm on the seat and staring at Henry.

"East Hampton! Christ, don't you understand English?"

"You got money for this?"

"Yes, I got money for this," Henry snapped, aping his accent.

He sat back and stared out the window. The cabbie didn't move. After a couple of moments, Henry looked back to him.

"Well, what the hell are you waiting for?"

"I see money, please."

Henry stared at him, openmouthed.

"Money please or you get out," the cabbie repeated.

Henry shoved his hand into his pocket and pulled out the eight hundred, and, before he could lower it, the cab screeched away from the corner, throwing him sideways on the seat.

"You don't be so nasty with peoples, is not good," he added as Henry tried to pull himself up on the seat. He glared at the back of the cabbie's thick head.

"No luggage, sir?" the bellhop asked as Michael walked past him into the suite.

"That a problem?" he asked, looking steadily at him.

"Oh, Michael, look at the flowers." He heard Lisa's voice behind him.

He shoved a five into the man's hand.

"There still bar service?" he asked.

"Yes, sir," he said, and walked out of the room, closing the door.

"Michael, really, this is so expensive," she said, walking into the bedroom.

He smiled after her and dropped his coat on the couch. He looked around the suite. Pale gold with green satin striped upholstery covered the couch and chairs. The white and gold coffee table had a glass ashtray on it. Long, filmy white curtains covered a somewhat grayed linen blind with a small gold rope tassel on it.

The front room of the suite looked as though it had been decorated in the early 1960s and not touched since. It was gaudier than he'd had in mind. And it was more run-down than he expected. He picked up the phone and waited to be connected to the bar as the sight of Lisa bouncing on the bed caught his eye.

"Oh, Michael," she repeated, and he watched her get off the bed and disappear out of sight.

Jeez, didn't the bum she was living with take her anywhere in New York? The line clicked and he got the bar.

"Order," the voice said, and he paused for a moment.

"Stone!" Lisa's voice came from the bedroom. "The bathroom is stone!"

She stared at the brown stone floor, polished to a mirror shine. The stone went halfway up the wall and dark wood paneling took over from there. His and her sinks, and sinktop-to-ceiling mirrors looked onto the most elaborate tub and shower Lisa had ever seen. She stood at the entrance to the bathroom and suddenly took her shoes off. She walked slowly across the cool stone and stared at the shiny gold-finished faucet and hot and cold water taps for a tub large enough to swim in. But it was the shower that really intrigued her. Three wide shower heads were lined up vertically on either side of the cornered wall. Six shower heads, just to make sure you really got rinsed off, she imagined. She darted a glance at the door, then carefully stepped into the tub. Maybe she should take a shower, she thought.

No, that would be rude. She got out of the tub and slipped her shoes back on. Well, if she was going to leave the city on Monday, at least she'd seen the inside of Maude's—and this shower.

"A bottle of champagne," Michael said quickly, looking up at the ceiling. Jesus, what was he doing, he thought as he gave the room number and listened to the selections.

Well, she wouldn't drink scotch, after all. And what woman doesn't drink champagne? he speculated, trying to rationalize what he was doing.

He chose a decent bottle and hung up as Lisa came out of the bedroom. She looked a little flushed.

"Oh, Michael," she said for the third time, pressing her hand to her chest. "I mean, when I said someplace safe, I thought, you know, we'd go to a friend's house."

"I don't have any friends," he said quietly, and threw his jacket on the couch.

"Well, this is so . . . expensive. You know, we could just go someplace cheaper. There's a Ramada Inn on Eighth Avenue—"

"I'm not checking out of here to go to a Ramada Inn," he said, unbuckling his shoulder holster. "I've had a bad day. Have you had a bad day?"

She nodded emphatically.

"So where would you rather be? Here or at a Ramada Inn?"

"Here."

He slipped the holster off his shoulder, carefully put it on a chair, and then covered it with his jacket. He swung his arms around in a circle and then moved his shoulders back and forth, trying to get some circulation back. He'd been tensed up all day. He looked at the lump in the jacket where his gun was. He hated that thing. He really hated it.

"Well, I'm going to have to owe you. . . ." she began.

"Owe me? For what?"

"For the room."

"Don't worry about the room," he said, staring at her.

"But really—" she said, and put a hand on his shoulder.

He stared down at her for a moment and she silently looked up at him. He cleared his throat and took a step away from her hand. "It's okay."

"No it's not," she continued. "I owe you—"

"You owe me nothing," he said, annoyed. "For God's sake, Lisa, I kidnapped you today, remember? Tied you up, held a gun to your head? Threatened to kill you?"

"Oh, but you wouldn't have killed me." She dismissed the thought and sat down on the couch.

"Yeah, but you didn't know that."

"Sure I did—"

There was a knock at the door, and Lisa sprang off the couch and crossed her hands over her chest, staring at him, frightened.

"Oh my God, who's that?" She took a step toward the bedroom.

"Don't worry," Michael said, and walked to the door as she ran into the bedroom.

After he paid the guy, he walked over to the coffee table in front of the couch and stared into the bedroom. He looked down at the champagne bucket and ice and felt truly embarrassed by it.

The nice hotel room, a bottle of champagne—what a bastard he was. He hadn't even been near a woman in the past two years. No woman had been near him, and this was not a good idea. He could see her on the stand after this was all over. Murder and rape, that's what she'd think of it as. He'd go for life.

If she'd just stop touching him. . . .

He was about to take the thing and throw it outside the door when Lisa walked back into the room. His eyes looked slowly over her body. He looked at what she was wearing, at the pair of white jeans and the white shirt with the small flowers on it. It accentuated her hips and made her waist look small. He felt himself swallow, and he looked up at her face. A small smile moved across her lips, and he looked away quickly.

She walked up beside him and looked down at the bucket.

"Champagne?"

"I didn't . . . I didn't know what you drink, and—"

She sat down.

"Are you going to open it?" she asked, and he looked down at her and breathed out a bit as she smiled.

Maybe this was all escaping her, he thought as he carefully held on to the cork and twisted the bottle. It gave a muffled pop as he held it against the rim of the bottle. He filled two glasses and handed her one, then sat next to her.

She kicked off her shoes and held the glass up and they

both took a long drink. She finished hers and held her glass out. He downed his and refilled them both.

"So you're a lawyer?" she asked after awhile.

"And then ve hear over radio. General Jaruselski has declared military law all around Poland. . . ."

Henry groaned and sank lower in the seat. Out of all the cabbies in New York, the thousands and thousands of them, he had to get a new, enthused immigrant. He could just scream. He tried to focus in on his watch but couldn't see it in the darkness. He couldn't figure out how long he'd been in the cab. His eyes darted to the meter.

Ninety-eight fifty.

"Lorenya, ve must flee, flee to America, I tell my wife. But she does not vant to go. She vants to stay in Poland. So I say—"

Henry fell supine across the entire backseat and tried closing his eyes. If he could just get out there, he could go to his mother's house and hide out till the wedding.

Tony walked down the ramp of the parking garage underneath Angela's building. In his left hand, he swung a crowbar. There was a bulge from a sack of sugar in his jacket pocket. The sounds of his footsteps echoed and he watched his shadow stretch longer before him and then shorter as he walked under the wide slats of fluorescents. He'd made it here in thirty-eight minutes flat from his house. He could still taste the sauce in his mouth.

He got to the lowest level and turned right, over to the G section, down two long rows. Across the floor, in the distance, he heard a motor start and rev up. He continued walking, not speeding up his pace but just walking like he belonged there. Behind him, he heard the car pull out and he watched the beams from the car headlights move along the white brick garage wall in front of him.

Section One Hundred G. He stood, breathing deeply until he heard the car pull up the ramp. He stared at the car sitting in his old spot and listened until the sound of the car behind him faded away into nothing and only his deep, angry breathing could be heard.

He stood in front of the black Porsche, parked in Angela's spot, the spot he used to park in. He raised the crowbar like a baseball bat and swung as hard as he could, feeling the pull across his shoulders and then the shock back through his arms as the crowbar shattered the windshield. He walked around the car, swinging again and again, feeling the shock to his upper arms as, one by one, every window in the car was broken.

He walked along to the gas tank's top and opened it with ease. He took the sack of sugar out and neatly poured it into the tank, screwed the top back on, and slowly walked back up to the main aisle. He stood in front of the car, looked over what he'd down, and exhaled.

He turned and walked back to the center, toward the ramp.

He could eat now.

He'd been reasonable about this. He felt light, as if he'd had a weight lifted off of him.

Now he could microwave the meatballs.

"So that's what happened," Michael said as he poured the last drops of champagne into her glass. He spilled a small amount on the rug and bent down to wipe it up, then sat back up, realizing that he didn't have a napkin. He was feeling pretty relaxed and he leaned back on the couch, slipped his shoes off, and looked over at her, sipping on her drink.

She was lovely. Her high cheeks were flushed from the champagne, and her lips were wet, and the freckles dotting her nose gave her this clean, girl-next-door innocence. She reminded him of the girls in college—girls who would spend the evenings discussing classes and professors and politics, not hairdressers and hits. That's what most of the women he'd come in contact with in the past two years seemed to talk about. She wouldn't have fake-looking hair, teased three feet above her head, or wear several layers too many of makeup, he thought. She didn't have large clawlike nails painted blood red or wear jeans two sizes too tight and sweatshirts that for some reason someone had spent hours embroidering with pearls and lace.

His nose felt itchy. He rubbed it and sat farther up. He really had to get a grip. He'd already talked too much. It was the booze. The triple Glenlivet he'd poured at the apartment, and now the half a bottle of champagne he'd sucked back in the last twenty minutes.

"And you couldn't get her to tell the truth? Tha's terrible. I think that's the most terrible thing I've heard," Lisa said, and finished off her glass.

She leaned over unevenly and put her glass on the table. Then she sat back, curling her slim legs alongside of her on the couch.

"You want me to get another bottle?" he asked.

She sat still for a couple of moments, thinking about it.

"No, I'm fine, but if you want some more," she said,

leaning over to him and placing her chin on his shoulder, "you can order more."

He found himself gazing at her for God knows how long, and he watched her look up at him, at his lips, his face, and he began to get lost somewhere, imagining taking her and kissing her all over slowly. He sat up suddenly and then got to his feet.

"I think I'll order another bottle," he announced, and walked over to the phone.

He picked up the receiver and watched her jump up unsteadily and walk over next to him. He began to shake slightly as she stood so close, he could feel her against his chest.

"No," she said, pulling the receiver out of his hand.

"No?" he repeated, barely above a squeak.

She dropped it back on the hook, looked up at him, and pressed herself against him.

"I'm a real loser, Lisa."

"I don't think so."

"You're just doing this to get back at the guy you're living with," he said, and took a step away from her.

"Would that make you feel better?"

"No," he said honestly.

She took a step toward him and he backed away again. She stopped and her eyes dropped. "I'm sorry. This isn't right. I just thought maybe. It's just been so long since anyone . . . even seemed to look after me, you know? I mean, I've been here for four years. I don't have any real friends. Andrew hasn't introduced me to anyone, except for . . ." Her voice faded away as a flash of pain showed in her eyes, and Michael saw again the woman on the man's lap in the club. He knew exactly what she was thinking.

She came out of it, and their eyes met as she continued. "We haven't gone to the clubs or out, and I just . . ." Her eyes began to turn red, and she looked away. ". . . sit at home each night, Michael, waiting for him to come in. This is the first night in a year I've been out to dinner, the first night I've had a glass of champagne or just sat and talked to someone. And look at me—this has been my life." Her voice began to get stronger. "And if I'm crowding you, it's because you, a guy who kidnapped me and tied me up, has shown me more compassion and respect than I've even shown myself in all this time."

She walked over to him and looked up.

"And," she said, staring at him as if something had gone off in her head, "I want you . . . to kiss me and . . . and hold me and look at me the way you've been looking at me, because I'm . . . lonely. Do you know what it's like to be lonely?"

God, it sounded like his life.

He stood there for a moment and then grabbed her, wrapped his arms around her, and kissed her. She rubbed her hands up and down his back, pressing herself as close to him as she could. He stooped over her and began kissing her neck and face, quick and hard, then slowed down and pulled himself back, shaking a bit.

"What?"

He caught his breath.

"I haven't done this in awhile. I need to slow down," he said.

She nodded and backed away, and he watched her walk over to the light next to the couch and turn it off. She shut off the other one.

"Do you have something?" she asked quickly.

He looked over at her, puzzled for a brief second, and then quickly walked over to his wallet.

He dug around inside and found one condom, which he had put in there almost a year ago. He stopped for a moment. The foil was still intact.

He saw her outline walk over to the bedroom door. She stood there, leaning against the wall, staring at him, until he straightened up. He walked over and took her by the hand and walked into the bedroom and over to the bed. He lowered her down onto it, staring at her face in the light from the window.

Outside, over the hum of the air conditioner, he could hear the pinging sounds of raindrops on the metal box as a light rain began to fall.

He slowly began unbuttoning her blouse, feeling her loosen his tie and pull it off, then struggle with the top button of his shirt. He kissed her slowly, working his way down her neck, pulling her shirt open gently and letting it fall to her sides on the bed.

She pulled his shirt open as he continued to work his way down. He was kissing her breasts and she couldn't reach his shirt anymore. He looked up at her for a moment.

"I think you're really beautiful, Lisa, and I have been looking at you like that all day and it's been driving me crazy, 'cause . . . I'm lonely, too," he whispered, then continued to caress her body.

It was noon. Tony Mac was standing in front of the bathroom mirror, carefully shaving his wide, flat face, when he heard the phone ring in the living room. He rinsed off the spots that still had the cream on them, then opened up the medicine chest. His eyes roamed over the two shelves of after-shave.

Every Christmas, all the women in the family gave him the same stuff—shaving lotions and after-shave. Normally, he wouldn't be caught dead wearing perfume—he didn't care what they called it, it was still perfume as far as he was concerned—but today was gonna be different. Today, he was going to ask Michigan for a date.

It had come to him in a dream, in the middle of the night. They were in the union office and out of the corner of his eye he had just seen her struggle with the gun and Giuseppe, and right there, in his dream, she did him. There was a big stain of blood on her dress, but suddenly the blood lifted off the dress and turned into roses; Tony was giving her great big bunches of red roses. And then her little dress turned into a beautiful wedding gown and they were walking up the aisle in the chapel of Our Lady of Precious Poverty.

He knew what that meant. Red roses are from the heart. She'd saved his life, for which he would always be grateful, and he'd always owe her, and here it was—God's answer to how to pay her back.

Marry her.

She'd make him a good wife.

She was a good shot.

She cared what he did but understood it.

His hand reached for the Old Spice, which he generously doused on his cheeks, then waited for the sting to subside.

"Anthony!" he heard his mother call from the kitchen.

"What, Ma?" he yelled back.

"It's your cousin Michael on the phone; he wants to talk wid you."

He opened the bathroom door, taking a small bottle of talcum powder with him, and walked down the hall to the living room. His eyes scanned the sofa for his gun.

He picked up the holster, took the gun out, and lightly sprinkled some of the powder inside.

That kept the holster from getting sticky in all this heat. He put the holster on.

"Anthony! You gonna get the phone or what?" his mother screamed from the kitchen.

"I'm coming! Fahcrissakes, let me put my gun on!" His voice roared through the walls and seemed to bounce around the entire house.

He always felt undressed without his gun—vulnerable.

He picked up the phone.

"Mikey?"

"Yeah, listen, I'm at the Plaza. Pick us up there."

He stood still for a moment, feeling his eyes begin to cross slightly.

"You got Michigan at the Plaza?" he asked slowly.

"Yeah," Michael said, and heard Tony exhale on the other end. He waited for a moment.

"Tony?"

"Yeah," he said more slowly. "Why you took Michigan to a hotel?"

Michael rolled over in bed and put his hand over his eyes to shade them from the light.

"She didn't want to stay at her place. It wasn't a good idea, anyway. What if the guy she lives with showed up?"

"The guy she lives with? She married?"

Oh Christ, Michael thought as he felt her move next to him, pulling the covers across him.

"No, she's not married. Just pick us up here. Then I

want to stop at my mother's house for a change of clothes. Okay?" He waited. "Tony, you there?"

"Yeah, yeah, I'll be there at one."

Tony stood holding the receiver and felt his hand tighten around it.

He didn't like this. He didn't like this one tiny bit.

Michael hung up and stared over at Lisa's shoulder. Tony would come and get them at one. Hopefully, by the time he showed, Michael would have some plan. That's all he needed to do—come up with some way to get them all off the hook.

A lock of blond hair fell across her cheek and he just lay there, watching her breathe. He'd forgotten how nice it was to wake up with someone next to him. He'd frozen himself out for two years.

His eyes shifted to the wall across from the bed. For a moment, he listened to the sound of the air conditioner and stared at a dusty slat of sunlight that had peeked through the blind of the window.

He rolled over and put his arm around her and kissed her shoulder. She made a slight noise and he kissed her ear.

"Lisa, we have to get up."

"Ummm," he heard as he lifted himself off the bed.

He walked over to the bathroom.

"I'm going to take a shower," he announced, looking back at her.

He stood, staring at the bed for just a moment longer, and walked into the bathroom. He turned on the shower and watched, entertained by the silly sight of six shower heads going off behind the glass doors. She could get a couple more minutes sleep, he thought, stepping inside.

Lisa covered her head with the sheet and didn't move a muscle until she heard him in the shower. She lay there, cringing.

She should make a run for it. Lisa slowly sat up, and the room spun around. The taste in her mouth was awful—pasty champagne, mingled with whatever that other stuff was that she'd had.

Tasted like cough syrup now.

She felt slightly nauseous and her head felt fizzy. She sank back down.

After all, they had kidnapped her, she thought. Well, Tony had kidnapped her; Michael was trapped in the situation from what he told her last night.

No, she should just get on her clothes and run this second, right now.

She stared at the bathroom door and the thought suddenly occurred to her that if she did make a run for it, what would happen to Michael? Would they hurt him? That would be awful. He didn't deserve that. Last night, he'd been so nice and honest. . . . She cringed again.

At least she'd asked about condoms, she thought, pulling the cover up over her head, embarrassed that she felt it was a point in her favor.

What was she turning into? She still could not conceive that she had done this. She had never done this—met some guy and slept with him the same day.

She heard the shower go off in the bathroom.

Well, it was too late to make a run for it. She felt herself push down farther under the covers, as if disguising herself as an unmade bed would make him forget she was there entirely and he'd just go on his merry way with Tony.

Her body tensed and she stopped breathing as she heard the door open again.

"Lisa? We have to get going."

She didn't answer.

"If you want to take a shower, you have to get up now," his voice said, closer now.

In a second, the whiteness of the sheet was lifted, and she pasted a stiff smile on her face and looked up at him.

He stood over her and she could see him reading her thoughts. His smile dropped and an embarrassed expression moved across him like a large cloud in the middle of a clear sky. He looked away and dropped the sheet.

"I, uh . . . I'll get coffee," he stammered. "Tony's going to be here at one." His voice turned cold.

She listened as he left the room. She sat straight up and grabbed her head as the room did a small jig. She stumbled to the bathroom and turned on the water. When it was lukewarm, she stepped under it.

She spent a long time lying in the bottom of the tub, letting the water run over her.

She heard a knock at the bathroom door, straightened up, yelled that she would be out in a moment, and stood up. She let a blast of ice-cold water run on her, then got out.

By the time she walked into the living room, Michael was sitting there, watching TV and sipping on a cup of coffee. His eyes darted to her and then away. She walked over to the coffeepot and poured herself a cup. She sat next to him, and they both stared at the set in embarrassed silence.

"I got some rolls if you want them," Michael muttered into his cup.

She choked back the nausea that came with the idea of a roll and nodded, then finally looked at him. He gave her a small smile, then looked back to the set.

"Michael—"

He stood up and put down his cup. "We have to get downstairs; it's five to one," he said stiffly.

They left the room in the same uneasy silence. Michael felt himself brooding and tried to snap out of it. They rang for the elevator.

Lisa stood still in the hallway, looking at Michael's back. She felt silly at having pasted that smile on her face. His eyes had this hurt look to them, which had grown worse over coffee. It had been her idea, after all. . . . Well, that wasn't true. It had been both of their ideas. She wanted to say something that would ease the situation. Just as she opened her mouth, the doors to the elevator slid open.

There were several people in it, and they had to squeeze together slightly to get in. Michael stared up at the floor-indicator light as they stopped on every floor.

God, what had he done? She really hated him, he could tell. And she'd go to the cops and tell them that he'd forced himself on her. He'd been drunk and lonely, he began thinking.

Just as Michael felt he was going to burst if he didn't say something before Tony showed up, he felt her slip her hand into his and give it a squeeze. He felt himself smiling as she stretched up and kissed him quickly on the side of the neck.

"It's okay," Lisa said quietly. She looked at the smile on his face and felt herself relax. There was something about him looking embarrassed and hurt that she couldn't stand. And, as odd as it was, it made her decide that it was okay. She also decided that if she did get an opportunity to run, she should take him with her.

They both relaxed and exhaled as the door slid open to the lobby.

Rosa Morelli was pacing in her bedroom, rolling her head from side to side, trying to get the achiness out of it. She'd fallen asleep on the windowsill and had awoken just as it was getting light out. Her arms felt heavy from the position they'd been in, folded under her chin when she'd come to.

She marched back into the kitchen, poured herself a cup of brown coffee, and sat on a folding chair. She couldn't believe Tony hadn't shown up. Hadn't Solly taken her seriously *this* time? She had half a mind to go out to his house and get his wife on him.

A shiver went down her spine. Then she'd have to talk to that pig Gina. Solly's mother had never liked her, and Rosa knew she was behind it whenever Solly didn't do as she said. Gina, wid her big Neapolitan garden, she thought, disgusted.

She hated Neapolitans. They thought they were the best in the world and the Sicilians were nothing. Look at the company she keeps. Rosa smirked. That snob Sophia Bonello. High Italian, Piedmontese, with all that fancy food she serves. Cream sauces, like the French. That's what killed her husband, she thought, all that rich food. That's why she lives in church now. That pig.

If Rosa had had a man like Vincent, she would have served him decent. Pasta 'ncaciata, properly draining the eggplants so they weren't bitter, using only the finest tomatoes and the best olive oil. He'd be alive today if he had been with her. Rosa's venom was full force now.

Maybe that was who had changed Solly's mind, that snob Sophia. After all, it was her son that Tony'd been with yesterday. Little Michael, the "smart one." And of course this type of life was too demeaning for Sophia's precious son, the lawyer! That must be it. It was all Sophia's fault.

Maybe she was jumping to conclusions, she thought, in a tiny rational moment. Maybe she should just be patient. Maybe the boss was just hard to find.

She stormed back over to the window and looked around for her cigarettes. She didn't see them anywhere. She leaned out the window, thinking that they dropped during the night, and the sight of the car hit her.

The tires had been stripped off of it and all the windows had been smashed in. The hood had been jimmied, and Rosa knew from experience that there was probably no engine left in the thing. She shook her head, knowing also from experience that this ugly shell would be sitting out in front of her building for months now, littering up her block.

She walked into the bathroom to throw some water on her face. She stared at her reflection in the mirror. Her face was wide and old. Big circles were under her eyes and deep slashes of wrinkles separated her mouth from her cheeks. Several black hairs stuck out under her chin and the mustache on her upper lip was heavy, the way her own mother's had been. She used to pluck and dye it, years ago when she'd still entertained some notion of finding another man. But the years had slipped by with very few opportunities, leaving her old and alone now.

The only thing she still did was her hair. That was the line over which she refused to cross. She had gained weight and stopped taking care of her face, but she would always have her hair done. She threw the water on her face.

She felt herself begin to get teary as the retirement condo she'd dreamed of came into her mind and then vanished.

Where the hell was Tony?

Six

The cab ride to East Hampton cost Henry $368, and he'd had to endure the constant ranting of the cabbie, who he swore had told him the entire history of Poland.

It was sunrise when he watched the cab dustily bounce back down the highway. He turned and stared at the large electronic gate to his mother's house and cringed.

Of course she'd be there. Mater would not miss the Sonders' wedding. He looked around at the empty road and listened to the sound of the beach.

His limbs were stiff from trying to sleep on the cramped backseat. He had to pee.

He leaned on the buzzer box until the butler's voice finally came over the box.

"It's Henry, George. Let me in," he said tiredly.

"I can't." George's English accent came across the box crisp and clear.

"What do you mean, you can't? Let me in. This is Henry."

"I know who it is, sir, and I can't. I've strict orders not to allow you in the house."

"Orders? Orders from whom?"

"Your mother, sir."

The box clicked dead, and Henry stood with his mouth open, staring at the box.

He leaned on the buzzer again.

"Yes?"

"You let me in the house this second, you dumb fuck! I've come a long way and—"

"I am turning the buzzer box off now, sir."

"No! Wait! Don't you dare, don't—" He listened to it go dead, then leaned into it and kept leaning until his shoulder hurt.

He screamed, picked up a rock, and hit the box with it.

He stood still for a moment, thinking back, and finally he remembered.

He'd missed his grandfather's funeral, last year.

He took a step back.

"Well fuck you, too, George," he bellowed. He unzipped his fly and peed all over the electric gate.

An hour later, he'd made it into town. He was grimy and sweating and the sizing from the new shirt and suit was making him itch. He tried to run his fingers through his hair, but they stuck halfway in the matted, snarled mess.

He stood on Main Street, watching the bakery open up.

The smell of fresh bread made him nauseous.

It was too early to buy clothes. He walked down the corner to a pay phone and dialed the only person he knew would still be up at this hour: his coke dealer in East Hampton.

Tony drove up to the main entrance of the Plaza. He leaned on the horn and watched Mikey and Michigan walk down the carpeted front steps. She was wearing jeans and a shirt. That meant that she must have gotten undressed. His eyebrows nearly met in the middle as he frowned.

He didn't like this one bit.

Michael opened the door for her and she got in the back. And then Tony watched Michael walk around the car to the front seat and get in next to him.

Tony felt his face relax. Naw, he was being stupid, he decided. Mikey was like a fuckin' Boy Scout. He would never . . .

Tony pulled away from the curb.

"Your mother's?" he asked.

Michael nodded to him.

"Can we stop for some coffee?" Michigan asked, leaning forward. Tony grunted and pulled away. They stopped short at the light and Michael sniffed for a moment. He looked over at Tony and discreetly sniffed again.

The nutmeggy odor of Old Spice filled his nostrils. He leaned back over as Tony shot him a glare.

"Ma?" Michael yelled out as he opened the front door.

He heard the sound of her footsteps running out of the kitchen.

"Michael? Where have you been?" Her voice was frantic.

"I'm fine, Ma. Don't worry," he said, walking down the hall toward his bedroom.

"Whatta you mean, you're fine? You stay out all night; you don't tell me where you've been. . . ."

He stood in front of his dresser and took his tie off.

"And who is that girl in the car with Tony?" she continued as he threw his tie on the bed.

He watched her reflection in the mirror as she immediately picked it up.

"I been up since five—" she continued, opening the door to the closet and placing the tie on the rack.

"You always get up at five," he countered, taking his shirt off.

She turned and remained rigidly still for a moment.

"I go to church. Confess my sins," she said with an edge in her voice, which stopped Michael. "Who is that in the car?"

"Lisa's nobody—"

"Lisa? You got a girl?" His mother's eyes were round.

"No, Ma, it's not—"

"You got a girl? How come you never told me you got a girl?"

"She's not my girl. She's—"

"You gonna marry this girl? Is she Italian?" His mother was rattling away as she took the shirt off the chair. He watched her walk around him to the hamper, looking down at her white hair as she moved about.

"No it's—"

"She's not Italian?" she interrupted.

He took her by the shoulders and grabbed them, turning her around to look at him.

"Ma, she's not my girl. I don't have a girl, *capisce*? She's just—" He cut himself off, realizing that there was no good way of putting it. "She's just nobody. She's from outta town." He nodded down to her and let go of her small shoulders.

"Whatta you mean? Why you got some girl from outta town in your car?"

He opened his mouth, but she continued. "Where were you last night? How come you didn't come home? I want to talk to you, Michael Antonio. You come inside to the kitchen."

"I don't have time. I have to—"

"You don't gotta do nothing but talk to me," she said in the same quiet, icy tone she'd used a moment before. "Inside," she added, and left the room.

It was too early for him to keep up with her. He changed into a fresh suit and walked into the kitchen. She was busy filling a kettle of water on the stove. He sat down and looked at her as she turned on the fire under it.

"I want to know what you been doing with Tony. I want to know now."

"Ma, I can't—"

"I know what you been doing," she interrupted, and he looked up at her, startled.

"What do you mean?" he asked slowly.

"I know what you been doing for Solly," she said, opening the refrigerator.

He leaned back and stared at her for a moment.

"You don't know."

She glared at him, took down a creamer, and filled it.

"Since when do you doubt your mother's word?" she snapped at him, then put the milk back in the refrigerator. "I been keeping up with everything you do. What, you think I don't care? Or I don't see what you're turning into?" She opened the cabinet. "Black coffee or brown?" She was angry.

"Whatever you want," he said carefully.

She pulled out a can of espresso and put it on the counter.

"I'm making black coffee. You look tired," she added,

and turned off the water on the stove. She went over to the espresso machine with the coffee, and he waited. He waited until he couldn't stand it anymore.

"Okay, Ma, what do you think you know?"

"I know you been riding with your cousin Tony, acting like some big-time wiseguy for that jedrool, Solly. I know he wants you on the inside now, and you gonna start making you bones. . . ." She measured the coffee into the small strainer, tamped it down with a teaspoon, and screwed it back into the machine.

"I'm right?"

Michael felt his breath stop. He tried to organize his thoughts, but he was working on too little sleep. He cleared his throat.

"And how do you think you know this?" he asked, trying to blow it off.

Another icy glare from her eyes caught him off guard.

"You think I don't know? You think nobody talks to nobody else in this neighborhood? What, you think 'cause I'm an old woman and you're some big-time wiseguy I don't know what I'm talking about? You think I don't know Solly's mother for all these years? And you know what I felt when she comes over to me yesterday before mass and congratulates me on you making your bones?"

Michael felt a chill up his spine.

"This I hear from a stranger? This my own son won't tell me? How did you get so stupid? Eh?"

"Ma, I didn't—"

He barely saw her move across the floor, she did it so quickly. He barely saw the back of her hand as she swung it into the side of his face, giving him a stinging smack. He held his jaw and stared up at her, stunned.

"Ma-a-a-a," he heard himself whine in a voice he

hadn't used since the last time she'd slapped him, when he was ten.

"Stunadze! Ah-fah-nab! An-baffa-fongoule!" she screamed in a deep Neapolitan accent, imitating her dead husband and brushing the underside of her chin quickly with the back of her hand, then cutting the inside of her elbow—essentially, giving him the finger in Neapolitan as she continued telling him to go to Naples, go to hell, telling him what a fuck he was.

He sat holding his jaw, staring frozenly at her. He'd never seen her explode like this. Her accent became softer, Piedmontese, as she began her own scolding. She was playing both parts. She was all over him, waving at him, and he felt himself press into the back of the chair. As he tried to glance away from her, he caught sight of Lisa standing at the doorway of the kitchen, silently staring at them.

His mother yanked his chin back, so he faced her, and began asking him questions.

"English? Ma?"

"Why? Now you some big-time hoodlum, you gotta learn your Italian, no?" She raised her hand above her head and was just about to whack him again when she froze, looking at the doorway.

"Um . . ." He heard Lisa clear her throat.

His mother stepped back, embarrassed, and looked at the floor. She grabbed her apron.

"I . . . gotta . . ." she said, rushing past Lisa.

Michael stood up from his chair, looking at his mother's figure disappear down the hallway.

"What's going on?" she asked, looking at him.

"Excuse me," he said, darting around her.

He made it up the stairs in almost no time. He walked

down the hallway and tapped on his mother's door. There was no answer. He tapped again.

"Ma?"

"Partire!" Her voice came back to him as stinging as the smack from her hand, and he could hear her crying.

He opened the door and walked in. She was sitting in her rocking chair, rocking back and forth with intense force. It creaked on the floor, and Sophia began breathing in time to it, fast and angry.

"Ma, please . . . I'm sorry, I'm sorry," he kept saying over and over.

She finally focused on him.

"You're spitting on your father's grave. You're spitting in both our faces."

"No. I didn't mean—"

"The only thing your father ever wanted, ever worked for was you being a good man. An honest man. And you wait until he dies to show this disrespect to him? A good man like him?"

"My father was a hoodlum, Ma. My father was one of them. He wasn't a goddamned bookkeeper!" he blurted out, and he watched her stop, stunned. And Michael knew he'd just broken a big rule.

Sophia stopped rocking. It was over. The whole lie was over. She stared at the tiny lines in Michael's face, around his eyes. It was like looking into Vincent's face. In fact, she thought, Vincent was probably Michael's age the first time they'd fought about him being a wiseguy.

She stared deeply into Michael's eyes, suspiciously, and he looked away. She looked down at the floor. Was that the answer? She was going to have to go through the rest of her life now having this same fight with her own son? If he'd figured out that Vincent couldn't have been a bookkeeper, then what must he have been doing in the last twenty-four hours to come to that truth? She stared back up at him. She slowly stood up and crossed her arms over her chest. She was not going to go through this again.

"Yes. Your father was not a bookkeeper, and we fought about it for thirty years. I hated what he did." She stared him straight in the eyes.

"Then why didn't you leave him?" Michael asked, staring straight back at her, testing.

"Because I loved him and I couldn't," she answered angrily. "But why I did or didn't leave your father is none of your business. What is your business is what he—what we—wanted for you, and that was not to have to do what he did. And he worked hard to make sure you had that choice. Your father didn't have that luxury. He wasn't sent to good schools. Your father could barely read English," she confessed, then stopped herself, realizing that she was using Vincent's own words about what he did for a living to defend him to his son.

"Why are you doing this, Michael? You're not stupid. You got brains . . . you got a college education," she said, coming at him, holding her hands out.

"I blew it. Don't you understand? I can't get into another law school with my record," he said, and began to feel the lump in his throat grow big and painful.

"So you do something else. You could be . . . you could be an accountant—"

"No-o-o."

"There's no shame in being an accountant."

"But you wanted better—"

"No, we wanted honest. There is no shame in working—even if you never make much money, there's no shame in it as long as it's honest work. That was the one thing he wanted so badly for you. To get away from the Sollys of the world. Don't you understand?"

He sat down on her bed, staring at her.

"I know I been all wrapped up in grief over your father these past two years, and I ain't been keeping an eye on you . . . but you gotta stop this, Michael. Before you get in any deeper."

"I want it over, too, Ma, believe me." He stared at her and slowly nodded.

She felt herself exhale and take in a more relaxed breath. Then she frowned at him.

"Then stop playing around. Take the nice girl from outta town and get the hell away from that big stupid cousin of yours," she said. Then she walked over to the window, waiting for him to leave.

He nodded to himself and quietly left the room. Well, everything was out in the open for the first time in his life. She was right. It was a choice, and he'd been given the tools to make it. He suddenly felt strong inside, a feeling he hadn't had in several years. He had the choice. He still had a choice.

But just run off? No.

As Michael walked downstairs slowly, he dangled one leg off of each stair for a moment before putting his weight on it. Lisa was standing at the foot of the stairs, watching when he came down.

"Are you all right?" she asked after a moment.

He nodded and kept staring at her.

"Why aren't you in the car?" he asked, finally focusing in on her.

A confused frown swept over her face. "Tony's . . . acting weird."

"Uh-huh," he said quietly.

Michael stood there, turning over everything in his mind. He didn't know exactly what he was going to do. Tony was a big problem. He was not going to stop stalking Lisa's boss just because Michael wanted to turn over a new leaf.

Solly wasn't going to throw his hands up and go along with the new-leaf theory, either.

Geddone—well, he didn't know what to do about that, either. He was in on it. Sooner or later, the body would turn up. Probably sometime Monday morning. Maybe that would appease Solly.

He doubted it.

"Let's get in the car," he said, taking Lisa by the arm.

She stopped and began to pull back.

"We have to stop him," she said quietly.

"Yeah."

"Talk to him," she said, pulling back again.

"Look, he's not going to stop just because we say so. This is revenge for Rosa. Fuckin' Rosa," he muttered. "Tony's not going to stop until she calls him off."

"Well, let's talk to her, then."

Michael looked at her and chuckled.

"You know anything about Rosa Morelli? She once tried to have Solly kill her grocer because the onions he sent over weren't big enough."

"Well, what do we do?"

Rosa Morelli and her blood lust. Everytime she was upset, guns were supposed to come out to make it all right. Rosa and guns, guns and Rosa! He stood still and caught sight of his mother at the top of the stairs, staring down at them. He looked back at Lisa and took her by the arm.

"I don't know. Maybe we can throw him off the track, you know?" His mother had disappeared.

They both stood in silence, and suddenly a big grin crossed Lisa's face.

"We'll go sit in front of Henry Foster Morgan's apartment! Just like Tony wants to," she said.

"What, are you kidding?" he said as a blast from the car horn outside rang through the house. He opened the door and gave Tony a nod. Tony leaned on the horn again and looked annoyed.

"No. He won't be there," she said, and continued walking past Michael and down the front steps.

"What do you mean?"

"I mean, there's a big society wedding out in the Hamptons this weekend and I know he's going to it."

"So?" he asked, and grabbed her by the arm, pulling her back as Tony blasted them with the horn again.

"He's going out there early. At ten. I know because he had me book the limo. So you see, he's already gone. He'll be gone the whole week," she said, smiling at him.

He felt a smile run along his face from ear to ear and he walked with her over to the car.

It was going to be a real bore sitting there in front of some loft in SoHo, but it would give him time to think about getting to Rosa.

He opened the back door and Lisa began to slide inside.

"Why don't youse sit up front here with me. Mikey can sit in the back. You don't mind, do you, Mikey?"

Cool air from the AC floated out, down around his legs, and the annoying *bong, bong, bong* of the door went off. He looked at her and shrugged. "No."

She reluctantly got out and slid in next to Tony Mac, giving Michael a look.

He stood at the car door and gave one last glance at the house. The curtain in his mother's room moved. His eyes stuck there for a moment until the strange electrical buzz of locust in one of the trees shook him out of it.

He looked around the yard. The air smelled of damp earth and fresh-cut grass. It was going to be hot again. The rain last night obviously hadn't done much. He lowered himself into the backseat and closed the door quickly.

He sat back, glancing at Lisa in the mirror for a moment as Tony started the car.

They went to the corner and turned right, then drove straight ahead. They got to the ramp and Tony suddenly turned onto the Shore Parkway going east.

"What are you doing? You're going the wrong way."

"No I ain't."

"City's back in the other direction."

"We ain't going to the city," Tony said, and pressed down on the accelerator, picking up speed.

"What do you mean? We have to stake out his apartment. That's where he'll be, right, Michigan?"

"Yes," she answered quickly.

Tony smirked and looked at him.

"There ain't nobody in his apartment. I stopped there on the way to pick youse up."

"Maybe he was asleep."

"He wasn't asleep, 'cause he wasn't there. I know where he is."

"Where?"

"East Hampton. Says so right in the appointment book you give me yesterday."

* * *

Sophia watched the car until it was out of sight. She shook her head. Too fast, they drive too fast. She turned from the window. Well, she'd said something. There was some relief in that, that and the fact that Michael didn't want to be in the situation, either. She felt a huge weight off her now just knowing that. The frightening thought that he actually might like being a hoodlum had hit her at about three o'clock that morning. She'd paced and paced, and found herself pacing into his room. She'd sat there in the dark, empty place until almost dawn, going over in her mind what she would do when . . . or if . . . he ever came home.

The previous morning came into Sophia's mind. She relived again walking down the church steps with Gina the way she had for the last two years.

Sophia's eyes stayed unfocused on Gina as she rattled on and on about her daughter-in-law, Val. Gina had never liked Val, and deep down Sophia really had no opinion of her, since all her knowledge of the woman was secondhand. She had met Val only briefly at the shower before the wedding, and then in that passing way you do with distant relatives you see only at funerals, weddings, or christenings. Like any good friend, she was honor-bound to commiserate with Gina over her problems with this woman, which were real, although Sophia suspected that Gina would find no woman on the planet good enough for her son, Enrico.

The car slid up in front of Café Egidio, and Paulo, the driver, got out. He helped Gina, then walked around and opened Sophia's door. She shooed away his hand as he tried to help her stand. He did this every morning, and

Sophia always was tempted to yell out to him that she was not Gina's age, that she was not some ancient old thing—she was 66, not 106.

"You be back here in one hour exactly," Gina warned him sternly, the way she did every morning, even though the man sat parked in front of the café, watching the door and the street.

The air was damp and still and comparatively cool considering what it would be in a couple of hours. The sidewalk in front of the café had been washed down, looking almost waxed and polished and reflecting the early-morning light. It made Gina's face almost appear rosy and young-looking.

The tinny bell on the door rang out as it was hit by the edge of the top of the door as they entered the café, and the smell of brewing espresso and chocolate surrounded them. Gina and Sophia nodded to Isabella, behind the counter, and they took their regular seats.

"He's making his bones," suddenly echoed again through Sophia's head and she felt dizzy and breathless for a moment. She placed her hands on the cold marble tabletop and took a deep breath.

"Sophia, you don't look so good," Gina's voice echoed.

"I'm just tired," she said as she lifted the cooled palms of her hands and gently pressed them against her face.

She sat with her hands on her cheeks and her eyes fell on the painting above Gina on the wall. The hooked nose and fierce eyes of Cesare Borgia seemed to stare coldly back down at her even though it was a profile. He was dressed up in his regal best, boxy flat orange and pale yellow velvet hat, a wide fur yolk, spreading out to the tips of his shoulders, gashed split sleeves, yellow on the outside, with the same orange used to gore the inside.

Around his neck, a wide blue ribbon hung, held flat against the puffed chest by something resembling a medal. In one hand was a feathered quill, in another a large book. A man of letters, the portrait seemed to say.

It didn't fool Sophia. She could still see what a cold-hearted murderer the man had been. She shifted her eyes, feeling paler. She concentrated on the shiny dark green walls with the busts of Roman and Sicilian emperors as Isabella silently set down two cappuccinos.

"Sophia, you drink some water," Gina said.

She nodded and looked up at Isabella. Her throat was dry as Gina's news echoed in her head.

"And I lost a pound this week, so I think I'll have a cannoli," Gina ordered.

Every Thursday, Gina lost a pound so she could have a cannoli, although, as far as Sophia could see, she was the same weight she'd been since she was forty. Sophia put her hands back down on the table as Gina continued talking. It was the first morning she'd ever noticed that Gina never looked directly at her, and she supposed that she could just turn to stone in front of this woman and she would still be rattling away about the goings-on in her house. And it was exactly those bits of gossip that Sophia had originally come for, but this morning, knowing that her son was going to be "taken care of" by Solly, the gossip seemed sordid and was making her sick.

Isabella placed a glass of ice water in front of Sophia and she immediately drank it. She could feel the cool water go all the way down to her stomach. The café's bell rang out again, and Vittorio appeared, the same way he did every morning.

He was a man Sophia's age, a widower who owned a rather successful travel agency, the kind advertised on late-night television. The agency specialized in tours of Italy and Sicily.

He was impeccably dressed in a three-piece linen suit and he carried a newspaper folded under his arm. His hair was silver-gray and glinted in the sunlight coming in from the windows overlooking the street. He had a sharp pointed nose and watery ice blue eyes, which were large and kindly-looking. He was very handsome, Sophia realized.

He nodded to Sophia and sat down at his usual table. She watched him unfold the paper and hold it up as he sipped the espresso that was waiting for him.

She stared at his paper. The puffy, slightly italicized letters of the logo for *Corriere Della Sera*, the daily paper of Milan, appeared at even more of an angle because of the way he was holding the paper. Her eyes looked up at him, somewhat startled. She had never noticed the Milanese paper. A Piedmontese . . . and suddenly her eyes took in the whole wall, what she had always assessed as his side of the café. Above him was a painting of Leonardo da Vinci.

Somehow it seemed fitting that Gina would choose to sit under Cesare Borgia and this legitimate businessman would sit under da Vinci. Reading his Milanese paper as though he lived there, dressed impeccably in linen, the truly regal silver in his hair, the almost-Swiss blue eyes, which shone and smiled at you, delicate pinkish skin, always clean-shaven—he was the very image of the dashing Piedmontese man Sophia's mother had had in mind for her to marry and grow old with.

She had loved Vincent very deeply—but God, she would give her soul to be sitting across the room with Vittorio. How unfair it was that his sons would wind up hawking tours on late-night television and worrying about their income-tax deductions, while her Michael was going to spend the rest of his life ducking bullets in Solly's nightmare world.

Her eyes focused back on Gina. She watched her devour a cannoli, still talking through the food in her mouth.

When had she noticed all these things about Vittorio?

She took a drink of water and cupped the cold glass with her hands. She had never consciously thought about him, and the truth was, he was as oblivious to her. She darted a glance up and was taken aback.

He was staring at her, lost in thought.

For once, she kept his stare. She let go of the glass and felt her hands begin to smooth her black dress. She watched his eyes focus on her, and he watched her hands, smoothing the dress, as if she was polishing her armor. She thought she detected a sigh from him, disappointed, as if the thought *Oh well* was going through his mind, and then he looked back at his paper.

Her eyes focused back into Michael's bedroom as she realized her hands were smoothing her bathrobe. She had dressed like a Neapolitan widow. The thought did not sit well with her. She got up and slowly walked to her bedroom. She sat on the edge of her bed, staring at her closet door. At last, she got up and pulled the string to the light. She searched through the closet of clothes, black tops, black skirts, black sleeveless dresses, and way in the back she found what she was looking for—a dress. Carefully, holding the hanger up, she took it out and looked at it. Delicate nosegays of violets with deep green leaves and tied with blue and pink ribbons decorated a white background. It was made of a silky rayon material, with a small lace collar, a matching belt, and short sleeves. She held the dress up to herself and looked in the full-length mirror attached to the inside of the closet.

It was such a pretty dress. It had been her favorite. She placed the dress on the bed and slipped her bathrobe and nightgown off. She pulled the dress over her head. It was baggy. Very, very baggy, she thought, amazed as she buckled the belt around her waist. Almost afraid, she slowly walked back to the closet mirror, keeping her eyes on the floor. Sophia stood in front of the mirror and gave a good long look.

Cinderella, she wasn't. But she was pretty, and comparatively slender since the time she'd bought it. She walked away from the mirror and quickly pulled the dress over her head. She hung it back up, turned off the light, and lay down on the bed.

One morning, when Gina was sick or busy with holidays, she was going to put that dress on and she was going to take the train to Café Egidio and she was going to sit under the picture of Leonardo da Vinci and she was going to wait for Vittorio. She was going to sit on the normal side of the room, the place where people utterly unconnected with the Sollys of the world sat, she determined in her head. She lay there, her eyes partially closed. .

Five A.M. came and fear hit her as she went to church, knowing Michael hadn't returned. It temporarily went away as she concentrated on the mass. She thought she saw Father D'Amico grimace at her from the altar. The fact was confirmed as she and Gina left the church.

Father D'Amico stood at the front door, shaking hands with his parishioners as they walked down the steps. Gina went first and continued on to the waiting car. Father D'Amico shook Sophia's hand, frowned, and looked her in the eyes.

"I hope, Sophia, you are planning to do something good today. Get out, maybe go on a little trip," he said.

She nodded and continued down the steps. She knew what he meant: something away from the church. She climbed into the car next to Gina and they began to drive to the same place they always had pastries and espresso. Yes, she was going to do something good today. She was not going back to the church.

Her mind returned to the current moment. She was home. What was the good thing she could do today?

She could wait for Michael to come home and tell her that he'd gotten it all straightened out and was going back to school. She walked slowly down the stairs.

Yes, that would be very nice. Her heart sank. And very unlikely. Solly wasn't going to let him off the hook, she knew that. In all the years she'd known of Solly's doings, he'd never let anyone off the hook. And Sophia knew her son was going to be no exception.

Panic began to overcome her as she realized that she'd made a terrible mistake. If Michael asked to be let out of it, she knew what Solly's reaction would be. He'd have him killed. God knows what Michael had seen over the last two years—that was one of the things that had kept Vincent tangled up in the mess—he knew too much and now she'd insisted on him asking to be let out.

Would Michael be that naïve?

She stopped, shaking on the last step.

Of course he would. She'd raised him that way.

What was she going to do?

Henry staggered out of the coffee shop. He'd had five cups of coffee and some eggs, which were making him sick. Most solid food made him sick. There was a rusty squeal and he stared across the street at a clothing store as a woman opened up the gates.

Well, at least he could get something clean.

He was just about to cross when a car caught his eye coming around the corner. He froze for a second, then quickly ducked back inside the coffee shop.

The shiny black Jaguar with the vanity plates MORRIS1 roared down the street and past the coffee shop. He stood there for a moment, until it screeched around the corner. He cowered and waited to see whether it was going to come back. After a moment, he walked stiffly toward the phone booth in the back of the coffee shop.

"Mother, let me in the house!" he screamed over the phone.

"Now really, lower your voice. I told you last year, you miss grandfather Foster's funeral and you're out—"

"I was working," Henry whined, thinking fast.

"Oh please, you haven't done an honest day's work in your whole life, Henry. This is your mother you are talking to."

"I was . . . covering an event for my magazine—"

"You were parading around New York. I know, I bought you that magazine. God knows, at least it keeps you out of the house. I know exactly how much work you do and when you do it."

"I was covering an event—"

"You were in bed with some tart who can't keep her clothes on in front of a camera. Don't lie to me, Henry. Why do you want to get into this house so badly, anyway? You haven't called me in three years."

"I just . . . I miss you."

"Henry, this is Mother. You haven't said 'I miss you'

since you were ten and wanted your own charge cards."

"All right, look, there's someone . . . here, in town. I just don't want to see right now."

"Why, what have you done to them?"

"I haven't done anything to them! Maybe they've done something to me."

"I doubt that."

"Anyway, so all I need is someplace to stay until the wedding. So what do you say?"

"I say you should have been at your grandfather's funeral."

"He's going to kill me."

"Well, then, I'll be at your funeral."

Click.

"So what time did youse get to the hotel?" Tony said, staring out as they drove.

"Around two," Michael said quietly.

"And why you go there?"

Michael glanced up to the rearview mirror at Lisa and she leaned forward.

"Because I wanted to leave. So I changed my clothes and we left." She said with a hint of annoyance. "Is that all right? I mean you've dragged me around for a day now, my car—" She sat back. "Oh my God, Michael, the car. It's still sitting up there."

"I'm sure it will be okay."

"But it's not even mine. What if they tow it?"

"I don't think—"

"What do you mean, it's not yours?" Tony interrupted.

"It's . . . a friend's."

"Where's your car?"

"I can't afford a car, Tony."

This was his chance, the in he'd been looking for. He cleared his throat.

"You can't afford a car! That's the worse thing in the world! Not having a way to get around."

"Well, it's not so bad—" she began.

"Oh yes it is." He looked over at her and took a deep breath. "You want a car? I'll give you a car," he said, presenting it to her proudly.

"What?"

"Tony—" Michael began.

"Any kind you want. You want a Lincoln?"

"No, I really—"

"Tony, you can't just give people cars."

"Why not?" he said, sneering at him.

"I—"

Lisa looked back at Michael and motioned him to be quiet. She would take care of this. She turned around toward Tony and began slowly.

"No, Tony, but thank you, anyway. I don't want a car."

"You don't want *my* car," he said, and his eyes narrowed.

"No, no, it's not that." She thought fast. "Where would I keep it?"

"The street."

"They'd tow it, then what would happen? I'd owe money on it."

"So . . . keep it in one of them places, whatta they—garages. You throw 'em fifty a month and—"

"Not in my neighborhood. Garages cost up to four hundred dollars—"

"A *month?* You gotta be kidding! You could rent an apartment in East Harlem for that."

"I know."

He was quiet for a moment.

"So, you could park it on the street next to one of them meters. Then they couldn't tow it. You just throw in change now and then and no problem. They never check them things."

"They do in her neighborhood."

Tony turned around and stared at Michael.

"Was anybody talkin' to you?"

"No, he's right, they check them a lot," she interjected. "And besides, I'd be out there every thirty minutes."

"Thirty minutes? How much you gotta give them?"

"Fifty cents."

"For thirty minutes? That's robbery. I don't know who your assemblyman is, but someone's on the take down there. Jeez, fifty cents for thirty minutes! Whatta racket they got going."

"I know. So you see, I couldn't have a car because I have no place to put it. It would cost me hundreds, just in meter quarters alone," she said, and Michael smiled at her.

"Jeez, I didn't think it was this much trouble, givin' somebody a car . . . fifty cents . . ."

"Yup," she said, sitting back.

They sat in silence for awhile, staring out at the drive along Long Island. Even though the air conditioner was blowing directly on her, the sun through the windshield was strong on her arms. She leaned back on her seat. The fuzzy maroon upholstery was soft on the skin on the backs of her arms.

She looked out. The L.I.E. was full of cars with surfboards strapped to their hoods and station wagons filled with kids and dogs and Styrofoam picnic baskets. They slowed as the traffic began to cram up around the first big beach, and the highway looked shimmering and liquidy in the heat. Lisa stared at all the cars, listening to the whir of the air conditioner, and thought about how nice it would be to be in one of those other cars with Michael on their way for a lovely day at the beach.

"Madonna!" Tony said, hitting the top of the steering wheel. "I know, I'll steal youse a parking meter!"

"What?" she said, then glanced in the mirror at Michael.

"A parking meter. I'll buy you the car and then steal youse a meter to go with it."

"What are you talking about?" Michael asked, leaning on the seat back.

"Jeez, don't you see nothin'? Look, when she puts out the meter next to the car, she can just keep the same quarters in it. . . . And here's the beauty of the plan, when she's using the car, she keeps the meter out so she can collect on all the dumb bastards puttin' in quarters every thirty minutes, *capisce*? She could make enough for gas. She might even make the insurance, who knows?"

"Tony, you're talking about stealing something that's *cemented* into a New York City sidewalk."

"Yeah," he said, not following what the problem would be.

She turned to Michael, who gave her a shrug. She was on her own with this one. She faced forward again as the vision of Tony tearing a parking meter out of the sidewalk filled her head. She glanced over at the girth of his upper arms.

He probably could do it that way, too, she thought. Then she got an idea.

"Well, don't you think the meter maids would notice an extra meter, kind of . . . chained next to a car?"

"Well . . ." Tony began, and gave a loud exhale.

This was beginning to get on his nerves. Why was this so complicated for Michigan? Angela'd have snapped this deal up. Didn't this one have no brains? Here he offers her a beautiful new car and she's gotta get all wrapped up in the details of the thing.

"You could take it in when they come around," he offered finally.

She sat in silence.

"Well, they're a little bulky to carry around . . . parking meters," she squeaked.

"Look, you just think about it and get back to me, eh?" he said tiredly.

They all fell silent again.

He'd have to think of something else with this one. Jeez, maybe Angela wasn't so bad.

She stared out the windshield at a station wagon. A little boy in the back had caught her eyes. He was busy playing with a little girl. She could see that they were laughing. After a few moments, the little boy noticed her and he smiled and waved at her. Lisa smiled and waved back, and they began to play peekaboo, with the little boy ducking under the window and then after a few seconds shooting up to the window and giggling. Lisa would give an exaggerated, startled expression and he would burst into laughter.

She kept this up as they inched along behind the car, and Lisa made her expression grow and grow as a kind of sadness swept over her. She leaned her back against the car door and she darted a glance at Michael.

Michael was gazing happily at her playing with the child, and the sadness seemed to lift as she let her eyes rest there for as long as she dared with Tony in the car. It had been an unspoken agreement that Tony should not be told what had gone on. Michael's lips moved with words she couldn't understand and she looked puzzled. He shook his head, mouthing that he would tell her later.

She looked back to the little boy, to find that he had busied himself with another game.

The road alongside the Sonders' home was mobbed with reporters. Like a large cancerous growth, vans, trucks, and cars clogged the highway running alongside the beach. Out, over the water, helicopters dipped and darted and hovered as bathers on the public stretches of beach looked overhead, pointing and trying to read the logos on the sides.

Security had been hired by the Sonders, who had stated in interviews and press releases that this was a sacred, private affair. The caterer had been sworn to privacy; the dress designer and even the groom's barber were forbidden to talk to the press.

Delivery vans had been pulling up to the Sonders' house for several days, unloading boxes and bags covered in a peculiar lilac shade of paper to provide even more privacy—and also to whet the appetites of photographers who had been camped out on the roadside for several days.

The large house looked as if it was under siege. Security checkpoints had been set up along the outside gates, and anyone not showing an invitation was cordially, or physically, escorted down the road and away from the house.

This being a public road, and the only one with beach access, all traffic had been successfully snarled in either direction for miles. Anyone unfortunate enough to own a beach house on that stretch of road was also totally inconvenienced. Several of the Sonders' unamused neighbors got caught up in the overzealous security measures, along with an entire tour bus of Japanese car manufacturers who wound up stuck on the dead-end road. After an hour, they had gotten out and were busy taking pictures of the whole mess, and laughing at it all.

Morris sat behind the wheel of his Jaguar, listening to the music blast. He'd bought a system with four speakers, capable of blowing the windows out if it was cranked up full.

He adjusted his sunglasses, trying to ignore the brightness of the sun and the pounding sound of the surf alongside the car. He couldn't figure out why people had houses on the beach. It was so fucking loud and bright.

He glanced down at the clock, coughed, and began leaning on the horn.

He'd been sitting out here on the highway forever. He had to get to that dimwit's wedding.

What was the fucking holdup?

He stood to make excellent money on this. He figured he could clear forty grams minimum in an hour.

The guest list read like his client list. . . .

He continued leaning on the horn, and began cursing out loud in that tight, clenched-teeth voice he'd developed over the last three years. Morris always sounded like a kid, ready to explode.

That prick, Henry.

He'd show up, sooner or later. Morris rubbed his stubbled chin with his free hand.

He'd cut his fuckin' balls off.

"That botherin' you, Michigan?" Tony asked, staring at the black Jag next to their car.

Lisa was holding her ears with her hands, trying to insulate herself from the horrible blast from the car in the next lane.

"There're a lot of assholes in this world," Tony muttered.

A man in a red sedan in front of the black Jaguar got out of his car, and they watched him walk back over and slam on the guy's window.

Morris looked up at him, gave him the finger, and went back to the horn.

The driver of the sedan began screaming into the car, and Michael watched Tony unlock his door.

"No—" Lisa's chest tensed.

The car ahead began to roll slowly forward.

"But—"

"Look, we're beginning to move," she added quickly, pointing to the car in front of them.

Tony sat back down fully in his seat and began to inch along the highway, and she relaxed.

Twenty-five minutes later, they inched their way past the Sonders' house as security waved them on. Michael looked back in time to see the Jaguar roll up to the front gate and unroll the window. He passed a piece of paper to a guard and the gates opened, allowing the Jaguar and several limousines to slide inside.

Henry sat in the back of the cab, carefully. The seat was burning hot from the sun and the new tuxedo he'd just bought felt itchy from all the sizing, and smelled of it. It was pearl gray, a color that almost exactly matched his skin shade at this point. He'd bought a brush and run it through his hair, which was now greasy, and he put it back into a ponytail. He looked at his face in the rearview mirror of the cab. He needed a sauna and a rubdown, and a shave. He noticed that his cheeks were sunken and realized that he was losing weight rapidly. He should go to a gym. . . .

Mother. She was going to get a piece of his mind. Who the hell was she to treat him like this? She was the one who'd insisted he take this lousy job. She was the one who'd threatened to cut off his trust if he didn't. So why the hell should he have to go to some eccentric old fart's funeral? He barely knew Grandfather Foster. The man never came out of this kind of odd greenhouse he'd built. A hundred and seven degrees and humid as hell, and this loon was always sitting in the center of it, bundled up in blankets, like Nanook of the North.

"Hurry up!" he barked at the back of the driver's head.

Let his sister get dragged off to these things. She loved them. Tiffany had always been an ass-kisser. Always there when Mother sneezed. He glared out the window at the beach.

All right, she wanted to play it like this, he'd play it like this. What exactly would he do?

He sat up on the seat as the idea came into his head.

He felt the corners of his lips curl up in a grin. A scene. The one thing that would make his mother's skin crawl. A nice big, screaming, embarrassing scene in front of all her society friends.

The cab pulled up to the large front gates of the house he'd remembered playing in as a child.

He'd actually always hated the Sonders. They were assholes. Most people were assholes. That's why they weren't permitted to all the places he hung out.

Morris. That scuzzy little bastard. Threatening *him*. Another person he'd settle with. He should be happy just supplying him, a leading New York magazine publisher.

If there was one thing he'd learned from his family, it was this: The rich don't pay for anything.

Hell, Henry's family was one of the 2 percent of this country who owned 90 percent of the wealth, and his father had to pay only one hundred dollars in taxes last year.

A guard rapped on the window and Henry rolled it down.

"Wedding invite, sir?"

He grumbled, dug into his pocket, then handed the man a crumpled, ripped invite. The gates opened and Henry pulled in.

Tony grabbed at his necktie and pulled on the knot to loosen it around his collar. He flexed his thigh muscles, trying to get some kind of circulation back in them.

Michael sat in the backseat, staring out at the road from the shoulder onto which they had pulled. He kept going over things, deals he could offer Tony to offer Solly to get him off the hook, deals to stop the hunt for Lisa's boss.

Lisa sat rigidly still every time Tony looked over at her. There was the strong smell of after-shave, which added to her fear of him. Even when she wasn't looking directly at him, even when she was trying to block him out of her mind, the scent refused to allow it. She looked over at him. He had an odd expression on his face that she couldn't quite read. She didn't like it at all. And she'd just noticed that his nose seemed to point at her even when he was looking straight ahead.

At that moment, she felt the tips of Michael's fingers brush the back of her neck as he leaned forward on the backseat. As they touched her, the zinging pulses that went through her body seemed overwhelmingly large for the lightness of the touch. Short memories of the night before went through her like small thunderbolts going through her legs, making the muscles on the tops of her thighs twitch and a tightness start deep in her pelvis. She felt her breathing becoming shallower and shallower, and her eyes began to close as the memories of him being all around her, the softness of his tongue as he explored her mouth, and the shaking—he shook—overtook her, making the car melt away for a moment.

Tony coughed and she snapped back to alertness, and Michael's hand quickly pulled away. Her body now felt stiff and scared. She looked around at Michael, wondering whether touching the back of her neck had set off the same pulses in him. Or was it only her?

What was she thinking? This man had kidnapped her. Then the terrible thought reoccurred to her. God, maybe she was one of those crazies who liked that kind of thing?

She ran it over in her mind. She had certainly never

asked anyone to tie her up and stick a gun in her face before going to bed. She hadn't slept with that many men, to tell the truth. She'd had a boyfriend in high school, there were two guys before Andrew, and then there was Andrew, and she had been faithful to him for almost five years.

When had she first had thoughts about Michael? What could possibly have attracted her to him?

Her eyes looked at him. He was sitting on the seat, looking . . .

That was it. That was when she knew he was safe. He had looked embarrassed by all this.

Then she had the odd thought about what it would be like to spend her life with Michael, away from all this. There was a twitching in her as she thought of Michael in Michigan. She would march into the newspaper office and get a job. Look, she would say, I have four years of experience on *Smug*. I can proofread; I can write blurbs; I know what to do.

And Michael would go to school and find a career. And they would go to dinners with people, and live in a big house, and they would go to PTA and lodge meetings. And she would not be stuck getting humiliated day after day by this jerk of a man, coming home to listen to her answering machine, praying Andrew would show some human compassion and call.

And no one in Bliss would ever even imagine this life. No one would know about him or how they met, and it would be a secret that would bind them together.

"How did you meet Michael?"

"He kidnapped me with a gun, because he was with the Mafia and was ordered to kill my boss." She could see the faces twist up confused at that, and then, as they giggled at the absurd idea, he would wink at her.

It made her chest tingle. There was something erotic about having this dark secret that they would look back on from a safe distance. It was dangerous. She was still in grave jeopardy; they still had to stop Tony. She felt a zinging in her pelvis again, and she suppressed a smile, because this was the first time in several years she'd felt excitement in her life.

Two nights ago, she'd sat, weeping by the front door, wondering when her life was going to change.

She really felt alive. And yes, she had been kidnapped, and yes, she had killed a man—in self-defense, she thought quickly—and yes, she had made passionate love to this man, because it might have been her last night on earth, and yes, she was still in the clutches of this robotic killer. Her eyes slid over to Tony. But strangely, somehow it seemed as though things were finally looking up in her life.

The sensation of a full bladder finally was persisting so much that she couldn't ignore it any longer.

She squirmed in her seat.

"I have to find a bathroom," she announced.

Tony grunted. He started up the car again and headed off for a restaurant up the road a bit.

Michael got out with Lisa and they walked over to the place that looked closed. They walked inside in silence and closed the door.

Behind the bar, a bartender was pouring ice into an ice bin. He stared up at them.

"We're closed."

"I know. You have a bathroom the lady can use?" Michael asked.

The man nodded toward a long hallway they were standing in front of and went back to pouring the ice.

"You okay?" Michael asked quickly.

"As long as there are no parking meters delivered to my building."

They both chuckled, and Lisa exhaled, realizing that this was the first time in a long time she'd made a joke.

"I better go back out," Michael said, and turned quickly.

She grabbed him by the arm and spun him around suddenly, catching him off guard. She gave him a long hard kiss, then turned and walked quickly down the hallway.

She'd always wanted to do that to someone.

He stared after her, finally getting his breath back. He quickly walked over to the men's room. He stood staring at the machine on the wall. After a moment, he dug into his wallet and shoved several coins into it. Two small boxes slid down the chute and into the bin. He grabbed them, took the foil-wrapped condoms out of them, shakily put them inside his wallet, and tossed the boxes. He walked back out quickly, putting his wallet into his jacket.

It was just . . . with all these diseases out there, who knew? And of course he knew Lisa would be fine, but who knew about that lowlife she'd been living with?

The feel of sheets and her body against his the night before flashed through his mind and made his skin tingle. He'd been having these flashes all day, being with her in the car, and he'd finally had to touch her, if only to brush the back of her neck. Michael stopped in the hallway. He had to get a grip on himself. He was not some breathless schoolboy who'd been kissed for the first time.

But it was very difficult being so near to her and not

being able to touch her. If he could just keep his mind off the night before—the sound of her moaning as he'd kissed the side of her neck when he was on top of her flooded his mind.

A small smile came over him as he opened the door to the restaurant.

It was—good—needing something like that again.

He exhaled and walked back outside. He glanced at Tony's face in the car, and wiped the smile off his face.

"Got to stretch my legs," he called over to the car.

It was even hotter than he'd thought. He walked over to the restaurant's deck, overlooking the beach, and leaned down. It smelled of salt water, with a tang of dying shellfish and the perfumed smell of suntan lotion.

He could feel his shirt begin to stick to him under the jacket.

Tony came up next to him and leaned over in silence. They watched people sunning themselves on towels, walking up and down, splashing in the water. In the corner, a volleyball game was in hot play.

"You think I should get married?" Tony's voice breezed by.

Michael stared over to him.

"What made you think of that?"

"I dunno. Maybe being around Michigan these past few days. It ain't easy, meetin' women, you know?"

"Yeah. Who you thinking of marrying? Angela?"

"Naw, she ain't right. . . . I dunno, someone don't want to talk too much."

Michael turned around and stared at the building, leaning his elbows on the rail. The stretch across his chest felt good.

"Maybe you should write to one of the agencies, you know, sends women over from Sicily. . . ."

He grunted and stared over at Michael.

"I don't mean *can't* talk, fahcrissake. I mean someone don't wanna talk."

"They *can* talk, Tony, just not in English."

"Naw, I get enough of that shit from my grandmother."

Michael shrugged and straightened up. He looked over at Tony, who was leaning on the rail and frowning, as he rubbed his clasped hands together.

"Tony, what about getting me off the hook?"

"What?"

"What I asked you in Forlini's last night. Getting me off the hook with Solly?"

Tony shook his head.

"Solly ain't so happy right now, Mikey. You saw him last night. Look, you do this guy for Aunt Rosa and maybe we can do something—"

"No. Don't you understand? I don't want to make my bones, Jesus!"

"You don't gotta raise your voice, here. Look, it ain't so bad. Solly takes good care of you. Look at what I got. I got a nice car, got good clothes, I got money." His voice stopped as Lisa came out of the restaurant.

They both watched her in silence.

"So what do you think about me gettin' married?"

A ten-tier lilac-colored wedding cake festooned with gardenias sat on a white linen table fifteen feet long. Twenty thousand white and rare silver-purple roses had been entwined into a thick garland, which hung around a long tent made of yards and yards of the same shade of lilac silk. The tent wrapped around three sides of the huge garden, enclosing the wedding area, overlooking the beach.

Folding chairs, cushioned with satin lilac pillows, were lined into thirty rows of ten on each side of a center aisle. A lilac silk carpet, specially woven in China for the occasion, ran the distance of the aisle. Another gracefully draped garland of gardenias ran up the aisle of seats along the inside and outside, creating pews.

An altar of lilac-colored marble had been erected at the head of the aisle. This, too, was covered with lilac-shaded flowers, sitting in silver pots.

Women in couture gowns of silk and linen, protected from the rays of the afternoon sun by elaborately designed hats, stood poised, talking to men in hand-tailored tuxedos and sipping Dom Pérignon from crystal champagne flutes. Others daintily bit at small toasts of beluga caviar or morsels of Maine lobster covered with dollops of dilled hollandaise. The music of Vivaldi, from a pared-down Boston Symphony, played out of sight behind the tent.

The guests were a match for the exquisite decor, not a hair out of place, not a paunch of a belly, nor a thigh spreading from having to sit at a desk day in and day out. These were the tight-muscled, perfectly sculpted bodies of the idle rich.

And then there was Henry.

Ashen and rumpled in his gray tux, Henry sat slumped over in a chair, guzzling from a champagne flute. He finished off the glass and dropped it under the chair, at the same time picking up the other glass he'd deposited there. He knew these events. If you didn't follow one of the waiters around, you never got a drink. His eyes didn't meet any of the people. He was going to be bored to death until the reception.

Ushers began walking people over to their designated seats as the orchestra finished "Spring" and began tuning up for Pachelbel, which was going to be the wedding march.

Around the other side of the building, in the pool cabana, Morris sat, doling out packets of coke to most of the groom's ushers.

He hadn't even seen the garden. He'd made two thousand dollars in thirty minutes. The ushers shuffled impatiently around him as the lookout announced that the wedding-march music was beginning, and Morris began to work double time.

The room soon cleared out quickly and Morris, wobbly from lack of sleep, walked out and around to the wedding area.

Henry's mother and sister were led over to their seats, next to Henry. His mother had red hair these days, he noted, and she was wearing a deep green sequined sheath over her skeletal body. Her eyes had that startled look to them, and Henry knew she'd had another face-lift. In fact, since the new face-lift, Tiffany looked more like her sister than her daughter.

Tiffany, Henry's sister, was now a blonde. Her nose was short and sharp, the result of an early nose job, and her body seemed to have changed drastically from the last time he'd seen her. She was now as skeletal as her mother. He'd heard a rumor that she'd had all kinds of tucks and pulls and nips right after her thirtieth birthday, and now that seemed to be confirmed. She was wearing a very short skirt, gathered at the bottom and pouffed out almost like a tutu. She looked like a floral bonbon.

He glared at them, but they did their best to ignore him. He finished the second glass of champagne and dropped the glass.

"For God's sake, can't you just once not get loaded at one of these things?" his sister whispered, and pulled her pouffed gown as far away from him as possible.

"Give me a fucking break," Henry said aloud, which made an old woman in front of him turn around and glare.

"Lower your voice," Tiffany snapped.

"Why? You weren't barred from Mother's house; you didn't have to pay for a cab to bring you out here—"

"That's right. I came in my Ferrari and Mother would have taken you in the Rolls, if you'd just shown up at the funeral."

"Well, tough shit!" he bellowed, and the woman in front put out a *really* under her breath and fanned her face with her clutch bag.

The chords of Pachelbel rose out as a ring bearer and flower girl walked down the aisle, followed by ten ushers and the groom. After a moment, ten lilac-gowned bridesmaids appeared, then the bride, wearing white lace from head to foot, with a ten-foot train embroidered with gold strands and decorated with lilac-tinted pearls. Next to her, her father walked stiffly, his arm wrapped around hers.

As soon as she appeared, helicopters hovered close, drowning out the ceremony, the music, and creating such a wind that it was like trying to sit out a tornado. At last, there was a flap of wings and a flock of lilac-dyed doves was released into the air—only to be blown back over the house by the force of wind created by the copters. The front row stood, clapping, and everyone followed, ducking the poor birds as they were knocked back.

As Henry rose unevenly and gave one clap, his eyes

glanced over to the right, then back, then immediately returned to the right. His hands began to shake and he froze in the middle of a clap as the equally ashen, sunglassed face of Morris stared at him from across the aisle.

In a moment, Morris's clenched face was hidden behind the wedding procession.

"Henry, I'm cutting—" his mother began as Henry slammed into the person next to him.

"Get out of my way!" Henry yelled, knocking over the woman on the end.

He made it to the tent on the right side, slamming into a waiter with a tray of champagne flutes. As they smashed to the ground, Henry turned around and caught sight of Morris, entangled with the same woman he'd just knocked over. He saw Morris look up, saw his lips move, and turned and ran.

The parking lot was filled with chauffeurs leaning against cars or playing cards on the hoods of their limos. Henry ran down to the end of the first row, when he caught sight of his sister's vintage 1965 red Ferrari.

He dodged over to the car and pulled on the passenger-side door. It was locked.

He could faintly hear Morris yelling after him as he ran around to the other side and tried the driver's door.

It pulled open, and Henry threw himself inside.

Morris grabbed onto the trunk handle as Henry backed it out of the spot.

"I'm going to kill you, Henry, you son of a bitch!" Henry heard as he shifted into forward and floored it.

He got to the gate and stopped short, throwing his chest into the steering wheel. He glanced in the mirror and saw Morris picking himself off the ground. He slammed on the horn and leaned out the window.

A man in his sixties sat in the small guard box, reading the paper.

"Open the gate, you moron," he screamed, and the man slowly looked up and frowned at him. Henry leaned back on the horn as the man lethargically turned the key to the gate. He sped out, only to be blinded by the combined flashes of waiting press cameras. He slammed on the brakes again, gave out a yelp, and began rubbing his eyes.

When enough of the spots had faded away, he started up again, turned right, and sped off down the road. Henry's eyes were still tearing from the lights.

After a couple of miles, he began to slow down, and glanced in the rearview mirror.

Morris's black Jag was a mile back and coming right at him.

"Shit," he cursed, looking ahead on the road.

Signs for a restaurant on the beach side met his eyes.

Lisa came walking out of the restaurant. She stared at Michael as he frowned back at her. She'd stayed inside a couple of minutes extra, hoping Michael would talk to Tony.

She could see by his expression that it hadn't helped.

She was right near the front bumper when the searing red sports car tore into the lot, swerved, and came to a stop, facing the highway.

In the dust stirred up by the maneuver, she saw the foggy outline of a face popping out of the window.

"What are you, fucking crazy? You could kill somebody doing that!" Michael yelled toward the red car.

A black car roared past on the highway, and Lisa

looked back to the sports car as the dust cleared enough for her to get a good look at the man's face.

"Oh my God, it's him," she said as Tony walked up next to her.

Henry stared up at her in the puzzled way you do when you see someone you associate with a specific setting and who is entirely out of place for where you are currently. Tony took a step toward the car and began reaching inside his jacket to his shoulder holster when the black Jaguar, which had blown its horn for a half hour on the road, came roaring into the parking lot.

Henry's head disappeared back inside the car and the car pulled out, kicking up a cloud of dust in their faces.

"I'm gonna kill you, Henry Foster Morgan!" a man yelled from the black Jag, as it, too, took off.

Tony grabbed Lisa by the arm and literally threw her into the backseat. Michael barely made it into the car as Tony pulled out of the lot in pursuit of the two cars.

"Look, you can't do it, Tony. You can't. I don't care what he did to Rosa, you can't kill him," Lisa was pleading.

Tony kept speeding and they began to gain on the Jaguar.

"I'll fix it. I'll give her my whole salary. I'll work for the rest of my life—"

"Shut her up, Mikey," Tony growled.

"No. You've got to stop it," he began, and Tony shot him a glare.

Michael sat, staring dumbly into the dashboard as Tony floored the car, and was hit in the face with the awful truth.

He was going to have to kill Tony.

His eyes looked out dazedly onto the road as the car

sped to catch up with the red Ferrari. Tony was leaning on the horn now as he tried to pass the black Jaguar. The Jag kept cutting him off again and again as they swerved across the road, until Tony whipped the wheel around, slamming the Caddy's front fender into the side of the Jag.

It knocked Morris across the lane, and he swerved back into the Cadillac, pushing the car off the road, into the center divider, and they both came to a stop.

Before Michael could say anything, Tony jumped out as the Jag pulled out and up on the divider. Morris rolled down his window and looked up as Tony approached.

"What the fuck's wrong—" he began in his clenched voice.

Tony shot him in the forehead and watched Morris slump sideways across the seat. Keeping the gun low and blocking the view of it with his body, Tony leaned in as if he was having a conversation and shot Morris again in the ear for good measure. He tucked the gun quickly back into his holster, pulled himself back up, and walked steadily back to the car.

He slammed the door as he got in, shaking the whole car. He started the motor quickly and pulled off the center divider and back onto the road.

"What happened?" Lisa asked as they went by the car.

"He said he'd be more careful on the road," Tony answered, pressing his foot back down.

Michael glanced in the sideview mirror at the driverless windshield of the black car, then looked back to Tony.

"Anybody hungry?" Tony asked.

A chill passed through Michael as he put together what had happened during the conversation.

Seven

The water lapped against Solly's private docks off the garden of his house in Mill Basin and gently rocked his boat back and forth. He sat, taking in the late-afternoon sun, sipping on a Campari and soda, and staring out over the water. His grandchildren were making a racket in the pool, so he'd moved down, closer to the canal off the back lawn.

He was sweating from the heat and grabbed a towel and rubbed his stocky middle above his bathing suit, then dropped the towel beside him and leaned back, closed his eyes, and breathed in. The air smelled of the sea, gasoline from his boat, and newly mown grass.

The silence was broken by the sound of Ralphie coming up next to him. Solly picked his head up, opened one eye, and stared up at him. Ralphie's tubby Bermuda-shorted middle stuck out from under a North Shore Bowling League shirt. His hairy naked legs sank into a pair of black shoes. Black socks rose up from the shoes to midcalf, held there by garters.

Made Solly's skin crawl, the way Ralphie dressed. He closed his eyes to cover up the sight.

"Solly," Ralphie said quietly, crossing his hands in front of him in a show of respect.

"The days go so fast now, you know, Ralphie? Summer's gone," he said, leaning back into the chair.

"Solly," Ralphie repeated, and waited for him to open his eyes and sit up.

"What?"

"Someone's here to see you."

He looked straight up at him and exhaled for a moment.

"Yeah? I ain't expecting nobody."

"It's Sophia Bonello."

The exits from the Jones Beach parking lot were backed up right and left, with families finished with their day at the beach.

"I can't fuckin' believe it! What kinda person would take little kids out in this heat." Tony was cursing and shaking his head back and forth. "I mean, they could get burnt all over, those little kids, you know what I mean, Michigan?" he added, and looked back at her, smiling.

She nodded and stared out the window. They had moved about seven feet in thirty minutes.

She couldn't imagine why anyone would go near Long Island. From what she'd seen, the beaches were crowded, with no room to walk, there was garbage all over, and getting out here was a nightmare.

Michael stared out his window silently.

He glanced over at Tony.

Tony was like a shark. He killed and ate, and swam on to his next victim and his next meal. Michael was going to have to shoot him. That was the only way to stop Tony.

Kill him.

Michael stared out the front window.

This got him back to the big problem, though. If he couldn't shoot some little accountant, how the hell was he going to shoot his own cousin? Yes, Tony was a killer, but he was also his cousin—someone he owed his life to. His own blood—family.

He watched Tony flex his legs.

No, he wasn't like a shark, either, Michael thought. He was more like—a Neapolitan mastiff. They were dogs some of the old-time wiseguys had. Dark as night, and big—some weighing more than a hundred pounds—with wide viselike jaws. They were large and stupid, fiercely loyal and incredibly effective at violence.

But Tony wasn't a dog or a fish. He was a member of his family. Michael clenched his teeth and felt himself frowning.

Say he shot him. Then what? What would happen? He'd have to leave New York, at the very least. The police would be all over the place on this. The police, hell, Solly. He didn't suppose that he could just shoot one of Solly's made men and then forget it all and go back to school. Solly would track him down. He wouldn't be able to do anything else.

Michael looked at himself in the rearview mirror and watched Lisa smile a quick smile at him, and the memory of the kiss in the bar came into his head. He let his eyes linger on the mirror until Tony began to hum, and he watched Lisa look away. He then took a good look at his own face.

He could have it surgically broken and rearranged to keep away from Solly. At least it would be clean, and certainly better than Solly having his face rearranged for him.

His mother. What would happen to her if he killed Tony? Would she still be able to go to church with Gina every morning to bend the priest's ear at her skimpy confessions and then go have espresso and cannoli?

She probably would have to move out of Brooklyn.

And where could he go? His eyes stared at the back of Lisa's head. Could he survive in Michigan? In school? With his face all broken up?

All right, so if he didn't shoot his cousin, then what? His eyes focused back on Tony and he began at his legs, then looked up, over his wide chest and thick neck. He stared at the bulges in the arms of his jacket from carefully worked arm muscles, at the bulge from his holster.

Maybe he could just maim him somehow.

Shit, his mother was right—he went to college. He had brains. Violence wouldn't solve anything . . . except in Tony's world. In the street, violence solved everything. That was all they knew. All Tony knew. Because no matter how many brains Michael had and no matter how much better skilled and educated he was, none of it would matter. Because Tony was a killer and would do what Solly said, even if it meant killing Michael.

And that was why Michael had to kill him.

"So, what can I do for you?" Solly asked, spinning his big white leather chair around so he could sit.

Sophia heard the click of the door behind her and did not even have to turn around to know that Ralphie was there.

Behind Solly was a big window overlooking the back

lawn of the house. That was the only familiar thing in the room. Sophia looked around, startled, and realized it had been a very long time since she'd been in his home.

Huge light gray Formica and chrome wall units with inset mirrors ran most of the length of the walls. The floor was carpeted white, and a white and gray couch sat in the middle of the room. Embedded in front of the couch was a large white stone coffee table, which Sophia estimated must have weighed three hundred pounds. It was polished to such a high sheen that it mirrored a three-foot glass sculpture that sat on top of it. It was of two dolphins flying out over a wave that looked as if it was just about to splash on the table. It looked like pictures she'd seen of big suites in gambling casinos in Reno, not like the dark wood-covered library of Solly's father's. All this white in New York, it must be a mess to keep clean, she thought. She watched Solly sit in the chair behind the glass desk. He placed his elbows on the chair arms and with his hands opened he touched his fingertips together, signaling that he was ready to hear her.

She cleared her throat. She was not going to let this new light decor throw her. He was still the same old snake, just like his father had been a snake before him. The way he was holding his hands proved it. That had been Enrico senior's habit, too. Her eyes narrowed and her hands twisted themselves around and around the heavy bag sitting in her lap.

"I want you to let my son off the hook," she said, clutching the bag.

"Now, Sophia, what are you talking about?"

Her knuckles were white on the heavy purse, and she felt small in the large white and gray room.

"Don't give me this crap, Solly, I watched you grow up. You leave my son alone," she continued.

Solly smiled at her.

"I don't know what you're talking about. I don't even know where Michael is, Sophia," he said smoothly.

"You know where he is and what he's doing because you sent him there. You leave my son alone. He's all I have left." She pursed her lips, wishing Vincent were alive.

He would know exactly how to handle it, whether coming here would be the way to approach it. . . . He would have taken care of this.

She was guessing.

"Don't you think you're embarrassing your son by interfering in his affairs like this? Sophia, he's no kid."

"I know what a snake you are, Solly. You let my son out of whatever this is that he's doing for you—"

"He's not doing anything for me," Solly insisted tiredly.

Off in the distance, she heard a phone ring, and she watched Solly nod to Ralphie. She heard the muted click of the door closing behind him and knew they were actually alone in the room.

Should she do it now? Her hands were damp on the purse.

"If he ain't doing anything for you, then who for?" she asked quietly.

He stared her in the face blankly.

"It's really none of your business," he said, then suddenly smiled at her and stood up.

"Look, your husband was a good friend of my family's. Why you come here, embarrassing his memory and his son, by interfering where you women don't belong?"

She stopped for a moment, thinking about what he'd said. The weight in her purse seemed to be getting heavier as she felt the metal bulge through the soft side of leather, and she began to feel that this was a big mistake, coming here like this. But she continued, anyway.

"Don't give me this crap, Solly. Every woman in this family knows what you're up to, when you're up to it. You call him back in."

"I'm tellin' you, I—"

The door clicked suddenly and Sophia watched Solly glance behind her once, then quickly again and frown.

"Solly," she heard Ralphie's voice, "someone did a job on Joey D.'s car last night."

"I'll be with you in a moment, Ralphie." He stared back down at Sophia. "Look, I got business to attend to here. You have to go now." He put his hand on her shoulder, and she pulled away.

She stood, defiant, clutching the bag.

"I swear, I'll make big trouble for you, Solly. Now who is Michael doing something for?"

Solly eyed her with annoyance. Another one going to make big trouble for him. Every fuckin' time he talked to a woman these days . . . She was not going to leave until he did something. He debated what that would be. Behind her, Ralphie was glaring at her. Solly's eyes went back to her.

Send her in a circle.

"Rosa Morelli," he said, then took her by the shoulders and led her to the door. "You want to know what Michael's doing? You go talk to Rosa."

She nodded, shook his hands from around her shoulders, gave him a defiant smile, and slowly walked out of the room.

Behind her, she heard the big door slam and she shakily walked out to the large front hall. Two men were standing there and one opened the front door silently.

She couldn't do it. She couldn't do what she'd come here to do.

She stood very still for a moment and glanced down the hallway toward the kitchen, wondering whether Gina was in there.

She began to feel her legs go on her slightly, but she took a deep breath and, as strongly as she could, she walked through the hall down to the kitchen, slowly, as she was supposed to, as if she belonged there in this house.

Gina Soltano was sitting out by the screen door, fanning herself with her apron while her cook was busy frying paper-thin pieces of veal. She must have just been to the beauty parlor, because her hair, still salt and pepper–colored even though she was almost seventy, had been coiffed and was looking fresher than it had at service this morning. The leathery skin on her face was wrinkled beyond belief, but there was still the echo of what a beauty she had been in her day. Her usual small pearl earrings dangled from her ears. The only other jewelry she wore was a gold cross around her neck, which shone against the blackness of her dress.

"Gina," she began, and the woman gave her a big smile and stood up.

"Sophia, what are you doing in my house?" she asked in her thick Neapolitan accent.

Sophia glanced toward the cook and then back.

"English?" she asked.

"She don't speak it. Comes from Palermo this past month," Gina said, switching back into English, the way they did with Italian when their children were young and they were discussing something that was not for little ears.

"You come out into the garden with me? I want some roses for the table tonight."

Gina was a good friend. When Sophia finally faced the fact that it might take her a long time to get Vincent into any other line of work, she had become friends with Gina. At first, she supposed it was because she felt she could keep an even closer eye on what Vincent was up to just by listening to Gina's gossip about the doings in her home. But as the years went by, she struck up a true friendship with her. The fact was, there weren't that many women who she could talk to frankly about her life. Her childhood friend Maria had married an honest grocer and moved to Arthur Avenue in the Bronx, so Sophia was really alone, except for Gina.

Sophia followed her out into the garden and turned right down a mossy brick path, toward a high boxwood hedge. They walked through a trellised entryway into a wide rectangular "room" of glorious rose varieties in full bloom, separated by the same brick paths. A rickety wooden table was set up at one side, and Sophia waited as Gina went over and pulled on some gardening gloves and a hat. Gina picked up a small basket with a pair of clippers in it and smiled at Sophia.

Sophia followed her down the center path to the tea roses. This garden was Gina's pride and joy, and she remembered when they'd put it in. It matched an old daguerrotype of the garden Gina's mother had had up on the hills above Naples.

"So, what you doing here?" she asked, snipping a half-closed bloom.

"I come to get Michael Antonio off the hook with your son."

"Why?"

She gulped, not wanting to offend Gina about her son's lifestyle.

"He ain't cut out for this kinda life, Gina. He should have been a lawyer."

"Things change," Gina said, cutting off several more blooms.

"You know Michael—he can't do the things Tony does for the family. He's gonna get himself all shot up, and he's all I got left, Gina."

"He know you're here?"

"No."

"He wants out?"

"Yeah. There's a good one," Sophia said, pointing to a large yellow bud.

She followed Gina back down to the bud. It wasn't working. Maybe she should go talk to Rosa.

No, that wouldn't work. Rosa hated her worse than she hated Gina. And Gina hated Rosa worse than anyone. Sophia felt her eyes open.

She knew how to goad her into action.

"Of course, it's all Rosa's fault."

Gina stopped and turned to her, and Sophia could see her nostrils flaring.

"What's Rosa got to do with it?"

"That's who Solly's having Michael do something for. For that pig."

It took a moment for Sophia to get the reaction she was hoping for.

"I bet your daughter-in-law put Solly up to it. It's a shame—the woman looks after Rosa better than her own family."

"Disgradziad," she heard Gina mutter.

Perhaps it wasn't fair, putting it this way. Everybody knew Gina hated her daughter-in-law. And Sophia personally knew that she hated Rosa Morelli almost as much, because the daughter-in-law used Rosa.

"So now, my Michael, who don't want no trouble and will go away"—she paused as she said that, knowing that it was as good as a solemn promise—"he's got to do something for that pig Rosa."

Sophia watched Gina snip another bud and drop it into the basket. They walked back silently toward the rickety table.

"This garden always makes me homesick," Gina said, taking off the gloves. "You find out what this is all about, and I'll take care of it," she added, giving Sophia a pat on the shoulder.

Sophia walked out the front door and into the generous driveway.

Out of the corner of her eye, she could see Solly and Ralphie through the big window of his office. They seemed to be arguing. As she stood waiting, Sophia watched Solly glance out the window and do a double take. He glanced down at his watch, then back at her, and he went a little pale. She looked away confidently.

The black car she'd hired drove up, and she stood staring until the driver finally got out. He grimaced as he walked around and opened the door for her.

She clutched the purse tightly and, as she got in the car, she could feel the bump against her thigh as she sat. She was sticking to the black double-knit dress. The pearls she'd put on were clammy against the back of her neck. She waited for the driver to get back in the car. When he did, she stared at his face in the mirror.

"East Harlem. I want to go to Pleasant Avenue and a Hun' nineteen," she said quietly.

The car began to pull out and she looked back over to the window of Solly's study. There was no one in the room. She let out a breath and suddenly there were butterflies in her stomach. She was shaking uncontrollably, with her hands still wrapped around the purse. The weight of the gun in it rested heavily in her lap.

She'd almost made a big mistake with him. Vincent would have been proud that she'd caught herself in time.

She felt herself smiling. Always do things the way you know they'll get done. It was like when she tried some new cleanser and then just had to go over the place again with what she knew worked and had worked for years.

Going to Gina was like using a good, old, reliable cleanser.

The sun had set when they pulled up in front of Tony's mother's house. Michael and Lisa were silent as they listened to Tony mutter. He unhooked his safety belt and opened the door.

"Youse wait here," he ordered, then gave Lisa a quick smile.

They watched him slam the door, and Michael was just about to say something when he heard the screech of a car behind them. They watched a white Lincoln turn hard in front of them, watched it bounce up onto the curb and run over three garbage cans, then drive onto the lawn, almost hitting Tony, before it came to a stop.

"YOU SONOFABITCH!" Angela screamed out the window as she slammed open the car door.

"What the hell—" Tony had just turned to face her

when they watched her take her purse and swing it into the side of his head.

"You—stupid bastard! You shit! What do you think you are!" she said, slamming him again and again. He grabbed the bag. Michael and Lisa watched as they wrestled with it, both grunting like prizefighters. Tony succeeded in pulling it out of her hands and the purse went flying into the shrubs next to the front door of the house. They watched her raise her hands and try to drag her long bright red nails across Tony's face. He grabbed one of her wrists. Michael watched her begin a roundhouse with the free arm.

He opened the car door.

Tony ducked the blow and turned her around, holding her arm behind her in a lock grip.

"What the fuck's wrong wid—"

"You're gonna die, Tony! I swear it! I'm gonna make big trouble for you. I called my father! He's gonna get you, Tony!"

"What the hell are you talkin' about?" Tony yelled back at her.

She kicked him in the shins with the spike of her high heels, and he gave a scream and let go of her, dropping his hands down to grab his shin. She gained balance, and Michael watched her back off, as her spikes sunk down in the wet lawn. In a flash, he knew what she was going to do.

"Oh, Jesus." He got out and grabbed at the door as he watched Angela begin to run back to Tony.

Her stone-washed jeans were so tight that as she raised her back leg to kick Tony in the head, like you would kick a football for a touchdown, the material held her leg back, giving Tony time to sweep his arm around and pull her remaining leg out from under her.

He shook his head at Michael, who was running up onto the lawn as Angela went down. Lisa had gotten out of the car and was staring at what she could see in the light from the street lamp. The outline of Tony's mother behind the screen door caught Michael's eye.

Tony quickly fell on Angela, pinning her shoulders to the damp lawn as she struggled. He leaned down over her as she screamed and spit in his face, and Michael, who had been coming to his rescue, realized that there was a grin on Tony's face.

He leaned over her, watching her blond hair get matted and seeing a leaf stick to it as she struggled underneath him.

"My father's gonna get you, you rat-fuckin' bastard."

"You should watch your mouth, Angela. You father know you curse like this?" He chuckled at her, which made her struggle even harder.

"Now, what's your problem?"

"I'm gonna make big trouble for you, Tony Macarelli."

"Yeah? Why?"

"You know why, you sonofabitch!"

"No. Why don't you tell me?"

"What you did last night."

"I didn't do nothin' to you last night."

"You fuckin' liar! You did a number on Joey D.'s car parked in my garage."

"I don't know what you're talking about."

"My father knows what you did—"

"Yeah, what the fuck was Joey D.'s car doin' in your spot?"

"It ain't none of your fuckin' business."

"Yeah? Your father know what kind of lowlife you been hangin' out with? You wanna tell me that?"

"You don't own me, Tony Mac. You broke up with me, remember? Huh?"

"I don't know nothin' about no car. Maybe it was one of Joey's business problems. The guy's scum."

"Yeah, you wish. You're so low and stupid, you wouldn't know a real man if you fell over one—"

"Oh yeah, takes a real man to sell junk to kids—"

"He don't do nothing like that, he's a restaurateur," she said, raising the tone of her voice as though she was referring to the Pope.

"Who's being stupid now, Angela? I break up with youse and what do you do? You tell your father I was gonna marry you. I never said nothin' about marriage. Then you go out with scum, and you come driving in here, saying I did a number on some lowlife's car and wrecking my front lawn. I don't know about you, Angela. You better straighten out here," he said, staring down at her and lying on her with his full weight. He could feel her trying to squirm out from under him, the way she used to do when they'd just done it. She began to turn red from the pressure. He let her gasp once or twice and then slowly got off of her.

She got up, crying. She looked around for her purse and finally stomped off to the car. Her shirt and the rounded ass of her jeans were muddy and grass-stained, her hair was disheveled, and Lisa couldn't take her eyes off her.

Angela teetered slightly as her heel sank down and stuck in the lawn. She tried to pull it out, then finally stepped out of the patent-leather pump, leaned down, and unevenly ripped it out of the lawn. She stood still for a moment, then whirled around, holding the shoe.

"I'm gonna get you for this, Tony Mac."

"Yeah, yeah."

"I don't know how, and I don't know when, but I'm gonna make you pay for what you done."

"I didn't do nothin'."

She stared up at him and a smirk came across her face as she held the shoe like a gun and bobbed up and down on one heel. She slowly began to walk toward him. He stood his ground, watching her look over his body almost hungrily, up and down. He felt a warm flush across his body as he looked over hers, and he licked his lips. He knew he'd won this round. There was one thing Angela could not resist, and that was muscles.

"I know what you think and when you think it, Tony Macaroni, and if you think this is it, you're wrong. There ain't too many women out there know what you do and how you do it. I waited a long time for you to come around to me. I had to watch you go through everyone else, and I waited, and then you shamed me. . . . I'm gonna get you for this." She was so close to him that he could just feel her.

After all the wrestling, he could've fucked her on the spot.

She gave a sneer, watching his eyes roam over her body.

"So you just watch out." She turned and bobbed up and down with as much dignity as she could muster, then got back in her car.

She pulled out quickly, leaving two tracks in the grass, backed noisily onto the street, and as she drove off she gave him the finger out of the car window.

Tony stood still, watching her go, then looked down at Michael.

"She's crazy. The woman don't know nothin'," he said, and then walked into his house.

Henry walked into his apartment and collapsed on the bed. He'd managed to lose Morris somewhere out on the Island. His eyes hurt and he could barely see from lack of sleep. The room began to spin as he heard the phone ring in the living room. It rang three times and then the machine picked up.

"Henry, this is your mother. Your behavior today was unacceptable, and you taking your sister's car was outrageous. You've finally pushed it to the limit. I'm calling to inform you that by Monday afternoon I intend to cut you off from this family . . . that includes the money. I certainly hope you'll be able to get by on what you make."

Click.

He lay there staring at the ceiling. That was all he needed, idle threats from his mother. She never appreciated how difficult his life really was. Tiffany was probably responsible for this. As he lay trying to figure out a way to get back at her for this, the phone rang again.

He stayed still and waited for the machine to pick up.

There was a deep man's voice he didn't recognize, asking whether he was there. After a moment or two, the man hung up.

He had to catch some sleep, he thought finally, and then rolled over and passed out.

* * *

The lights from the police cars lining the street bounced off of the dark brick buildings. Static, followed by voices over radios, echoed in the quiet as men moved about, ducking under the yellow crime-scene tape they'd used to mark off the building. Upstairs in the third-floor corner window, the light was on, the only one for blocks in the closed downtown Brooklyn business district.

Two detectives were leaning over the body as the duster dusted for prints. Rough chalk markings outlined the body. Officers and detectives milled about, poking into things, pulling open drawers, looking about in files.

Another two men were taking inventory of the safe behind the desk. One wrote down every item the other pulled out.

In the outer office sat the cleaning woman, shaking and sick from what she had stumbled and fallen over in the dark. A young officer handed her a cup of tea, and another officer sat with a tape recorder on, asking her the usual questions.

She'd been cleaning the building for twenty years.

No, she'd never seen anything like this.

Yes, she'd actually fallen over it. . . . Well, she'd run out of the office so fast, she might've moved the body a bit, but she wasn't sure, and she wasn't going back in there to check.

It took ten minutes before she *could* dial the phone. She felt another wave of nausea come over her as they asked more questions.

"It's gotta be a hit, George—it's too clean," she heard one of the officers opine in the other room as someone handed her a pack of cigarettes. She lighted one shakily and informed the officer with the tape recorder that she was going to quit on Monday.

* * *

Rosa Morelli had been sitting in her kitchen when the buzzer rang. She'd quickly jumped to it, pushing it without asking who it was. She sat back down at the table and lighted a cigarette in anticipation of what she knew was going to be a nice fat check and the gory details of how Tony had done the number on Henry Foster Morgan.

The door swung open, and Rosa's face dropped as Sophia Bonello stepped inside.

"Sophia—" she began as she watched her close the door behind her.

"Rosa Morelli, I come here about my son. I don't know what you got him doing, but I want it to stop now."

"What the hell are you talking about?" Rosa screeched.

Sophia held on to her bag tightly and stepped toward the woman.

"You lower your mouth—I'm not Solly here. You can't push me around. Now tell me what you got my son doing."

"You get out—" Rosa began, and started to stand up.

Sophia pushed her back down in her chair.

"You gotta big mouth, Rosa, and you been driving everyone crazy since that *stunadze* you married got himself all shot up. Now you got Solly convinced he gotta look out for you—and that's fine, but you're dealing with me now. . . . Gina and I wanna know what's going on here."

Sophia stood very still, looking down at Rosa. She knew Solly's mother would enjoy seeing this. Rosa was the biggest pain in the ass she'd ever met. She watched Rosa go slightly pale at the mention of Gina's name.

"What's going on with my son and Tony?"

Rosa sat still, then slowly drew in a breath.

"They fired me," she began, and Sophia actually watched tears come to Rosa's eyes for the first time since they'd buried her husband over thirty years ago.

They'd been sitting in front of Henry's apartment on Grand Street for five hours; now it was after midnight. Every time a cab had come down the block, both Michael and Lisa had held their breath, waiting for Henry to appear and for Tony to go through with Rosa's orders.

Lisa was stuck in the backseat the entire time and kept meeting Michael's eyes in the mirror. They would look at each other for a brief moment until the memory of the night before flushed each of their faces and then they would automatically shift their vision before Tony could notice.

She had stretched out across the backseat after a while, but now she was staring at a restaurant and bar across the street. People walked in and out, oblivious of the car and of them, and she wished she was one of those people, blissfully going out to dinner and then to a club. . . .

The sight of the woman on Andrew's lap flashed through her mind and she felt oddly numb to it now. She remembered the dinners she had sat through with both of them. How they must have been laughing at her. The naïve good little woman who never asked questions and never interfered. She tried to think back to the first night he had brought her over. She wondered whether he had been sleeping with her at that point or if it had started later. Cynthia was introduced as "someone who works with me." After dinner, Andrew insisted on walking her home because, he had told Lisa, "New York was a dangerous place."

Yeah, it was dangerous all right, dangerous for the trusting.

That was probably why Cynthia had never returned her phone calls about getting together, Lisa thought. For the longest time, she had thought Cynthia just didn't like her. Now the whole thing made perfect sense. The woman was sleeping with Andrew. Of course she wouldn't want to become friends with the woman he lived with, or maybe she had enough human compassion not to do that.

They must have laughed over it, watching her trying to make friends with Cynthia, trusting Andrew with her. Oddly enough, she felt hollow inside when she thought of Andrew. It was as if she were erasing him from existence. She would think back over all the times he hadn't shown up or all the times he'd been inexplicably late, and then she would let them go. Michael was right about her having no self-respect.

Tony looked at his watch. He knew Joey D.'s hangout on the East Side. He wanted to cruise around there just to make sure Angela wasn't with him. He stared in the rearview mirror. He couldn't go looking for Angela with Lisa in the car. He stared over at his cousin. He knew it wasn't fair, but he'd just have to stick Mikey with her for another night. He still wanted to get Michigan out on a date, but his mind kept wandering back to Angela.

She'd finally shown him a little respectability, trying to attack him on the lawn that way. And he liked the way her body had felt underneath him again. She'd dropped a couple of pounds, he could tell.

He stared up at the building and began to rationalize leaving his post. This fruitcake wasn't coming home tonight, anyways. He'd called awhile ago and got one of those machines. And besides, his Aunt Rosa couldn't cash a check in the middle of the night.

"Mikey, I got something to do," he said, staring over at him. He watched Michael blink. "You want me to take youse back to the Plaza?"

Henry rolled over and opened his eyes to look at the clock. Andy Warhol's head was on four, and his other head was on twelve. He yawned, debating whether or not he should get up. He could go to Downtown Beirut, a club in the East Village. He sat up and the room began to spin from lack of alcohol.

He lay back down. His mother must be joking about his trust, he thought, and began to pass out again.

The same bellhop who had been on duty the night before opened the door to the room.

"No luggage, sir?" he'd asked, knowing full well there was none. Michael didn't even bother to answer. He shoved a single in his hand and closed the door behind him. He leaned against the door and gazed at Lisa.

She slowly walked over to him and ran her hands along the smooth, stiff lapel of his jacket. She slipped her hands inside and ran them up, lifting the coat off his shoulders. He felt it slide down his arms, and he let it drop to the floor next to his feet. She ran her hands across his chest—avoiding his holster—and up to his tie. She silently began to loosen it. He grabbed her hands for a moment, then pushed them away and undid his own tie.

He was going to be strong.

He pulled it off around his neck and she took it from

him and dropped it on the floor, on top of his coat. He quickly unbuckled his holster and it dropped to the floor with a thud. He stared down at it as her hands went back to his chest, and he felt himself begin to tingle as she touched him. He let her hands wander down to his waist, and then he grabbed her wrists again. She stared up into his face.

"I am not going to touch you. Do you hear me, Lisa?"

She nodded.

"Last night was . . . a mistake. And I'm not going to touch you."

As soon as the words were out of his mouth, he knew in twenty minutes flat he was going to have his shirt and pants unbuttoned, and she was going to kiss him as she did it, going lower and lower, making him shake and tingle, and he was going to pull her up and undress her the same way, but slowly and carefully tonight. He was going to spend the night making love to her because he'd spent the whole day thinking about it, about why he shouldn't, and how if he was stuck with her again tonight he'd be strong and not lead himself on, all the while imagining what it would be like to touch her again.

He was screwed.

"I am *not* going to touch you," he added one last futile time as she wrapped her arms around his neck and began to kiss him.

Tony stared at the dance floor. He watched Angela lean over the bar, looking for something, as the music beat so loudly, Tony could feel the floorboards vibrate through his shoes. Smoky lights danced around, zooming up and down and changing colors every thirty seconds or so, it seemed to him.

It made him dizzy, watching them whirl. He stood silently, watching her through the crowd.

It wasn't good she was there. He looked around and couldn't see Joey D.

Scumbag was probably in the bathroom somewhere.

Angela was lighting herself a cigarette, when she turned and waved, and Tony watched Joey D. slip his arm around her.

That was enough for Tony.

He'd missed dinner at his mother's two nights in a row, for what? he thought, getting hungry.

He turned and walked out, down the dark back corridor, and out to the back lot, where the owners parked their cars. A bouncer walked over to him, asking him what he was doing.

"I'm looking for Joey D.'s car. Could youse point out which one it is?" he asked, staring down at this man who was supposed to be the new muscle at the club.

"I'm sorry, I can't give out that information. Would you please leave now, sir?"

"Look, I just need to know which one it is—" Tony began as the usual security guy came down the corridor.

"Fred—" he began and then stopped as he caught sight of Tony. "Mr. Macarelli, what can I do for you?"

"I was wondering if you could point out Joey D.'s car for me."

"Of course, anything you want," he said, walking out the door and into the lot.

Tony was led to a rented town car, and with much apology the security guy backed off into the club.

"You know who that was?" Tony heard the regular bouncer explain. "Tony Macarelli."

"Tony Mac? Aw jeez," the second one said, and then they both were out of earshot.

Joey D. must be dumb, he thought. After what happened to his car last night, anyone else woulda gotten the hint. Tony turned his full attention to the car. He stared through the side door, and saw the keys, hanging in the ignition. He opened the door, got in, and drove it out of the lot. He drove it over to Ninth Avenue to the Westside Car Shop, and pulled it in back. He sat and honked the horn twice, until Gus, the night guy, came out.

Gus was in his usual mechanic suit and he gave Tony a big smile as he walked around the car, appraising it and chewing steadily on a fat cigar he always had in his mouth. He got back to the driver's side as Tony rolled down the window.

"Tony, I ain't seen you for how many years now?" his deep, raspy Louis Armstrong voice rumbled as he held out his hand.

"I dunno, Gus, five, maybe."

"So you back in the car business?"

"Naw, this is just a special case," he said, and turned off the ignition, took the keys, and got out.

"How much?" Gus asked after giving the car one last going-over.

"This one's on me, for all the times you took what I had," Tony said, dropping the keys into Gus's hand.

He watched Gus stare at the key ring.

"Avis, huh?" Gus said as Tony walked toward the front.

"Top of the line. Not many miles on it, neither. See

youse around," Tony added, and walked back out to Ninth Avenue.

He stepped off the curb and hailed a cab back to the club to pick up his car. Gus would probably have the thing stripped down to nothing in twenty minutes. Now he wanted to see what fuckin' Joey D. would do about this here thing he'd just done.

He drove straight back to Brooklyn. Tomorrow, he was going to track down this fruitcake for Rosa if it was the last thing he did. He couldn't waste no more time on this.

He hummed, clicked on the radio, and listened to the early-morning news.

Maybe there was some of that stuffed veal left he could heat up.

Sophia walked into her house and down the hall toward the kitchen. She tapped on Michael's door and waited for a moment, then slowly opened it up. He hadn't come home tonight, either. She carefully closed the door and continued into the kitchen. She put the bag down on the table and took Vincent's old gun out of it. She put it back in the drawer with the string and scissors, muttering to herself that she should just get rid of the thing.

She put a pot of water on the stove for coffee and sat down tiredly. She was not used to being up this late; she was too old for this. She rubbed her chin with her hand and stared at the old enameled kitchen tabletop.

She remembered Rosa's face as she wept about her pension and her retirement and not being able to go to Florida. It was true, she felt sorry and bad for Rosa about what this snake in her office had done, but she was hardly sorry enough to sacrifice her only son. No, there was another way out of this. Sophia glanced up at the kitchen clock, shaped like a teakettle. She couldn't bother Gina this time of night. She wondered where Michael was and what he was doing, and she was going to go to church in an hour or two and pray he hadn't done anything yet. And then she was going to have another long talk with Vincent, as she lit a candle for him, and try and find out what he would have done in this position.

The coffee water was boiling, and she was drowsy as she poured it over the grounds.

The next morning, Lisa was washing her hair in the bathroom and Michael was adjusting his tie when room service arrived carrying a tray with coffee and juice.

Michigan probably wouldn't be so bad, he thought as he paid the guy and closed the door. All right, it would be cold, but what the hell, it was better than going for the big chill here in New York. He poured himself a cup of coffee and heard the water in the shower shut off.

"Lisa, you want a cup of coffee?" he yelled in to her.

"Yes, I'll be out in a minute."

Lisa stared at her face in the mirror. She'd slept with him again. She'd thrown herself at him, something she had never done.

God, it felt good.

Michael sipped his coffee and looked out the window at the hot, steamy city. In the end of August in New York, a smoky film of haze always settled in, sometimes looking like fog, but all the time trapping hot, dirty air amidst the walls of skyscrapers.

He stared out at it and then walked over and switched on the TV. He poured a cup for her as she walked out, a large white towel wrapped on her head like a turban. She kissed him and took the cup, holding it in both hands like a precious egg. She took a sip and sat down on the couch.

"So I thought—" Michael had just begun when he heard a gasp and the sound of a breaking cup behind him. He turned and saw her, pale and shaking, standing up, pointing at the television.

His eyes immediately darted to it. The sight of the union office building, surrounded by police cars and reporters, was staring back at him. He grabbed the remote and turned it up just as the screen flashed back to the studio. He heard the anchor say, "And now for the weather."

"Oh God! Oh my God!" he heard Lisa say, her voice high and panicking. He shut the thing off and grabbed her, shaking her by the shoulders.

"Stop it! You've got to get a grip on yourself!" he said as loudly as he could, trying to bring her past the thoughts he knew were running through her head.

"Michael, they found him . . . they found him, oh my God! I should have turned myself in. I should have done it last night—"

"Stop it, Lisa. Just stop it," he said, and pulled her to him, wrapping his arms around her.

She was shaking all over and whimpering into his shoulder. He began to talk fast.

"Okay, they found him, they were going to, anyway. It would have been better if they had done it on Monday—we could have gotten out of town by the time they figured out—but they haven't figured out anything. Listen to me, Lisa. They don't know it's us. They don't have anything on either one of us. All we have to do is get out of town and away from Tony and all this crap."

The phone rang and Lisa let out a scream and jumped to her feet, staring at it, frozen. It rang again and Michael, who had been just as paralyzed, finally snapped to and picked it up. He stood still and nodded as he listened to Tony, then hung up.

"We're late. He's on his way up," he said, staring at her.

"He's here?" she squeaked at him, and he gave her a rough hug.

"Now, let's calm down. We have to stop him fast and get out of town."

"We'll never get away from this. We'll never get out. Why didn't I call the police? Why didn't I go back to Michigan last year? Oh God, why didn't I go to Connecticut, why—"

"Yeah, why didn't I just go back to school—but I didn't and you didn't. Now listen to me. I don't want to chance sneaking out. He'll shoot on sight if he needs to. We're going to have to shoot him," Michael said.

They stared at each other, startled.

"I can't shoot another person, Michael. For God's sake, I shot the last guy I—"

"Not kill him, just maim him, to slow him down," Michael said quickly, and they both stared at each other again.

It wasn't until he'd just heard it come out of his mouth that he knew it was the right thing, the only thing to do. No, he couldn't kill his cousin. But if he could just shoot him, maybe in the leg or the arm, and then run. . . . Michael thought this over.

Tony was there to pick them up and go back down to

the loft on Grand Street. They could wait until he was getting out of the car, then Michael could pull the gun on him and shoot him in the thigh or the arm. At that close a range, he could probably even hit him. He looked at Lisa. She was a better shot than he was. She had sunk down on the couch.

No, he'd have to do it. Then what?

Michael began to pace back and forth. He walked over to the door, bent down, and picked up the holster and his jacket. He dropped the jacket on the couch, took the gun out of its holster, and stood staring at it, feeling the cold weight in his hand. He felt himself exhale shakily, trying to reconcile actually using the thing, and he passed it from one hand to the other, almost as if he was trying to decide which hand it felt best in. He'd have to disarm him. He knew Tony. Even shot in the leg, he'd go for them. And *he* was a good shot, a real shooter.

He stared at his jacket. He'd have to keep it in his pocket. He couldn't take the time to reach into his holster if he was going to pull it on Tony.

Lisa walked back into the bedroom, almost in a trance. He walked in after her and watched her finish dressing.

"I'm going to try and get his gun and shoot him in the leg when he tries to get out of the car to get your boss," he began as evenly as he could. She nodded silently as she buttoned her shirt.

"When I do that, I want you to open the door and run as quickly as possible out onto West Broadway and try to hail a cab while you're waiting for me."

"What if—"

"If I'm not out on the street after two minutes, you get the hell out of there, cab or no cab. Go back to your apartment, pack what you can, and get on the first train out of the city—"

"But—"

"You take a train and pay cash, then fly from another city—it'll take more time to trace. You do what I say."

She stood still, staring at him.

"I don't want to leave without you, you've—"

"Look, this mess isn't your fault. You got stuck in the middle of something you shouldn't have. . . ." His voice dwindled away as she walked into his arms and held on to him tightly.

"Go back to Michigan, where you belong. Believe me, Lisa, if I can get away, I'll do it, if not, then maybe it's God's way of telling me that I belong in this kind of life. I don't know. I'm sorry for everything you've been through . . . I'm sorry for what I did."

There was a knock at the door, and slowly she let go of him.

"Be right there," Michael called out, looking at the door.

Lisa was standing at the small desk, writing something down on the hotel stationery, when he walked over to her.

"What are you doing? We have to go."

She folded the paper and stuffed it into his jacket pocket.

"What is it?"

"It's my address and phone number in Michigan." He opened his mouth, but she gently put her hand over his lips and gazed at him. "I'll wait as long as I can on the street. If something goes wrong and you don't get out within three minutes, I'll wait for you at the information booth in Grand Central two hours after we do this. If you don't show up, keep the address and join me later. You don't belong in this kind of life, Michael. Get out now while you have the chance. I'll be waiting."

There was a banging knock on the door, and they gazed at each other for the last time. Lisa nodded and Michael opened the door.

Tony was standing there, annoyed.

"Jeez, what the hell took youse so long?" he demanded as they walked into the hallway.

"You know women," was the only thing Michael could say as he pushed the button for the elevator.

Eight

Gina's black limousine pulled up in front of the church as Sophia came down the steps. She smiled and waved as Gina opened the door, then she got inside.

"Father D'Amico asked for you," Sophia said as the car turned onto a side street.

"What did you tell him?"

"I told him you weren't feeling well," she said, deciding that she'd have to confess that lie to him at the next confession. She stared at the street, a bit confused.

"Where we going, Gina?"

"My son's house . . . to deal with Rosa," Gina said in her gravelly voice. Then she exhaled and sank back into the velvety upholstered seat. Sophia watched a big smile come across her face, followed by a contented sigh, and she, too, made herself comfortable in the car. She had called Gina first thing that morning about Rosa. They were finally going to get rid of her—Sophia knew it in her bones.

* * *

Michael's eyes kept surveying Tony's body as they drove downtown. He kept staring at the bulky thighs and arms. He could see the bulge from his holster. He finally forced his eyes forward as they traveled down Fifth Avenue. The streets were nearly empty. It was too hot even for the tourists to be out walking.

Tony was humming to himself, and thinking about Gus tearing up Joey D.'s Avis. He was surprised he hadn't heard from Angela already. Even Ralphie had been cool on the phone, not letting on he knew anything when Tony called in for his daily check and to run down the day's schedule. He shot a glance sideways at Mikey and wondered whether he knew his mother had been out to see Solly. Naw.

He continued humming, then stared at Michigan in the rearview mirror. Maybe he should try one last time with her. They stopped at a light, and Tony's eyes landed on a block with nothing but fur-coat shops. He glanced back to her.

Should he even try it? he thought. God knows what she'd tell him about fur coats. This one was a total mystery to him. Her flat blond hair and freckly face faded into Angela attacking him on the lawn.

"Tony?" Michael said, and he looked out and saw that the light was green.

He stepped on the gas.

"You like fur coats?" he asked.

"Who?" he heard Michael ask, and he glared at him.

"Jeez, how many times I gotta tell you? I'm not talkin' to you." He turned back to Michigan. "You like fur coats?"

"You mean the ones where they kill all those poor little animals?"

No, this broad was a total mystery to him.

"Aw jeez, that's what they raise 'em for. You see, they treat 'em good *before* they chop 'em up."

"Yes, but then all they do is kill them for their fur."

"So?" Tony's eyes began crossing.

"Well, if we ate mink or sable, it would be different."

"Why? The thing's dead. Dead is dead, nothin' else. They don't care if they get eaten—"

"Well, if they raised you just to rip your skin off, wouldn't you be upset?" Lisa said, taking the bull by the horns.

"If I'm dead, what's the difference?" he nearly yelped.

"It's the principle of the thing. I just couldn't wear one, that's all."

"What do people give you for presents for God's sake?" Tony asked, his voice booming with frustration.

"Flowers?"

They all went silent. Tony kept shaking his head back and forth as they drove through the empty streets on the way down to SoHo. Flowers. Fuckin' flowers, no dead animal coats . . .

He looked over to her. Jeez, if he could get Angela to swallow a line like that . . .

"Sit down, Rosa," Gina said, carefully untying the black lace hair protector from her head.

Sophia watched Rosa stare uneasily at her and sit down. She wiggled uncomfortably in the chair, her eyes looking around Solly's office. Gina folded the hair protector and placed it and her black handbag on the desk.

"Is Val here?" Rosa asked carefully.

"My daughter-in-law is at church. It's none of her business, anyway. This is between us."

The three of them sank into silence as they waited for Solly. Sophia watched Rosa squirm, knowing Rosa wanted a cigarette but didn't dare ask whether she could smoke in the room. Everyone knew that since Solly had been on his health kick, smoking was forbidden in his house. Sophia hid a smile as she coughed into her handkerchief.

The door clicked and Solly walked in. He was dressed in white tennis clothes and he stopped for a moment and frowned disgustedly at the three of them. Rosa stood up as he continued to his desk.

"Solly, I—" Rosa began, but she stopped as she watched his eyebrow raise.

"Sit down, Rosa," Solly said, and they all sat down.

Solly cleared his throat and clasped his hands on the desktop.

"My mother," he began, darting a frown in Gina's direction, "wants this mess with your boss straightened out another way."

Gina gave him a crisp smile and folded her arms.

"Okay, your problem is that you don't got enough money to go live in Florida?"

"But he shamed me, firing me from the—"

Solly raised his hands and hushed her.

"The problem is that you don't got enough money to go live in Florida, right?" he repeated.

"Yeah, but—"

"Okay, then," he said, gritting his teeth as he stared at his mother. "In deference to your late husband getting himself all shot up on the avenue"—Sophia could see Solly wince—"my mother has pointed out to me that I ought to pay for you to go live in Florida."

"But what—"

"I buy the condo," his voice interrupted loudly and sharply, "and I throw in a yearly pension of twenty—" Gina coughed, and he grimaced again and corrected the figure. "Thirty thousand a year, tax free."

"Solly, he did—"

Solly glared at her and stood up.

"Look, youse take the fuckin' condo and the money and we call it even with this guy from your office."

"But—"

"That's the deal. You better take it"—he glared at his mother again—" 'cause this is the last goddamned time I'm makin' this offer. You understand me, Rosa Morelli?"

Sophia caught a glare from him and she stared at the floor. Tough luck, she thought, knowing that she was not going to be popular for this.

They listened to Rosa exhale loudly and Sophia watched her nod.

"All right, I'll take the deal," she said finally, and got up.

She glared at the three of them and walked out the door. They listened to it slam behind her.

"All right? You happy now?" Solly asked his mother tersely.

"Yes, Enrico."

"I'm goin' to play tennis," he said, and Sophia coughed.

"And Michael?"

"I'm gonna get Ralphie to call him off," he said, and walked over to his mother. "You don't ever do this to me again, eh?" he said fiercely, and Gina sniffed and gave him a look, as if he was being silly.

They listened to the door slam after him.

"I hope this didn't make no trouble for you," Sophia said gratefully.

Gina waved her hand after Solly and shook her head. "He got nothing to be upset about. He'll realize what a favor he just did himself once he ships her down to Florida. She isn't gonna call him every fifteen minutes from there."

She stopped and the two of them stared at each other and then began to giggle, first low, then getting louder and louder until they were bellowing.

"We did it, Soph'. Took us thirty years, but we finally got rid of her!" Gina said, grabbing her around the shoulders.

"Come inside. I got some pastries from Venieros, fresh. I'll make black coffee," Gina added, and the two of them walked out of the study.

"Why you want to know where they are?" Ralphie was saying over the phone.

"I just want to."

"You're not going to do anything stupid—"

"Pop! I don't do stupid things. You just tell me where he is, is all."

Ralphie took the phone away from his ear and covered it with his hand. Well, Tony was a big man and could take care of himself. Besides, he sure as hell didn't want Joey D. as a son-in-law.

"Grand Street and West Broadway, but—" he began, and there was a click on the other end as Angela hung up.

He stood still, and the sinking feeling that he'd just fucked up again came into Ralphie's mind. His eyes caught sight of Solly, stomping off through the main hallway on the way to his tennis match. He gave a wave, which Solly missed as he slammed the big front door.

Jeez, he was in another mood. Ralphie stood, watching the phone, and then walked to the front door. He opened it in time to see Solly's car drive past.

Solly glanced out at Ralphie as the car slid in a circle past the door.

"Jerry, stop. I forgot to tell Ralphie something," he said, pulling himself forward with one hand. His eyes fell on his watch. Now he was going to be late because of his mother's goddamned . . .

"What, Solly? I didn't catch that."

"Nothin', just drive. I'll do it later," Solly said, and leaned back in the seat.

He picked up his new tennis racket and spun it in his hand, feeling the weight. He'd call them off Rosa's guy when he got back. Who the hell knew what those two fuckin' morons had been doing for two whole days, anyway, he thought. Michael, he wasn't surprised at, but Tony? . . . It seemed like the more time he spent with his cousin, the stupider he got. Jeez, Solly thought, a college education can suck the brains right out of youse. Besides, as long as they'd done the important part, getting Geddone, everything was fine.

Henry had taken his shower, dressed, and was standing at the door, waiting for the elevator to come up. He put a dark pair of glasses on his puffy eyes as he heard the whir of machinery in the shaft begin. It was terribly odd being up at nine in the morning without having been up the whole night. It was the first time in a long while he'd done this.

Henry felt terrible. He needed a drink. His nausea quelled a bit as he heard the elevator start up. He'd go to one of the neighborhood places. He wondered whether they were open this early on a Sunday. Besides, who knew where Morris was.

A chill went through him as he remembered his mother's voice on the answering machine. It must have been a dream, he thought. He stared at the machine. He walked back over to it and hit the replay button as the elevator opened, spreading out a beam of fluorescent light across the dark floor.

The tape replayed and he listened to his mother's voice again as the elevator closed behind him. There was something disturbing in her voice. Something like . . . her meaning this.

He sank down on the couch, trying to compose himself. He didn't know why this time was different, but he sensed that it was, and as he heard the elevator begin its descent he felt strangely paralyzed.

Angela's white Lincoln ripped out of her parking spot and screeched up the ramp. She stopped just short of the red and white candy cane–colored gate and watched the big yellow bow tied to the rearview mirror shake from the force. She leaned on the horn, waiting for the guy to lift it. She watched it rise up and cursed him as she sped out of the garage and into the sunlight. She squinted and roared to a stop at the corner. She pulled a pair of sunglasses out of the glove compartment. Her eyes caught sight of the bow again and she angrily ripped it off the mirror.

Tony was going to get his today. Her thighs tensed exposed beneath a very short white miniskirt. Her chest felt flushed as she thought about having him on top of her on the lawn, and it felt itchy under the tight white middrift she'd thrown on. Men, she thought angrily, and she floored it.

They sat in the car listening to the radio, and Tony glanced up at the door every couple of minutes. He had turned on one of those stations that played back-to-back news, and they had now heard, for the third time, how the cops had found Geddone's body.

They listened to all the suppositions being put out by the cops, about how they figured it might be mob-connected, or a robbery attempt.

Tony listened like a producer listening to a good review of his movie and smiled proudly, shaking his head.

"Jeez, those guys, they don't know nothin', huh, Mikey?" He chuckled.

Michael gave him a weak smile and looked forward. He could feel his stomach begin to go on him.

"Hey, Tony, put on some music, huh?" he said, watching him grimace and then switch channels.

He waited for Tony to look back to the doorway, and then he slowly tightened his hand on the gun in his pocket. His hand was sweating around it and his shoulder was held slightly up in an uncomfortable shrug. He was going to have to keep it there.

His eyes faced down Grand Street. In the distance, he could see where the street turned slightly, just at Broadway, where it ceased to be SoHo and turned into Little Italy. At the turn, he could see in his mind the big red, white, and green sign for Ferrara's pastry shop. He sat there trying to remember the smells and sounds of the block that he probably wouldn't see again soon, if ever.

He wanted to try to etch it into his mind so he would never forget it.

They'd been sitting in front of the building for twenty-five minutes, and Michael's shoulder was hurting from holding it up loosely on the gun. Tony coughed and Michael glanced sideways. Out of the corner of his eye, he saw the door to the building open and Henry Foster Morgan stagger outside.

"Okay, let's go," he heard Tony say.

Tony opened his door and Lisa opened hers and jumped out. As Tony turned and looked behind, Michael grabbed at the bulge in Tony's jacket. His hand quickly slipped inside and he grabbed Tony's gun.

"What the hell's going on here?" Tony said as he turned back and his eyes fell down on the gun Michael was holding on him beneath the dashboard.

"Mikey," he began, and Michael watched a pained, confused look cross his cousin's face.

"I can't let you do this. I—" he started, and suddenly Tony got out of the car, as though he hadn't even seen the gun.

"He's gettin' away," Tony yelled back in as he quickly began to walk behind Henry toward West Broadway. Michael sat still, stunned for a moment.

He pulled himself up and sprang out of the car, waving the gun.

"Tony! Stop right now!" he yelled as he watched Tony almost put his hand on Henry's shoulder. Tony turned and stared at Michael, then his eyes stared down at the gun and back up to Michael's face.

"What are you doin' here?" was the eerie question that came from him. It was the same one he'd asked the Bronx league's tackle sixteen years before. Good, Michael thought, it'll keep me focused.

"I'm going to shoot you."

"Yeah?" Tony chuckled and turned around. "I don't think so," he said, and began walking away.

"I got a fucking gun on you!" Michael screamed indignantly.

"You got the fuckin' safety on."

People stopped suddenly and Michael heard gasps as someone yelled, "Look out, he's got a gun!"

As Michael struggled with the safety, he saw Lisa come up beside him. She grabbed the gun out of his hands as Michael reached inside to the gun in his pocket.

"Tony, STOP!" she yelled as Michael unhooked the safety.

Tony slowly turned around in the middle of West Broadway, staring at the two of them. They were both shaking and pointing their guns at him, their arms extended and tight. People on the sidewalks began scattering. A frown passed Tony's face as his arms rose up and the three of them stood staring at one another. Behind Tony, Michael could see the figure of Lisa's boss disappearing obliviously around a corner.

"What are youse doin'?"

"We're going to stop you."

"How?"

"We're going to shoot you."

"Yeah?" Tony asked, and then they watched this odd smirk cross his face. "How come I don't hear no gun goin' off? What are youse gonna do? Talk me to death? Go *bang bang* and hope I drop? You guys," he said, throwing his hands up at their incompetence. Then he turned his back on them.

Michael watched him take one step and he closed his eyes and gently squeezed the trigger. Beside him, he heard Lisa's gun go off, as well. Screams came from the crowds as people in the restaurants began leaning up against the windows. Michael slowly opened his eyes to what he knew was going to be a bloody sight.

They'd missed. His jaw dropped.

He stared openmouthed at Tony, who was standing in the street, facing them, shaking his head, and in the corner of his eye, behind Tony, out on the edge of Grand Street and Sixth Avenue, Michael saw the light change and a white Lincoln roar around the turn.

"I don't fuckin'—"

The Lincoln was not slowing down.

"Tony, look out," Michael heard himself scream as the car came at him.

There was a thud of flesh hitting metal, and Tony's body was thrown sideways from the force, landing in the crosswalk at West Broadway and Grand, motionless. Michael was holding on to Lisa—and for what seemed like an eternity, life stopped on the street.

"Get out of here," he said, pushing Lisa away from him.

"But—"

"I'll meet you at Grand Central. GET OUT NOW," he screamed, pushing her hard. He watched her stare at his face, then down at Tony, and run. He looked after her for a second, just to make sure she had gotten away, and then he ran over to Tony as Angela got out of the car. He knelt down to Tony, then glanced up and saw Lisa disappear up Sixth Avenue.

When the ambulance finally showed up, Angela was kneeling beside Tony, weeping.

"I wasn't gonna run you over, I swear, Tony, I swear."

Tony was staring up at the sky as faces pressed in a crowded circle looked down on him with curiosity. Michael helped the attendants get Tony onto the stretcher and into the ambulance.

"One person only," the man said, and Angela stared at Michael.

"Him," Tony's voice floated out to them.

Michael stared at Angela, who shook her head and nodded. Michael climbed inside.

"I'm comin' to the hospital, Tony," Angela yelled inside, "don't you worry! I'm gonna take good care of youse from now on." Her voice filtered through the ambulance doors right before they closed them.

"Fuckin' great, all I need," Tony mumbled.

Michael stared down at him as the ambulance lurched into motion toward Beekman Downtown Hospital. The plastic IV sac swung against the chrome rod as the emergency medic kept his eyes on the drip.

"Tony—" Michael began.

"Mikey," Tony interrupted, then he lay there for a moment. "You ain't cut out for this life," he said finally.

"No."

"You and Michigan stand less than ten feet from me, and the only one hits me is Angela with the car. You don't even remember about the fuckin' safety," he added. And as he tried to shake his head, he let out a low yelp from the pain.

"Don't try to move," the medic said quickly.

They were silent for a moment.

"You gotta get out of town, Mikey. Take Michigan with youse. Solly's not gonna like any of this shit."

"Okay," Michael said evenly, then added, "Tony, I didn't want to shoot you—"

"You didn't. You missed," he added, grimacing, an
the pain welled up in his face again. "You was right an
I was wrong—you're just not cut out for this line of work."

"No."

The ambulance came to a stop and the doors wer
pulled open by attendants. Michael saw them pull th
gurney out, heard the legs snap down, and watched a
they lowered Tony down as gently as possible. Michae
climbed down after him and walked alongside.

"Stop," Tony said as they were halfway through th
doors to the emergency room. "STOP A MINUTE," h
screamed out.

"Mr.—" one of the medics began, and Michael leane
down over Tony.

"Get out of here, *now.* I ain't kidding. I'll try and squar
it with Solly, but just leave," he was saying, and suddenl
they heard Angela's voice.

"You fuckin' let me in to see Tony or I'll make bi
trouble for youse, I swear!" she was screaming at one o
the attendants.

"Aw jeez," Tony muttered again, and Angela burs
through the doors. "Go. I'll let youse know when it's saf
to come back."

Rosa Morelli was busy packing her bags. She was goin
to leave as soon as she could, that day. Solly hadn'
squared it for her. She'd been shamed and disgraced b
this pig of a man in her office and no one cared. No on
cared that she had nothing.

She was going to go down to Florida and she was goin
to buy the best condo she could. Really soak Solly for th
money.

She walked to the door, carrying her bags, and looked around. She'd come back for the rest of her things, she thought.

She put the key in the lock.

No, she wouldn't. She'd let Solly buy her all new things! That would get Gina into hot water, the bills.

She made it down to the front of her building and stared at what was left of the station wagon—a dirty, empty shell. She looked up as her neighbor Mr. Ciccone came up beside her, shaking his head at the thing.

"It's gonna be here for months," he said.

"Yeah," she said, and turned to walk away. She turned back.

"You wanna get rid of that thing?" she hollered back to him. He looked up and nodded. "All you need is some gasoline and a match. You set fire to it and the fire department, they come and put it out and report it to them guys who tow cars." She nodded at him.

"All I gotta do is set it on fire?" his voice echoed after her. She made it to the corner of a Hun' sixteen and hailed a gypsy cab.

"Newark, and you make it fast," she warned the driver.

She sat back in the seat. She'd started spending Solly's money already. That should get Gina back for this.

Lisa ran up Grand to Sixth Avenue and hailed a cab.

She walked into the apartment stiffly. Then she marched into the bedroom and pulled open the closet door, banging it loudly.

Behind her, she heard Andrew stir, with a moan.

"Wha—" he began groggily. She pulled down the suitcase and began emptying her drawers.

"Lisa? Were we robbed? What happened to the window in the living room and all my liquor?" he asked, sitting up in bed and rubbing his eyes.

She emptied her underwear drawer into the suitcase she had originally arrived in New York with, and then went to the closet and began picking out dresses she wanted to keep.

"What are you doing?" he asked as she crunched her best dresses and skirts into the case.

She walked into the bathroom and remembered that her toothbrush and her face stuff were in the small bag she'd packed for the weekend and left in the car in Harlem. She walked back into the bedroom.

"You owe me an explanation," he said as she locked up her suitcase. She lugged it into the living room and then walked back into the bedroom.

"Don't give me this attitude—" he began.

"Listen, you jerk, I'm leaving. You can screw what's-her-name for the rest of your life. You can take anything that's left of mine in this apartment and toss it. You lying, two-faced—rat bastard," she heard herself say, echoing Angela.

She walked back into the living room as he followed.

"You owe me the rent for this month and—"

"Keys," she said, holding up her set. She promptly dropped them on the couch. "The car is parked on Pleasant Avenue and a Hundred and nineteenth Street," she continued.

"What is my car doing on a Hundred and nineteenth Street for—"

"Find someone else to pay for your co-op," she said, cutting him off.

She swung her purse over her shoulder and picked up her suitcase.

"And I'll tell you one thing else, if I come down with any kind of disease because of you, I'll break every bone in your body—and that goes for Cynthia, too!"

She heard him screaming about his rent as she rang for the elevator. She got on and rode down in silence. When she got to the lobby, she lugged the suitcase out to the sidewalk and stood still for a moment.

She looked back at the lobby doorway and a sudden feeling of relief washed over her: relief at never having to come back to this doorway each night; at never having to have that foreboding, as she walked in, that she was going to be sitting all alone waiting for the inevitable phone call. She looked up at the building and then down the block, searching for anything that felt like sorrow about all this. She was just . . . surprised by how pleased she was at not having to do this anymore.

Two hours later, she was standing at the information booth at Grand Central. The odd mix of smells of doughnuts and hot dogs and cookies wafted around the busy terminal. The large clock on top of the information booth showed one o'clock. She sat down on her suitcase and leaned her face on her hands.

He wasn't going to show up.

There was that sinking feeling she got when she knew something was going to go wrong.

She couldn't lose him. All she wanted to do was have him next to her. She wanted to spend the rest of her life touching him. God, what if something really bad had happened?

The terminal echoed with more announcements of trains departing and arriving. People poured out of the archways to the train platforms as others fought their way in. She should stay and wait for him. Maybe she should go after him. . . . That was the kind of thinking that had gotten her in this mess in the first place.

"Washington, D.C., boarding on track thirty-nine." The announcement blared out rhythmically and echoed around the terminal. She stayed there for three more calls and then slowly stood up. No, she should get back to Michigan as fast as possible and wait for him there. That would be the smart thing. That would be the thing Michael would want her to do.

She picked up her suitcase. As she reached down for her big case, she saw a familiar hand reach down and take the handle. She straightened up.

"I don't know if I can do it, but . . . you want a roommate in Michigan?" he asked.

She gazed at him and smiled widely.

"I won't screw around on you. I'll try and be good and honest, Lisa—"

She took his arm and they walked through the arch onto the dark platform.

"What happened?"

"I'll explain it on the train," he said quickly, and they walked down toward the first car.

"Is Tony—"

"I think he'll be okay," Michael said, and they both stepped onto the train.

They sat down quickly. She grabbed him so hard that he shook and she gave him another long, hard kiss. She felt him shaking. When she stopped kissing him, she watched him fall back against the seat, trying to catch his breath. She liked that. She liked watching him shake.

Epilogue

Tony pulled the car up to the American Airlines Terminal at Newark. He turned up the wipers as snow began falling harder against the windshield. He pulled his arm up to wipe the steam from the window and a twinge in his shoulder started.

"So after the viewing, I made reservations at Florio's," Angela was saying as he rotated his shoulder.

"Florio's? I hate that place. What's wrong wid Gargiulio's out in the Bay?"

"You listen to me, Tony Mac. I made them reservations where I want to eat. We always gotta go out to the Bay, and in this snow I don't wanna get stuck."

"Why, your mother's got the kids, fahcrissakes. I don't see what the difference is."

"I don't wanna go way the hell out—"

Tony tuned out Angela's voice as the terminal doors started opening. Passengers from the Detroit flight began pouring out and Tony's eyes scanned the platform. His shoulder twinged again, and it reminded him of that day in SoHo. His eyes fell on his cousin Michael, walking through the doors, carrying two suitcases. Beside him was Michigan, carrying their newborn son.

"And the antipast' at Gargiulio's is always rubbery and they never give you enough—"

"It's them," Tony said, and honked the horn as his cousin began looking around.

Michael stood on the platform and his eyes were drawn to the white Lincoln. Even before the door opened, he knew it was Tony and Angela. It was just as he'd imagined, right before the plane landed. The snow, the big white car, and Michael realized that even though it had been only five years, he and Lisa were at least a lifetime from their lives here in New York.

"Hey. Hey, Mikey," Tony said, getting out of the car. He took the bags from him, and Michael noticed a limp as he walked around to the trunk.

"Get that baby outta the snow!" Angela ordered Lisa.

"Yes, honey, get him into the car," Michael added, opening the back door for them.

"So, when did Solly die?" Michael asked as Tony made room in the trunk.

"Thursday night. He had a heart attack, joggin'," Tony added, and Michael sensed amusement at that.

"The word is, he had some woman on the side makin' him do all that shit," he said, lowering his voice, his eyes looking at the car. "So how are things in Detroit? There much accountin' work up there?" Tony asked loudly, and slammed down the trunk hood.

"I'm pretty busy."

"Good, it's good to stay busy. Aayy, your mother's been talkin' and talkin' about your big house up there since she got back from the baby being born," Tony said, and patted him on the back.

"I guess it all worked out, huh, Mikey?" Tony said, then grimaced at the back of Angela's head, and Michael heard a *jeez* under Tony's breath. Tony opened the door for him.

"Yeah, I guess, Tony."

"But you know, Mikey, I been thinkin'." Michael braced himself. "What with Solly gone, I got pull. . . . Maybe youse don't have to stay up there in that cold place. You know, I could take care of youse right here, just like I always done for my little cousin."

"I'll think about it, Tony." Michael smiled to himself, and shuddered.

Another favor from Tony. All he needed, another favor.